PRAISE FOR BEN STOLTZFUS'S *DUMPSTER, FOR GOD'S SAKE*:

"*Winesburg, Ohio* meets *Day of the Locust* meets *White Noise* meets reality TV in this satirical send-up of the year before the millennium in a small-time American city. Stoltzfus starts with the outrageous—a city so devoted to waste disposal that it creates a flag with the colors of the garbage cans—and ups the grotesque ante from there. Crows are methodically infested with lice, a city-wide poetry contest delivers white supremacist doggerel, followed by a banal sort of neo-liberalism, followed by an exquisite corpse, while a crew of homeless people determine to live upwardly mobile even if that means taking over the local parks. At the poetry festival one character feels a glimmer of consciousness and almost rises to action, but that moment is swiftly forgotten as things devolve further. Serial murders, mayhem, a sighting of the Virgin Mary (or is that two?), reflections on what is and what is not metafiction, killer bees, multiple crow deaths, and one large motorcycle. At once a parody and a novel of ideas, *Dumpster, for God's Sake* charms as it slowly horrifies, and then, despite everything, charms again."

–STEPHANIE BARBÉ HAMMER, author of Sex with Buildings
and The Puppet Turners of Narrow Interior

"Reading *Dumpster* is like taking a trip through a carnival funhouse. My advice: kick back and enjoy Ben Stoltzfus's unique vision as he leads you through a world of bizarre events, dazzling imagery, and unpredictable conversations."

–CARLOS CORTÉS, author of Rose Hill and Fourth Quarter

"*Dumpster, for God's Sake* fingers and elaborates on one of the great failings of sociological theory, perhaps it's greatest failing: i.e., to account for the recrudescence of primitive tribal passions in our complex, globalized societies. We know that human interdependence can produce hostility as well as respect across lines of difference. *Dumpster* captures this dialectic—the return of tribalism that tears us apart as fast as it brings us together. In fact it gives the contours and texture of this unanalyzed 'in-our-face' sociological mess better than any sociological accounting of it because it fills out the space between Durkheim and Tarde, the two nineteenth-century sociologists, in a way that could, perhaps, only be done by fiction. *Dumpster* is creepily, profoundly dystopian and completely believable. What happens to the good people of Loviers City is as bad as any imagined alien invasion. Only there aren't any aliens to blame. In Stoltzfus's light hand, this fiction gets us closer to the truth about 'community' than any sociological account I have read."

–DEAN MACCANNELL, author of The Tourist and The Ethics of Sightseeing

ALSO BY BEN STOLTZFUS

NOVELS
The Eye of the Needle
Black Lazarus
Red White & Blue
Valley of Roses
Cat O'Nine Tails (short stories)
Romoland (a pictonovel with artist Judith Palmer)
Falling and Other Stories

TRANSLATIONS
La Belle Captive (Alain Robbe-Grillet)
The Target (Alain Robbe-Grillet)

MONOGRAPHS
Georges Chennevière et l'unanimisme
Alain Robbe-Grillet and the New French Novel
Gide's Eagles
Gide and Hemingway: Rebels Against God
Alain Robbe-Grillet: The Body of the Text
Postmodern Poetics: Nouveau Roman and Innovative Fiction
La Belle Captive: A Novel. Alain Robbe-Grillet and René Magritte
Lacan and Literature: Purloined Pretexts
The Target: Alain Robbe-Grillet and Jasper Johns
Hemingway & French Writers
Magritte and Literature: Elective Affinities

DUMPSTER

for God's sake

DUMPSTER

for God's sake

a novel

BEN STOLTZFUS

39 WEST PRESS

39 WEST PRESS
Kansas City, MO
www.39WestPress.com

First Edition: April 2019

ISBN: 978-1-946358-17-2

Library of Congress Control Number: 2019930909

10 9 8 7 6 5 4 3 2 1

Book Design, Edits: j.d.tulloch

39WP-27-P

For Andrew

"What a quiet, civilized pleasure, to step outdoors of a morning in any season, sometimes before first light, and to find one's refuse collected for disposal."

–John Barth

"The garbage men are talking trash, deep in thought beside their truck: the job provokes reflection on essences and accidentals."

–Jeff Dolven

FOREWORD

DUMPSTER, FOR GOD'S SAKE is a novel about Loviers City—a city that believes *cleanliness is next to Godliness*. Reverend Peter Newell, Pastor of the First Unanimist Church, wants Godliness. David Goodhew, Mayor of Loviers City, wants cleanliness. Carmen Grace, Director of the Arts Council, writes and talks about identity and the self-consciousness of groups. These characters and many others inhabit Loviers City—the novel's main character. When Loviers Symphony Orchestra plays Beethoven's Ninth Symphony, the music melds the auditorium into joyful cohesion. A citywide poetry contest brings disparate units together, as women, the homeless, Latinos, and many others listen to the judges read the winning poems. Poetry molds the different groups into larger self-aware units. But Loviers City is also a town of contradictions: Godliness, the Virgin, Dianetics, a zorgone box, frozen heads, a cryonics center, and the suicidal impulses of Heaven's Preamble (a millennial cult) all lead an uneasy coexistence. These entities display a longing for fulfillment, happiness, and immortality. They—and others like them—highlight Loviers City's quest for soul. Events climax in one big comedic rock and roll gig of the Rolling Bones—the most successful display of collective soul and group joy.

The city's motto of cleanliness is soon subverted, however, by a miraculous sighting of the Virgin. Her shrine attracts undocumented immigrants, religious tourists, and zealots. Hundreds of people, followed by thousands, visit the spot where She appeared. The infirm pray for a cure. The faithful compare Her to the Virgin of Guadalupe. The Pope visits Mexico City and Los Angeles, and a Cardinal visits Loviers City. The Vatican sells holy water. Loviers City builds hotels, hospitals, and spas, and Ziad Khalid's businesses thrive. Meanwhile, hordes of visitors discard paper, plastic, and refuse. Loviers City's All-America vision is besmirched as all the vendors, squatters, curious, sick, and faithful leave their mark.

Despite the city's good intentions, its vision of purity and spotlessness is overwhelmed. Over time, the homeless, a plague of crows, a brush fire, serial murders, the shooting of the mayor by Bernard Mingus (an SPCA activist), and an invasion of Africanized bees compound the city's problems. From prison, Mingus, agitating for a new Reformation that will bring Catholics and Protestants back together, writes impassioned letters to Hazel Broom, editor of the city newspaper. Rudy Squazza, the red-bearded ringleader of the homeless, and Jasmine, a precocious teenager working on a high school project on the homeless, fall in love. Rudy is a dumpster diver and the victim of police brutality. Jasmine dresses in black leather, rides a red Ducati Supersport 750, and is known as the "Angel from Hell." She is also an aspiring writer, and when she wins a prize for her piece on the sighting of the Virgin, she and her creative writing mentor, Gregor Rissotto, discuss the differences between life and art. He, too, is writing a novel—a counterfeit one about Loviers City—named *Americus*.

Fiction or life, real or counterfeit, we want to know what will happen to Rudy and Jasmine. Will Rudy win his suit against the city and be compensated for his injuries? Will cleanliness give way to squalor? Will Godliness survive the apparition of the Virgin? Will Loviers City find its soul? Suspense mounts as the two lovers and Loviers City fulfill their respective roles. Jeff Dolven's epigraph sums it up: "The garbage men are talking trash, deep in thought beside their truck: the job provokes reflection on essences and accidentals."

Cast of characters:

Loviers City
The Reverend Peter Newel, Pastor, First Unanimist Church
David Goodhew, Mayor
Albert Speer, Sanitation Engineer
Ziad Khalid, Businessman
Kathy Konlon, Director of Environment, ardent conservationist
Alfredo Garcia, Chief of Police
Thomas Jefferson Ohr, City Ombudsman
The Sanitary Squadron (The SS)
Carmen Grace (or C.G.), Director, Arts Council
Tony Thatcher, C.G.'s husband
Bernard Mingus, SPCA activist
Rudy Squazza, a homeless person
Jasmine Khalid, Ziad's daughter, a teenager
Gregor Rissotto, English Teacher, City College
Paul Moser, a student
Cheryl Igo, a student
Nora Silber, English Teacher, Loviers City High School
George Wilson, Owner, Moby Dickens Bookstore
Nicole Sebastian, Ziad Khalid's personal assistant
Dorothy Khalid, Ziad's wife

LEILA KHALID, Jasmine's younger sister
CHIP BURGER, a serial killer
NURSE COGG
JUDGE OSBORNE
BART HOLCOMB, Owner, Three Lambs Mortuary
TYRUS ULLMAN, Rudy Squazza's lawyer
FATHER ORTIZ, Pastor, Our Lady of Loviers City
HAZEL BROOM, Editor, *Loviers City Sun*
NORMAN DESH, Leader of Heaven's Preamble, a Y2K cult
HORACE QUICKENDHAL, a sculptor

DUMPSTER

for God's sake

LOVIERS CITY IS A God-fearing town, a town where cleanliness is next to … well … you know … It's also a city on the move: people, business, trucks—particularly garbage trucks.

Monday through Friday, you see the yellow monsters careening around the corners of suburbia's streets, gathering waste from America's households. The dumpsters are motorized behemoths on the prowl. Brown trashcans for solid waste, blue ones for recyclables, and green for yard clippings and leaves. Every snippet is gathered, lifted, and dumped into the animal's insatiable maw. Day after day, week after week, year-in and year-out, these leviathans chase down the color coded receptacles and empty them with single minded purpose.

From a distance, you hear the monsters approaching. The noise of their motors, gears, and wheels moves from one block to the next, getting closer, stopping and starting at each driveway. At every stop, the mechanical arm darts out from the machine's midsection, encircles the trash can with its hydraulic hand—

two giant pinchers—lifts the receptacle high above the gaping aperture, tilts it on its axis, shakes the canister several times, and, after the refuse has fallen into the open throat, returns the can to its original position by the curb. The pinchers open, the arm withdraws, the innards clank and grate, the brakes release with a loud whoosh, and the animal on wheels moves on: stop, flashing light, arm, clasp, lift, dump, clank, release, whoosh, growl, and go. Curb after curb, intersection after intersection, from one neighborhood to the next, from early morning to midafternoon, the yellow trucks comb the city streets.

This cleanliness is what the people want. Every Sunday, they gather in God's temple to sing His praises, to beseech forgiveness, to pray, and to commune. Reverend Peter Newell, Minister of the First Unanimist Church, believes in communion, not only the soul cleansing-wafer-wine-transmutation of sin variety of communion with God—and His subsequent forgiveness for transgressions large and small—but also the communion of all souls, living and dead. It is a commingling of humanity— both past and present—that thrusts its mystical tentacles into the future. "The seeds of the future," says Newell, "are in the present. As ye sow, so shall ye reap. If you sow the wind, you will reap the whirlwind, but if you show mercy and kindness, your rewards will be multiplied on earth and in heaven. The angels rejoice over one lost soul redeemed, but one soul is not enough. God wants thousands, nay millions, to establish His kingdom. Therefore, I say unto you, act in the name of the Lord, and you will be rewarded. Manifest your collective goodwill, help shape the future History of the world, and you will bask in the glory of mankind. No soul is an island. We are all a part of the mainland, and our salvation will be unanimous or it will not be. The miracle is in the whole. Therefore, commune, wash away iniquity, and rally in the name of the Lord."

The congregation is inspired, and, after communion, it chants, "We Gather Together to Sing the Lord's Blessings." The faithful sing with rapture and abandon. The voices of the men and women mingle with the voices of the choir. They rise and fall, swelling in unison, in the united spirit of Christ. They fill the apse and roll toward the nave, gathering strength for the assault on History that will prove manifest destiny and the divine power of multitude. The voices of the adults blend with the high pitched voices of the Sunday-School children in the annex. The men, women, and children sing Reverend Newell's rendition of "Jesus Loves Me":

> Jesus loves me this I know
> For the Bible tells me so
> He is clean and we are not
> He will wash out every spot.

The church organ reverberates with deep booms and high tremolos. The spire aspires, and the sun shines on the faithful. They have gathered to sing the Lord's praises.

Properly cleansed and restored, the people return to their Monday jobs, if perhaps not always willingly, at least somewhat prepared to earn their daily bread ... and more ... much more: cars, appliances, smartphones, cereals, laxatives, shampoos, toothpaste, mouthwash, antacids, deodorants, dog food, pain killers, tampons, videos, detergents, liners, cleansers, bras ... you name it ... every product imaginable. The people want their products ... and on credit, even with high monthly installments. Isn't that why plastic was invented? What's an occasional bankruptcy, as long as the economy keeps rolling? Consume ... discard. It's like breathing in and breathing out ... or waving the flag. Without incentive, what is patriotism?

And, after consumption, what's the incentive of Loviers City? Cleanliness! Or maybe it's the other way around: cleanliness, then consumption. Like day and night, up and down, yes and no, good and evil, you can't have one without the other. If you buy, you must discard; when you pay, you throw away. It's inevitable. So, except for holidays, the trucks make their appointed rounds, scooping up the town's leftovers: Styrofoam, newspapers, fliers, magazines, cardboard, glass bottles, plastic containers, tin cans, and all the empties, with their wrappers and labels, that were once full of beer, milk, wine, soda pop, and soup or cereals, chickens, hamburgers, steaks, hot dogs, and buns, consumed and discharged into the blue recycle bins where they accumulate and wait to be scooped up by next week's arrival of the trucks.

The toters, as they are called, are four-and-a-half feet tall and made of plastic. They have two wheels and a cover whose hinge doubles as a handle. The bottom half is round, but it flares upward into a square section, two-and-a-half feet long by two-and-a-half feet wide. Both sections accommodate a surprising amount of garbage. Each toter has, in white, an identity tag: two capital letters followed by a series of numbers. The blue one, BS 26978, says: RECYCLABLES ONLY—NO DIAPERS—NO FOOD. The brown one, BS 26979, says: SOLID WASTE ONLY. And the green one, BS 26980, says: YARDWASTE ONLY. On the side of each toter, also in white, is Loviers City's stylized logo: a double-cross atop a mission belfry containing a bell. Above the logo, on each dumpster, are the words: LOVIERS CITY. And the mid section of each truck sports on a yellow background a giant, white double-cross belfry-bell, which is based on the Mission Inn. Built by a man who collected bells from around the world, the *fake* mission is the town's main landmark. Now, bells proliferate in every driveway, on every lamppost, and on every truck. And, on Sunday, church bells resonate from one end of town to the other. The *BLUE, BROWN,* and *GREEN* toters serve as weekday echoes of the Sabbath. So, Loviers City functions as one glorified and unified whole.

Mission bells, church bells, dumpster bells, and Saturday-night belles peal every day of the week, vigorously, ceaselessly, and with uncommon zeal, reminding the residents of the city's resolve. The bells can be seen, heard, and felt by all. The proud logo unites the citizens of Loviers City, whose self-esteem grows, even as the waste accumulates in the landfill. The mountain of garbage—their sign of solidarity—confirms the city's objective. There is unanimity, and the bells toll. Loneliness is a thing of the past. No one feels isolated. The spirit of communion reigns. People join hands, embrace, lift their faces to the heavens, and give thanks. Every load of refuse brings the faithful closer to salvation ... and to each other. They bask in the splendor of cleanliness. They believe as one, and their group soul tingles gloriously. It mingles. It is no longer single. There is no room for sadness or despair. Togetherness banishes filth, the stain of sin is removed, and the buff of happiness glows on every kitchen floor. It sparkles, it radiates, and it smiles, shouting the dirt away. Song is in the air. There is gladness everywhere.

In his Sunday sermons, Reverend Newell compares garbage with sin. "Sin," he says, "is the pain we feel when we have acted badly, when we have disobeyed God's commandments. It is a form of surplus, and if we carry it around long enough, it begins to smell. It contaminates the spirit, and it disrupts our lives. It is a weight upon the soul, an unnecessary burden we need not carry. Confess, commune, and conquer. Conquer your redemption. These are the three Cs of a healthy person ... and a healthy community. Repeat after me, all together now ... Confess ... Commune ... Conquer ... That's good ... God's spirit moves in mysterious ways. But if you meet Him halfway, He will take you all the way—all the way to Eagle Mountain, where you will feel cleansed and purified. Renewed, restored, revivified. You've heard of the three Rs? Reading, riting, and rithmetic? Well ... Renewed ... Restored ... Revivified. These are God's three, glorious Rs ... to go with the three Cs. Practice your Cs, and God will reward you with Rs. It's salvation's alphabet, the language of happiness. And it's that simple. Toss out the bad, and replace it with the good. Out ... In ... Out ... In ... Nature abhors a vacuum ... Out with the old ... In with the new." Reverend Newell's mane of white hair adds assurance to his words. His benevolent smile comforts the faithful, and they know the lines on his brow are the furrows of wisdom. He wears the robes of probity, and he walks in the paths of righteousness.

"Idleness breeds sin. And that's why God decreed that we should earn our daily bread with the sweat of our brows. There is dignity in work—in an honest job well done. But the devil exists. And he is here to tempt us, to lead us astray, to guide us down the slippery slope of good intentions. But good intentions are not good enough. Martin Luther once said that you can't prevent birds from flying over your head, but you can keep them from building nests in your hair. I say, discard the nests of evil, shoo away the birds of iniquity, work diligently in the Lord's vineyard, and you will not be burdened by the surplus, by sin. Sing God's praises and you will be rewarded on earth and in heaven.

"You have heard it said that it's easier for a camel to go through the eye of the needle than for a rich man to enter the kingdom of God. And I say unto you, it is not the accumulation of riches that is wrong, but what you do with them that must be questioned. The misers of this world will not be rewarded, not in the afterlife. To pave your private street with gold is to build a slippery slope. Its shimmer is illusory because it's the reflection of solitude. Remember, not alone, but together. Salvation is a collective goal. Heaven is for brethren. Again … all together … Heaven is for brethren. You have also heard it said that two abreast cannot enter through the strait gate. I say that the gate is wide enough to accommodate the multitude and that it will open widely when there are enough worthy souls ready to pass through it. It will always be too narrow for the miserly, for the selfish, the self-centered. They will never pass through it, no matter how thin they are. They could be skin and bones, and it would make no difference. Sin of any kind will always obstruct your passage through the gate. The gate narrows automatically whenever there is sin—the surplus. Therefore, as Unanimist Christians, cast off your burdens and work for the common good: live togetherness. Practice your Cs, and the Lord will give you Rs."

Reverend Newell is admired by all. He is a charismatic preacher, and, every Sunday, the First Unanimist Church is filled to capacity. His delivery is so confident, and his manner so reassuring, that the congregation hangs onto his sentences, believes his message, and envisions salvation. He is so persuasive that, in the middle of a sermon, women of a certain age see him as a reincarnation of the divine. They sit there enraptured, listening to words that fill them with fervor—a warmth that will sustain them through the solitude of another empty week.

MAYOR DAVID GOODHEW, ANOTHER leading citizen of Loviers City, has a solid body planted over two sturdy legs. When he speaks, his ruddy cheeks glow, and his walrus mustache quivers with the authority of salt-and-pepper hair. The mayor's words are as staunch as his demeanor. He walks with assurance and looks you in the eye, squarely, with his own hazel gaze. His laugh booms forth with jovial persuasion. At the Town Council meeting, Mayor Goodhew proposes a new city motto: *Waste Not*. Albert Speer, the Sanitation Engineer, proposes an alternate motto: *Haste Makes Waste*. But Ziad Khalid, Loviers City's most prominent businessman, points out that not consuming is bad for business. He says: "It is also more in keeping with the city's work ethic. Waste exists, waste happens, waste accumulates. We all know that, but that's not our goal. Above all, we want a happy city. Happiness is first and foremost. We want a city in which the residents feel comfortable, at ease, content. We want people to like each other, get along, and play together. If they are happy, they will consume—and *that* is good for business." Khalid emphasizes the word "that" with a knowing inflection of his bushy eyebrows. "We could even say, 'Your business is our business.' How's that for a motto?"

"No, that's too intrusive, too Big Brother-like," says Kathy Konlon, Director of Environment, running the fingers of her left hand through locks of blond hair. Blond curls hug her ears.

Alfredo Garcia, chief of police, seconds Khalid's ideas. "Yeah," he says with a slight Spanish accent, "getting along sure helps to reduce crime. All my men will support that—law and order. That's good. I'll endorse any measure that restores law and order." He removes a black comb from his shirt pocket and combs his hair.

"Jesus H. Christ," says Thomas Jefferson Ohr, the Ombudsman. "Alfredo's on the right track. If I'm okay, you're okay. And if we're okay, then the city's okay. And if the city's okay, I may be out of a job. But that's okay with me." He rests his chin on the clasped fingertips of both hands.

"What's the 'H' for, Thomas?" asks Garcia, chuckling. "Is that to bring you closer to the Jesus?"

"I'm all for that," says Ohr. "When everybody wants the same thing and thinks the same way, there will be less conflict. People will get along. And for the sake of law and order, we should encourage like-mindedness. That will make everybody's job a lot easier—Alfredo's particularly. That's why I think David's campaign and Peter's sermons emphasize the right stuff. We all want good things to happen." He taps his ballpoint pen on the table.

"You bet," says Alfredo, turning his head to the left and to the right. "Our motto on the force is *Crime Means Time*. People want to feel safe." He puts the comb back into the pocket of his blue shirt.

"Maybe we should spike our drinking water with Valium and Prozac," says Speer, wiping his steel-rim glasses. "We did it with fluoride. We could call it Cleanlium, or Cleazac."

Konlon shakes her blond head: "You *must* be kidding."

In the end, the motto *Waste Not* is deemed more appropriate to the city's image of itself. The Council votes on the proposal, and to cheers from the people in the audience, it is adopted unanimously.

The mayor calls the Council back to order. "I have an idea."

His hazel eyes sparkle and his red cheeks glow. "What this city needs is a flag—a flag that will unfurl with pride." The Council members exchange glances, waiting for Goodhew to resume. He says: "How about blue, brown, and green? To match the toters. Three bright horizontal bands of color with the double-cross and belfry-bell logo—in white, for purity of purpose—in the center." Speer shifts his glasses one notch up on his nose, Konlon runs fingers through blond hair, Khalid takes a sip of tea from a white mug with a green cedar on the side, and Ohr tries to assess the mood of the group. After a brief discussion of the pros and cons, and after deciding it's a good idea, the group focuses on the colors. They all agree that blue on top will represent the sky, that green in the middle will stand for the trees and leaves, and that brown at the bottom will signify the earth and walnuts. After all, Loviers City is the walnut capital of California.

"Hear, hear," says Khalid. Goodhew's proposal is adopted unanimously. Henceforth, on every letterhead of every mailing from City Hall, the printing will be blue, green, and brown, a reminder that the flag, waving in the smoggy sky, flaps with the consent of the people: *E pluribus unum.*

Blue, the color of group difference, for the *pluribuses*; *Green*, the color for common goals, for the *unums*; and *Brown*, the color of balance and harmony, for the *pluribuses* and the *unums*. As the flag waves, so does Loviers City. Its colors meld diversity into purpose, purpose into business, and business into happiness. Amen. Buy. Consume. Discard. A-B-C-D.

Once a month, the trash bills go out, and every resident pays their dues, knowing that the money serves a higher purpose. Waste serves as a reminder that only heaven is pure; in heaven, there is no haste. "Heaven has all the time in the world," says Goodhew, "unlike this impure, imperfect, and polluted planet that is sinking and soon will be a stinking hole. Only conscious effort will reverse the trend, only a collective will." Goodhew is eloquent, as always.

On Election Day, the people come together and vote with

their pocketbooks. Like trout to a fly, they rise to the occasion and elect Goodhew because of his appeal to their fiscal good. His opponent, Sally Spooner, whose cause is art and women's rights, has no chance and is roundly defeated in a landslide. After losing, she, naturally, disappears to lick her wounds in solitude. The citizens of Loviers City, as one, choose a mayor who will make them great again, give them heaven on earth, God in the home, and law and order in the streets while lifting every heart with cleanliness.

Mayor Goodhew is a genius. He speaks of a dream where he is a man on a mound, pitching hope, happiness, and humor. In his dream, every player hits home runs. Babe Ruth's and Roger Maris's records are broken, then McGuire's and Sosa's. "Life will be a holiday," says Goodhew, "while I'm managing the team—the home team. Practice makes perfect. And, my friends, you will win. I promise you a winning season."

Loviers City is now a ballpark, and everybody gets to play. But after all of the hot dogs, punch, and banners, there are mountains of discarded cups, napkins, straws, posters, and flyers. With the same urgency as the campaign, the yellow trucks, always ready to serve, waste no time in sweeping up the signs of victory into the Blue Toters, waiting to yield all that unwanted paper into the open jaws of the marauding colossi.

For the victory celebration, the environmental crew, under Konlon's direction, does its job: trimming trees, clipping bushes, and cutting the grass. If not yard waste, what are the Green Toters for? Leaves, branches, flowers, tomato vines, roots, tubers, and weeds—recyclable garden life that grows and dies and will regenerate as compost in its organic time. While not the metal, glass, or paper of the Blue Toters, it is useful in a different and important way. And it is unlike the solid waste—diapers, sanitary napkins, kitty litter, dishes, scraps of food, left-overs, peach pits, orange rinds, carrot greens, coffee grounds, tea bags, banana peels, bones, gristle, and fat—that is unusable and goes into the Brown Toters. All that stuff—surplus matter that comes alive and crawls, flies, and multiplies if not picked up—soon begins to smell. It breeds flies and maggots. Brown is indeed the color that must be at the curb on time. There is a certain urgency. *Blue, Brown*, and *Green* are more than a reminder of cleanliness. They are essential to community well-being, as is the weekly roar of all the trucks.

The trucks are a noisy part of the global enterprise. Export. Import. Buy and sell. Compete. Survive. The world is a store. Invest. Ingest. Digest. Stocks, bonds, futures, and derivatives. Consolidate. Divest. Look for higher interest rates. Dow Jones, Nasdaq, Amex, Standard & Poor's, Dollar Index, P.E., money markets, hedge funds, Asian contagion, and recession. High, low, dip, recovery. Bulls and bears. Oil, wheat, pork bellies, and more. Alibaba. Open sesame.

Loviers City is an octopus. The streets, roads, and freeway are its tentacles, and every house has lines—water, electricity, telephone, cable, and gas—coming in and going out. Trucks rolling in with produce from around the world feed the people's needs. A lifeline. What would happen without them? Or the sewer lines? For Loviers City, any backup or breakdown is disaster, a calamity. Like the truckers' strike that caused the stench of accumulated garbage. Soon after that mishap Reverend Newell compared garbage to sin, and his analogy struck a chord. The white folks nodded their heads, the African Americans said a loud "amen," and the next day, the Latina women swept their driveways with renewed determination.

So, the weekly disposal of *Blue, Brown*, and *Green* is important, essential even, because a breakdown in service disrupts the city's quality of life and threatens its salvation. Its commuting, communing, upward mobility, and channel surfing are challenged whenever the stench of garbage seeps into the nooks and crannies of offices and homes. And when the air conditioning fails … think of it. No, don't think. One whiff is enough.

Each truck gathers its quota of surplus with synchronized

precision. The Blue Toter Truck—full of glass, metal, and plastic—goes to the recycling plant. The yard waste of the Green Toter Truck becomes compost and is resold as mulch. The solid waste of the Brown Toter Truck goes into an abandoned copper mine on Eagle Mountain. It makes a thirty-mile bee-line through the desert to the gigantic pit where food, diapers, dog doo, and kitty litter are dumped into smelly mounds and then redistributed and flattened by yellow bulldozers. The food cooks in the sun. Crows recycle what they can. Sea gulls circle before descending to nip their preferred pickings. The wind blows plastic bags back and forth. Updrafts lift them above the rim of the landfill. They gyrate into the air toward the desert where the Joshua Trees, Yucca, and cactus grow; where the ancient tortoise walks, the rabbits run, and the coyote howls; where the ravens multiply, the range of the sea gulls expands, and the tortoise population declines. It's a small price to pay for keeping Loviers City clean. Out of sight, out of mind. What you don't know won't hurt you. Right?

Soon after the new city flag is unfurled, Albert Speer, Sanitation Engineer, writes a pledge of allegiance that is adopted and, in due course, recited by children and adults at ceremonial functions:

> I pledge allegiance to the flag of Loviers City and to our city that is clean, one asylum under God, lean, unified, indivisible, and mean.

Inspired by such a vision, Alfredo Garcia suggests to the mayor and the City Council that a school uniform would encourage conformity, a uniformity in keeping with law and order. A proposal is batted back and forth, and, after debate, it is adopted by majority vote. Brown shoes and socks, green pants or skirts, and blue shirts or jackets. The new school year imposes the mandatory combination for K through 12. Where once disparate colors prevailed, there are now blue, brown, and green uniforms. Khalid's clothing outlet thrives.

Each class organizes an ecology club, and Kathy Konlon,

Director of Environment, is invited to speak about the importance of conservation. She talks about the future well-being of Loviers City and of the planet. She discusses cancer and the depletion of the ozone layer, the proper disposal of toxic waste, the greenhouse effect and the melting of the polar caps, the need to recycle, and the dangers of asbestos, second-hand smoke, and lead. She discusses the contamination of ground water, food, and air; the unsanitary conditions in the packing plants, salmonella, e-coli, flesh-eating bacteria, and AIDS; the destruction of the tropical forests, the collapse of ocean fishing, and the extinction of species; the junk in outer space, poisoning the seas, drought, el niño, the rising seas, the depletion of the water table, and the imminent worldwide shortage of water; and the bomb, germ warfare (anthrax, ebola, small pox), terrorism, corruption, and fanaticism—all man made, man generated, and lethal.

The students listen thoughtfully, take notes, organize themselves into sanitary squadrons (the SS), and spread out into the community—two persons per squadron and five squadrons per district. The SS has the blessing of the school principal and the town Council. They have the authority to inspect the contents of each toter, and if the refuse does not conform to the color codes, they are authorized to place a yellow sticker on the toter, reminding the resident(s) of their civic duty: recyclables and yard waste should not be mixed, nor should solid waste be joined with other stuff.

The City Council of Loviers City is an unusual combination of people. It functions as one unit. There is little bickering. Disagreements, yes, but the members are reasonable people, they have no axes to grind, and their goal is the salvation of Loviers City. To that end, they inflect their minds and wills and apply their considerable skills to motivate the masses, to get them moving in the same direction, to engineer cooperation, and to make Loviers City a model for the nation. It is a marvelous thing—the well-oiled machinery of unanimity working for the common good.

The garbage strike is heaven sent, and the town fathers use it, capitalizing on the reactions of impatience and disgust, the unanimous revulsion against the previous administration, and the sense that things had gone too far. They reject the laissez-faire attitude of their predecessors. Indeed, the sanitary squadrons inspect not only the toters but also the demeanor of each neighborhood. If a toter has been left at the curb after 8:00 p.m., it's a ten dollar fine. If the grass on a lawn is too long, the SS leaves a note in the mailbox. If a dead tree has been left uncut, that is noted. If a house is in disrepair or needs paint, the SS leaves the names and telephone numbers of handymen and painters.

Reverend Newell implores the residents of Loviers City to think of the SS not as intruders but as good Samaritans, helping one and all. Editorials in the newspaper, the *Loviers City Sun*, admonish readers to act as responsible citizens, to take pride in a clean, well-ordered neighborhood, and to band together for the common good. The editor notes that a beautiful city is a prosperous city, that prosperity is a state of mind, and that the power of positive thinking can, in the united spirit of things, contribute to the ultimate development of Loviers City. In time, says an optimistic editorial, Loviers City will become the best city in the United States. It will top the charts, be the number one place in which to live.

The City Hall Sextet, as it is lovingly called, sings with one voice, and the people of Loviers City harmonize their collective rhythms in concert with the beat of their collective soul. Progressively, they find themselves more and more in tune with what is happening. Inspired by Newell's sermons, Goodhew's leadership, and the general spirit of cooperation, Thomas Jefferson Ohr writes a poem to celebrate Loviers City's newly-found harmony. He sends copies to Newell, Goodhew, and his other friends on the City Council. Goodhew likes it so much he arranges to have it published in the Sunday Arts section of the *Loviers City Sun*. An introductory paragraph tells the readers that this poem to cleanliness and Godliness was inspired by the residents' cooperation, goodwill, and unanimous diligence. It is a tribute to everybody's civic mindedness and was written as an "exploded" villanelle.

DUMPSTERS

Dumpsters make the trash go round
Truckers gather every pound
Eagle Mountain's where they're
Bound to go.

When the garbage overflows.
Blue Brown and Green
They're meant to keep the city clean
No refuse can be seen
To grow because
The mayor's on the go.

Truckers gather every pound
Dumpsters make the trash go round
Sanitation is the city's sound
Response to waste
In its proximity.

Dumpsters keep the city clean
Because no refuse can be seen
Godliness is what we mean
To prove
Loviers City's on the move.

The trucks take the green waste to the recycling plant where grass, tree trimmings, leaves, and scrap wood are ground into a yellow-brown mass that looks like wet hay. Fertilizer companies want it for fertilizer, electric cogeneration plants use it as fuel, and landfills sell it as cover material. Nothing is wasted. Konlon is proud of USBC's program, and USBC is happy to be paid for accepting the waste—and just as happy to sell it. Fees on the incoming side, sales on the outbound. The closest ecological example to self-contained perpetual motion. Inexhaustible. Greenwaste into greenbacks. Total profit. What efficiency. "It's so good it's sinful," says Newell, tongue in cheek.

A city ordinance mandates that old cars, boats, trailers, stoves, refrigerators, toilets, cabinets, and other such treasures be removed from front and back yards. The city promises to help with the disposal. Deadlines are set, and notices go out. There is grumbling, but a bounty on the old hulks oils the wheels of cooperation. "Operation Removal" begins. Compliance takes time. But eventually, the eyesores disappear, and the junkier neighborhoods begin to sparkle with pride.

Many neighbors who had nothing in common, and who avoided each other, connect in unforeseen ways. They greet each other while jogging or walking their dogs, and the pet owners, out of consideration for the joggers, carry poop bags. Whenever Rover poops, the doggie doo goes into the poop bag, and, in due course, it is emptied into the Brown Toter. The residents of Loviers City discuss the city's improvements, and they pause while mowing the lawn, or clipping an oleander, or trimming a liquidambar to discuss the latest proposal, be it the downtown mall, the planting of a traffic divider, or the design of the most recent sign. In addition to Washington and Jefferson, the large street names on the historic avenues that run between Walnut Hill and the river bottom also display the bell and cross on the left and a cluster of three brown walnuts and four green leaves on the right. The name Madison is in white on a blue background, the cross-and-belfry are in brown, and the bell inside is in green. The sign is carefully designed to incorporate the colors of the flag and the symbols of Loviers City.

At other times, imbued with the spirit of civic consciousness, individuals taking their morning constitutional, converge spontaneously on a sidewalk or a street corner, greet each other warmly, and, after exchanging pleasantries, discuss the economy, Wall Street, the sex lives of politicians, and the latest international crisis. Loviers City has a well-informed constituency. Invariably, they comment on the dynamics of group behavior and cluster psychology—the idea that the entity is greater than its individual parts, no matter how smart any one person might be. Collective influence is greater than isolated brilliance.

The local bookstores and libraries record a significant shift from biographies, how-to books, animal books, horror, witchcraft, and zombies to *The Psychology of the Crowd, Group Therapy, Mob Behavior*, and *The Collective Unconscious*. People are amazed to discover that the notion of utopia, so long discredited by cynicism, corruption, and the gridlock of political ideology, surfaces frequently during their discussions. They are amazed to learn that many residents now believe in happiness—that elusive entity so often associated with life and liberty. They believe that happiness is now perhaps within their grasp—if only they can exercise the necessary discipline and cooperation. That's why they lend their support to the City Sextet, not only because they agree with its counsel but also because they believe that leadership is necessary for the kind of concerted action that brings progress. They tweet with a newly found collective pride.

Every Sunday, Reverend Newell's *Hour of Power* is televised on LCRW so that whoever is not sitting in a pew at the First Unanimist Church may tune in to, and be inspired by, the power of positive thinking. Newell's mane of white hair, tanned face, fatherly smile, and urgent message can be seen and heard on thousands of screens. His message of Godliness, cleanliness, salvation, cooperation, unanimity, haste, waste, and consumption fills the hearts and minds of young and old. The choir sings: "He is clean, and we are not; God will wash out every spot." Newell's head fills the screen. He picks up a small brass bell with a wooden handle and shakes it. The metallic sound resonates in every Loviers City living room. "Whenever you shake it, you will hear the tinkling of God's love and compassion, and the sound will remind you of our unanimous purpose." All over Loviers City, thousands of bells ring. The bells are now screen size, showing the image of an eagle soaring over twin peaks. Two fingers hold the handle of the bell and turn it slowly to reveal the imprinted bronze scroll on the opposite side on which, in capital letters, is etched the word UNANIMITY. "You, God, and country united," says Newell. "This is the bell of your commitment—your promise to love and obey. Don't delay. Call UNANIMA now, text us, or email newel@ unanima.com. Visa, AMEX, or Mastercard. Your bell is waiting. All you have to do is send a check or ten-dollar bill to the First Unanimist Church. Or pay online." The choir sings: "Jesus loves me! This I know, for the Bible tells me so …" Newell rings the bell again, and its metallic tinkle echoes simultaneously in thousands of households. Loviers City reaches for its collective wallet. The *Hour of Power* is a city, and the people in it are one.

The following Monday at high noon, a man wearing a Grateful Dead T-shirt and faded jeans walks into the middle of an intersection in the heart of the city and stops traffic. His red beard quivers in the sunlight. Then, under the traffic light, in full view of the Mission Inn, the expanding First Unanimist Church, the Postmodern Library, and the Aggressive Bank of America, the man gesticulates and shouts: "Cleanliness is next to Godliness." At first, motorists and pedestrians are perplexed, but in time, despite the honking of horns and the snickers of those who are amused by this display of eccentricity, they are calmed by the words, "Cleanliness is next to Godliness." He repeats the message, turning militarily to face east, west, north, and south until, in due course, and with traffic backed-up and snarled for several blocks, two uniformed policemen arrive, cite him, and drive him off to jail.

The next day, Rudy Squazza is arraigned, and when the black-robed judge asks him to explain his actions, he answers that it was his civic duty—that cleanliness and Godliness were the messages he has been hearing at the First Unanimist Church and reading about in the *Loviers City Sun*. He produces a clipping of Ohr's poem in support of his argument, and although he admits that neither Reverend Newell nor the *Loviers City Sun* had used that exact slogan—cleanliness is next to Godliness—it was abundantly clear to him and to others that cleanliness was in the air, if not on the ground, and that Loviers City's enlightened policy required action—that the new city flag, the school uniforms, the SS, the color-coded toters, the sermons, and the editorials were all designed to clean up Loviers City and make it Godly.

Squazza insists that he is no crazier than the next person, that he is only repeating what is on everybody's mind, that he intended no harm, that he was in fact acting in concert with Loviers City's unofficial, although clearly understood, policy, and that in the spirit of raising the city's consciousness, he hopes the judge will understand. After explaining himself, Rudy—his homeless friends call him Rudy the Red—pleads no contest and throws himself on the mercy of the court.

Judge Osbourne, a satellite of the City Sextet and a good friend of Garcia's, is sympathetic. He releases the defendant with a reprimand for disrupting public order and interfering with the proper flow of traffic and, for the sake of protocol in keeping with the noonday message, sentences him to two consecutive weekends of freeway clean-up.

At 8:00 a.m. the following Saturday, Squazza reports for the day's detail to City Hall, where he puts on an orange vest and leather gloves and, in the company of drug offenders, petty thieves, and exhibitionists, rides the yellow bus to the designated freeway. There, with the roar of traffic in his ears, the smell of exhaust fumes in his nostrils, and the constant whipping of air currents around his body and legs, he picks up paper wrappers, Styrofoam cups, bottles, and cans. He drops them one by one into the plastic orange bag that he holds in his left hand. Hour after hour the crew picks up months of discarded refuse from a million cars: bags of pot, syringes, dirty pictures, guns, and money. Rudy picks up a one hundred dollar bill. Hot dog. Better than dumpster diving. He has never felt closer to God, and he is grateful to Judge Osbourne for the ingenuity of his sentence. The African Daisies growing along the sloping shoulders of the freeway are, once again, resplendent. They have never been cleaner.

Meanwhile, the *Loviers City Sun* picks up on the incident and runs a news item in the B Section of the paper. CLEANLINESS IS NEXT TO GODLINESS. The piece describes Rudy Squazza's arrest, the slogan, and the aptness of the judge's sentence. Since everybody in Loviers City reads *The Sun*, in no time at all the saying is on a thousand lips. Housewives, while scrubbing their kitchen floors, sing it with variations and tremolos. The SS makes its rounds with renewed vigor, the pooper-scoopers sweep more briskly than before, and the trucks whisk through the neighborhood with greater diligence. The city now manifests more cleanliness and a higher consciousness. These pockets of awareness commune with other pockets of identity, and the people in them feel an internal rhythm that expands and contracts. Depending on the time of day, groups coalesce and dissolve in keeping with habit, custom, and endeavor. They commute, they work, they eat, they exercise, they entertain themselves, and then they sleep.

Soon after the Squazza episode, the city experiences an enhanced sense of contentment—a feeling that God is in His heaven and that all is right with the world. The sanitary squadrons are now greeted cordially. The boys and girls are given cookies and lemonade, even as the roving groups make notations on their omnipresent clipboards. The people are grateful for these reminders that, despite early antagonism, have brought them closer together. They are no longer angry, and no trespasser has been shot. Indeed, the purchase of guns is on the decline, and one

NRA official, while being interviewed on LCRW, asserts that the residents of Loviers City have turned their backs on the second amendment and are no longer interested in individual rights.

Despite such remonstrances, the majority of Loviers City residents agree with the newspaper editorials, Goodhew's pronouncements, and Reverend Newell's sermons. God is watching, the SS is vigilant, beauty is sprouting, and cleanliness shines on the human condition. Nothing has been left to chance, and the word "oversight," which until recently meant to "overlook," now has only positive connotations. It means that no piece of trash will be overlooked, that God is an eye in the sky, and that the people, by their actions, have moved closer to Him and will now be rewarded by rays of divine love. Heaven and earth are indeed closer, the angels are singing, and the Kingdom of God is at hand. The label on Trader Joe's liquid hand soap says, "Next to Godliness hand soap is enriched with a gentle blend of lavender oil, chamomile oil, and tea tree oil with grapefruit seed extract and vitamin E."

CARMEN GRACE—A RED-HAIRED one-time cover girl, now in her thirties, Director of the Arts Council, and sometime essayist—has been trying to make sense of Loviers City's emerging self-consciousness. She has been keeping a journal in which she records her thoughts about events, encounters, incidents, places, and occurrences. Her entries are frequently personal and, now that she is married, describe her relationship with her husband, Tony Thatcher. Of late, however, the entries have assumed a point of view that is more group oriented. She believes that groups form, live, and die according to specific patterns and prescribed routines. For example, in the morning it's coffee, the newspaper, and the editorials that provide direction. Then, it's the labor force on its way to work that gathers momentum. After that, the meetings in the corporate chambers help to focus energy, and, in due course, a gastronomic consciousness prevails in the downtown restaurants during the noon hour. Meanwhile, email, voicemail, smartphones, texting, and Twitter and Facebook solidify the sense of oneness, and these clustered exchanges between people propel them toward a collective self-consciousness. Hungry mouths and ears gather to feed, chat, and gossip. In the afternoon, the business of making money eventually gives way to lassitude—the desire to end the day and return to the smaller entities of family, children, friends, lovers, or solitude. After a drink or two and dinner, zombied residents tune into their favorite television programs, and for several hours, the city oozes into the hazy oosphere of evening entertainment.

Although streaming and television channels serve different menus, for several hours Loviers City is both larger and smaller than itself. Its awareness drifts from one program to another. Nonetheless, whatever the venue, Loviers City communes indirectly with millions of viewers in other cities because every sitcom, movie, comedy, or newscast that generates laughter, musings, thought, or excitement is part of a larger psyche. Eventually, sleep dismisses the day's faxes, tweets, emails, gains, losses, and petty cares, and each dreamer is enveloped in their cocoon of unconsciousness. At dawn, when the alarm sounds and the nocturnal cocoon dissolves, Loviers City begins another day.

Every evening before turning in, Carmen Grace opens her journal and in looping cursive writing records her evolving observations about group behavior. "A group," she writes, "is born, lives, and dies. It exists as an amorphous being in a state of flux that is forming and reforming, sometimes conscious of itself and at other times oblivious of its existence. It can go in many directions. It may evolve, it may grow, and it may decline. The life of the group composes and decomposes. Basically, it's ephemeral, like condensation on your glasses, or on a windshield.

"For example, groups of people in the street form vague entities. They are unstable clusters going this way and that. Unlike the street, however, the line of customers at the Bank of America is more conscious of itself. The queue eyes its head and tail, advances slowly, waits, and perseveres in the knowledge that the last eventually will be first, that a deposit or withdrawal is imminent, and that once the transaction is complete and the teller says goodbye, the line is gone.

"Elsewhere, another group is forming. This time it's inside a department store where customers wander, looking at things, checking prices, thinking of the item they may or may not purchase. They eye the rows of merchandise, the display of objects, and they walk up and down the aisles, conscious of sizes, colors, quality, and cost. If a fire alarm disrupts the calm, the shoppers' haphazard order focuses on the sound. Men, women, and children run for the exits, shout, push and shove, and, after the confusion, gather outside on the sidewalk in small bunches— gesticulating groups that speak. When the red fire engines, with their sirens blaring, roar down the street in one long wail, the group turns its head in the direction of the sound.

"Elsewhere, a collision of two cars at an intersection arouses the curiosity of onlookers. They form a circle and gawk to see what happens. It is an accidental group whose interest focuses on the treatment of the injured, the overturned white sedan, and the blue pickup wrapped around a telephone pole. Flares sputter on the pavement and block traffic in both directions. Here and there are scattered fragments of glass and metal. One body lies on a stretcher under a green sheet. Another person in a neck-brace is lying on a gurney. She is being wheeled toward the open doors of an ambulance. The group thinks of injury, pain, and death. It is curious and subdued, reluctant to dissolve. It is waiting for something more to happen, without quite knowing what to expect. It frets and mills about, wondering whether to go or stay. When the police cars and ambulances leave, people exchange information and express opinions. Gradually, as the bond within the group decomposes, it disperses, and the street returns to its former unconscious state."

C.G. stops writing (her friends call her C.G.), closes her journal, turns out the light, and pulls the covers up under her chin. While falling asleep, she thinks about her life, Loviers City, and the lives of groups. She dreams of Tony with his light brown hair.

It is Saturday evening. Music lovers gather in the city auditorium for a performance of Beethoven's Ninth. Latecomers thread their way toward the few remaining seats. It is an elegant crowd, dressed to the teeth. The orchestra is tuning its instruments—violins, cellos, and oboes. There is the audible murmur of voices, and the eyes of the audience are on itself. The auditorium has identity and class. The crowd knows why it's there, and it glows with an expectant self-satisfaction, an air of superiority, anticipation, and contentment. When the conductor appears, all hands clap unanimously; he bows. And after he taps the baton on the podium and raises his arms, a collective silence envelops the hall. The music commences and the spirit of Beethoven reigns. Spacetime expands with the sound of strings, brasses, wind instruments, and drums. After intermission, when the human voices of the chorus join the symphonic roll, modulating its harmonies and rhythms, the words of Schiller's "Ode to Joy" rise and fall, amplified and reverberating throughout the hall. The collective soul of the men and women, the singers and the audience, resonates gloriously. Life's vicissitudes are forgotten. Death seems less certain, contingency disappears, and the people no longer feel mediocre, unimportant, or lost. Space contracts, and for the duration of the concert, the auditorium basks in the illusion of immortality. There is no past or future, only the present. Beethoven has suspended time. He is space itself, and he is a god. The Ninth Symphony reigns supreme.

The next day, Sunday, members of the congregation of the First Unanimist Church, having experienced the deification of the auditorium by Beethoven's Ninth, arrive early, sensing that Reverend Newell will have something important to say. He does not disappoint them. He explores the feelings generated by Beethoven's music the night before, and he talks about its contribution to the idea of social improvement. He says that philosophers from Plato and Aristotle to Nietzsche and Bergson have stressed the impact music has had on human behavior and social mores, how music has influenced, educated and directed human lives and the masses. Newell pauses, raises his eyes, and looks out over the heads of the congregation. He looks into the living rooms of Loviers City and many cities elsewhere, where his message is being heard. A vast audience reverently listens to what he is saying.

"In Athens," says Newell, "drama belonged to the people. Thirty thousand assembled there to celebrate Dionysus. Think of the Middle Ages and the artisans who built Chartres and Notre Dame. Think of the faithful watching the religious spectacles that took place in the square, in front of cathedral doors. What an impressive phenomenon: Greek tragedy, medieval liturgies, and later, the festivals of the French Revolution, all stressing group participation, the forging of bonds, and the celebration of an ideal. Beethoven's music does all this because it is a force telling us that life is to be lived. It manifests joy and sadness, pleasure and pain, happiness and despair, good and evil, and the alternating triumph of day and night. To the question, 'Should we?' Beethoven answers, 'We must … we must!'"

Newell stresses the role that men and women play in constructing a community. He emphasizes the importance of cooperation and goodwill. He says music can play an important role in bringing people together. He cites the symbolism of Beethoven's chorus and the melding of voices with the sounds of instruments. He says: "Together they erase differences between nature and culture, the unconscious and the conscious, the individual and the group." His white mane waves with comfort and wisdom. When he emphasizes the role of the church in modulating behavior, specifically the role of The First Unanimist in developing the higher consciousness of the group, the congregation nods in agreement. When he stresses Unanimist power and its work for the general good, the flock murmurs its approval. Newell highlights the role of music in bringing men and women together. He praises the arts in general, because they can provide order, direction, and structure to life. "Art," he says, "can be an antidote to chaos."

Having experienced the deification of the auditorium by Beethoven's music, Reverend Newell and Mayor Goodhew believe it is time to apply the dynamic of group behavior engendered by the arts to Loviers City. Carmen Grace, also a church member and ardent supporter of Loviers City's symphony orchestra, concurs. She and Goodhew both believe that modern art has lost contact with the masses.

"We need to harness experience," says Goodhew. "Music and poetry can be the leaven for social order and cultural progress. We need to encourage the creative efforts of individuals who can influence the psychic life of a group. If we succeed, Loviers City will have an awareness of itself that will give it cohesion, purpose, and strength … even beyond the colors of the flag and the tolling of the bells. Think of it, an entire city working together. If that can be my legacy, I'll die happy." Goodhew's hazel eyes beam joyfully, and C.G.'s smile dances ironically across the red highlights of her hair.

"And we can have a funeral procession with recitations by local poets, music by The Lost Wandering Blues and Jazz Band, and dramatic improvisations. We will rejoice over your coffin, sing Bacchic refrains, and commune with the collective soul of all mourners. How would you like that? I know I would. My death could energize a return to the origins of artistic experience, one that all could share in, not just a few. And we will play Wagner and pretend that music has its source deep in the collective unconscious of the Folk." C.G. gives her words a mock-heroic tone, and her red ringlets sparkle.

"Mock me if you will," says Goodhew, good-naturedly. "But the artwork of the future will combine music, dance, and poetry. It will be a total art form."

"Why don't we put it to the test," says C.G. "I'll organize a poetry festival, if City Hall will pay for it, and we'll see what happens."

"You're on," says Goodhew. "Let the festival stress freedom and love, and our city will be transformed."

After preliminary discussions, and with Goodhew's strong support, the City Council votes to increase the Arts Council's budget, and, to honor the occasion, C.G. proposes a poetry contest for the city and its environs, one that will focus on the group with attendant possibilities for collective engagement. All agree that the focus of the contest will not be on old chestnuts, such as unrequited love, nature, and a poet's agonized psyche, but rather, on the deification of a group.

In the Arts Council's flyer and in the *Loviers City Sun's* news dispatch, the contest rules, in addition to a first prize of five hundred dollars, stress Unanimist sensibilities: the street, the square, the church, the auditorium, the stadium—places where groups exist, places where the soul of collective consciousness manifests itself. The deadline for submissions will be November 1, in three months. The winning entry of five hundred dollars, and the runner-up for three hundred, will be announced Thanksgiving weekend—the day the turkeys are roasted. There is some opposition to this idea from people who say that you can't legislate art or morality, but for the most part, the idea of brotherhood and sisterhood overrides the objections of the purists and the legalists. The city's mood of goodwill prevails. The flyer is circulated and posted on street corners, bulletin boards, and the web. The word is out, and all poets, established and aspiring, are eligible to submit their work: three short poems or one long one, nothing longer than two pages.

C.G. appoints a committee of judges: Nora Silber, who teaches English at Loviers City High; Gregor Rissotto, a professor at City College; and Benjamin Wilson, the owner of the Moby Dickens bookstore. The decision of the judges will be final, and the date of the award ceremony and reading will be announced in the newspaper. Loviers City is abuzz. Never in its history has a poetry contest caused such excitement. The students in Loviers City high school English classes and the creative writing classes at City College—as well as the patrons of Moby Dickens and the three coffee houses where art and aesthetics are dispensed, inhaled, and swallowed with each cup of java or mocha—sharpen their pencils and their minds. The idea of the self, alone and isolated, recedes and is replaced by the idea of the group—the collective self.

Unfortunately, the first submissions extol mob rule. One poem is about lynching and white-robed Klansmen. Another is about rebellion and looting in the city, hateful grist for the poetry mill of Unanimism's prize. These early entries banish the individual, in accordance with the guidelines, but reason, moderation, cooperation, and the idea of brotherly-sisterly love are lacking. The tone is definitely one of bigotry and intolerance.

C.G. reads these poems, barely able to contain her dismay. They are no more than rantings of hate. She is outraged, and she adds her name to the panel of judges: two women, two men. That seems fair. She rereads one of the poems:

ODE TO GOOD AND BAD

White is good
They are bad
Pure a virtue
Tolerance so sad.

Hate is good
Black is bad
Misogyny has merit
Equality's a fad.

Might is good
Love is bad
Except for us
When we're not mad.

There are two more stanzas but C.G. stops reading. She wonders about the contest and what it may have unleashed. Where do such people come from, and how many are there? Where is the goodness to which Loviers City aspires? Are these poems a backlash to cleanliness? Clearly, the submissions are within the rules but not in the spirit of the contest. She calls the mayor to express her reservations, but he tells her that the contest cannot, and indeed, should not be canceled. C.G. tells him that the poems are politically incorrect and the mayor says that November 1 is a long way off. Nonetheless, C.G. sends the most egregious poems to Goodhew, and he, in turn, hands the names and addresses over to Garcia. Garcia wants to initiate strict surveillance of the goings and comings of the persons behind the most radical submissions, but the city lawyers advise against such measures. Wilson is also against surveillance because, he says, it smacks of censorship. He reminds the committee that there is no place for censorship in the arts. "Robert Mapplethorpe's homoerotic photos and the Piss-Christ sacrilege may offend Jesse Helms, but then you wouldn't want Jesse Helms judging this contest, would you?" Wilson strokes his white beard thoughtfully and looks at his colleagues with an expansiveness that is almost Whitmanesque. Although there is no consensus, the City Council, which has been buoyed of late by Loviers City's good will, is profoundly disturbed.

Garcia blames the Arts Council for unleashing the devil, but

Newell remarks that it's better to have Satan out in the open than lurking unseen in the river bottom. "The fact that you're not always aware of him doesn't mean he isn't there." Speer, Ohr, and Konlon concur.

"Where does that leave us?" asks Garcia.

"Where we were before," says Goodhew. "A hateful poem is not a criminal act. There's nothing to do except rely on the good judgment of the prize committee. When they come up with winners, we'll disseminate them vigorously."

The Post Office delivers more envelopes, and as time passes, arson, murder, and dismemberment give way to less violent poems, to more thoughtful renditions of group consciousness. C.G. no longer reads the submissions as they arrive but puts them in a pile for distribution to the panel of judges.

CARMEN AND TONY THATCHER have a long-distance marriage. He is Professor of American History at the University of Texas, Austin. She joins him every other weekend. He does the same in Loviers City. Although they love each other, a love enhanced by the obstacle of separation, they enjoy the advantages of two incomes: money and independence. Of late, C.G. has been trying to reconcile the distance between Texas and California and what it means to be a split couple. What is a unit of two, and how do separate people form a whole? She is beginning to understand the dynamics of group behavior, but how, she wonders, do two individuals fit the mold?

She likes being married. She feels more secure, less dispersed, and able to focus on her job at the Arts Council without worrying about her social life. She has friends, both men and women, and after a long day in the office, she enjoys their company. But contact with them is not essential to her well-being, whereas contact with Tony is. What's the difference? There's sex, of course, and shared interests. But these might be present with other men. What is so special about Tony? Yes, he is attractive, sexy, intelligent, and honest but so are many others. Why him? Can it be chemistry? The touch of his skin? Their backgrounds? Their genes? Animal magnetism? All of these, no doubt … and a certain commitment. She is always thrilled to see him, to hear his voice, to feel his arms about her, to listen to his ideas, and to laugh at his wry sense of humor, his play of language, and his irony. When they are together, she feels like a better person— more alive, more interesting, more complete, more curious, more of everything. Their shared intimacies round out her life, and their separate careers in no way challenge their identities. They are not jealous. Tony encourages her in her job, and she is thrilled that he likes his. For the most part, there is a meeting of their minds. Neither bullies the other. Disagreements occur, but they are not perceived as threatening. Each one feels secure in the knowledge of professional independence.

C.G. feels that their commitment to each other is not only intellectual but also visceral. They share a tactile link—the magic of touch—whenever their fingers, hands, and lips meet, whenever they embrace. She loves the smell of his body, the feel of his back, the pressure of his thighs. She believes that the fire in their lovemaking comes from a blue core of desire, from the earth itself, and when the glow of orgasm flows through every sinew, rolling, wheeling, turning forever, it seems, on the waves of his rhythm and hers, stroking, melting, and opening in slow motion, as though the petals of her love were dilating and her essence trembling like a vast cosmic rose. She feels the oneness and completeness of their union.

The range of their relationship both captivates and fascinates her, unlike the one-night stand with the photographer on a Bahamas shoot where, an aggressive camera, its hypnotic clicks, the sand, the waves, the sun, and her red hair spilled over into the night when the day was done. Sudden sex may have had its challenge and pleasure, a certain exoticism, but the brevity of the connection had all the anonymity and haste of two lonely pedestrians walking down a street. They barely existed, whereas she and Tony survive, even when apart. Despite the distance, their bodies retain a psychic bond, a life in hibernation waiting for the resurrection of their next encounter.

When she is with Tony, it is always summer, and the bushberries are plump and ripe and succulent. Sometimes they melt in her mouth, and at other times, they pucker her cheeks. But the flavor is astonishing, and the surprises are constant. When Tony is a resilient birch, she is the bluebird in the nest. When she feathers the wind, it sings through his branches. Their melody bends the forest and the animals it keeps, and despite their urban lives and the prosaic conveniences of technology, the metaphors of their lovemaking weave back and forth with natural design.

Is this what it means to be a couple? C.G. sighs as she writes, wishing Tony were with her. Her sentences fill the blank pages of her journal, and her thoughts gather the meaning of her words. Together, she and Tony are the smallest unit. Their bodies, together in love, are a god. There are other gods, larger ones, but they are harder to comprehend and even harder to control. How do you govern or patrol a street, an intersection, an auditorium, the church, the city, the state, Wall Street, the nation, the Internet? How do you regulate an entity when voluntary compliance fails? Each unit contains varying degrees of energy, but none, she feels, is as potent as her love or the bond she shares with her husband. She doubts that larger groups can somehow draw on the heat of the core and the vision of the cosmic rose, because she knows that people are decentered, that interests collide, that ideologies differ, and that power politics is blunt. "Nonetheless," she writes, "it's pretty to think so. No wonder people and nations fight."

THE SUBMISSIONS FOR THE poetry contest continue to arrive, and the piles of priority mail and manila envelopes are stacked high into four piles, one for each judge: C.G., Wilson, Silber, and Rissotto. C.G. wonders if the quality of the writing will have improved, if the idea of group consciousness will generate something beyond intolerance. She thinks of the Holocaust, of *Mein Kampf*. She thinks of the Nazis, the rhetoric of hate, and the megalomania of power. Hadn't Hitler himself conceived of the nation as a living organism and every citizen in it a cell within the body that was Germany? Hadn't Hitler also thought of the Jews as a virus, as pathogenic cells needing to be killed? C.G. thinks that sometimes it is easy to pervert the good, that language is malleable, and that people frequently lend their support to deranged leaders. She thinks that Hitler was able to galvanize a nation and lead it toward destruction. She thinks that leaders have always been able to mobilize the mob, tap into its collective energy, and exploit the unconscious loss of self. But not all leaders are bad. Some are good. Others, perhaps, are even divine. Indeed, every Sunday, in every Christian church, Christ lives. And His crucifixion, whatever the interpretation, is sufficient to animate the spirit of the congregation, be it Catholic or Protestant. For Muslims, Allah is present in every mosque whenever the faithful gather for prayer, and all eyes are turned toward Mecca, the city from which He calls. Money also speaks, and the world's markets rise and fall in concert with the vagaries of the economy. The force of Wall Street is as potent as religion. Sometimes investors are the only believers.

C.G. pauses in her reflections, pauses long enough to compare Loviers City's example with historical precedent. Where will it end? Will the efforts of Newell and Goodhew bear fruit, and will it be the fruit of righteousness? Who will be the judge? Is the Godliness of cleanliness the proper course to pursue, and is it right for Loviers City? Time will tell, of course. So far, so good. Maybe the poetry contest will illuminate something.

AUGUST WHIPS INTO SEPTEMBER, and September slides into October. The nights are cooler and the sun less intense, but the aridity of Loviers City keeps the river dry. The palm fronds flap against the sky. Tony and Carmen meet twice a month, love, fly, and work, reenacting the ritual of unity whenever the forest of their passion sways and the cosmic rose unfolds. Goodhew pitches his winning games, Newell spreads the gospel of the group, Garcia ministers to law and order, and Thomas Jefferson Ohr is still okay. Wilson tends shop at Moby Dickens, Speer perfects his truckers' gear, Khalid multiplies his profits, and Konlon protects the endangered butterfly. The Sanitary Squadrons make their rounds, the neighbors gather daily in little groups, the workers earn their weekly pay, and the poets of the city write, thinking they believe in what they say.

AS FAR BACK AS anyone can remember, the crow population in Loviers City has numbered in the thousands. The birds' black feathers gloss purple in the sunlight whenever they strut insolently across a back yard, turn over a sycamore leaf, or poke the grass with their beaks looking for bugs. When surprised, they fly into a Jacaranda where they perch and caw, flexing their necks and chunky bodies with a prolonged cah, kahr-r-r-cah. And every afternoon, at sunset, they leave their feeding grounds and fly west toward the river bottom where they spend the night in the cottonwoods. Their flights take them over Loviers City in loose formations of a dozen or more, the primary feathers of their wings etched fingerlike against an azure sky tinged with rose. Occasionally, one crow dives toward another, leaving the other bird to flap alone. New flights appear, always moving west toward the rookery. When the sun sets, shadows settle over the cottonwoods, the bushes, and reeds. The river bottom turns quiet.

At sunrise, the crows leave their rookeries and fly east toward Eagle Mountain. Sometimes, rival bands fly toward shamel ash trees or magnolias, and the angry cawing of warring factions becomes a loud and noisy confrontation. The tribes occupy the crowns, turning them black, as restless birds flap, ascend, circle, and caw. The cacophony is intense and the droppings substantial. Cats run for cover, dogs howl, and even the red-tailed hawks are no match for a murder of crows. Incensed swimming-pool owners draw canvases over the water, gardeners cover their heads and shoulders with plastic bags, and car owners drive their autos into the garage. The avian population is exploding, and bird droppings cover the sidewalks. Smog may be bad for your health, but a black sky and a shat-upon city make life intolerable. Goodhew receives daily letters from irate citizens demanding that city hall do something to alleviate the scourge.

The crows' eating habits are a problem. They raid the walnut groves, split the green rind, and fly off with the nut. Walnuts are now raining on Loviers City. Thousands of big, brown walnuts are falling from the sky. The shells break on pavements, sidewalks, and driveways. The streets are littered with broken shells and green husks. The chickens are scared. Every roof of every house reverberates with nutty hail. There are now walnuts in the flowerbeds, walnuts bobbing in the swimming pools, walnuts chipping the paint on cars, and walnuts bouncing off people's heads. Khalid's store experiences a run on hard hats.

The crows have blighted the community, and the City Council meets in order to discuss the problem. What to do? The birds are a source of noise pollution, and their droppings are unsanitary. They violate the city's code. They must go: extermination. For Kathy Konlon, a decline in the crow population means a reprieve for the endangered desert tortoise. She lends her support to a proposal to eradicate the birds. The Council asks her and Speer to formulate a plan. The war on crows begins.

Every evening after sunset, men armed with shotguns raid the river-bottom rookeries, shooting crows. At night, the residents on the bluff overlooking the river listen to the blasts. They also watch the beams of flashlights crisscrossing the branches of the trees. The men set baited cages. Soon, heaps of dead crows are added to the landfill. After that, batches of solid waste treated with poison are dumped on Eagle Mountain. Loviers City residents see the war as an extension of Godliness. Others say the cure is worse than the disease. Several weeks pass, and the draconian measures make no dent in the bird population. The complaints resume, and the Society for the Prevention of Cruelty to Animals rises up in arms. It asks for a moratorium on the poisonings. It wants an environmental impact study, but the City Council says a moratorium is premature and the study inappropriate. The eradication program stays in place.

Speer wants aerial spraying at night, but Konlon says that any poison strong enough to kill the crows will destroy other river-bottom species. "All the birds will die," she says, "not to mention snakes, lizards, rodents, and the like." She opposes all forms of spraying. She also has reservations about the landfill poison but rationalizes its use as a measure of last resort. The crow carcasses are bulldozed immediately, and the area is secured by a tall chain-link fence to keep the coyotes and wild dogs out.

Charles Gum, an ornithologist at City College, tells Konlon that a more efficient long-range solution to the problem requires the use of bird lice—lice that are selectively toxic to crows. He suggests Mallophaga, a particularly virulent bacterial mutant that will not affect other birds. Konlon likes the idea, and she persuades Speer to initiate the process. Sacramento authorizes the use of Mallophaga, and the state toxicology laboratory sends two hundred vials of the lice. Konlon, Speer, Gum, and his student assistants load the cannon and *boom*—it fires a large net over the crows on the Eagle Mountain landfill. One by one, each of the eighty-two crows is laid out on its back, wings spread on a flat wooden board, while lice are applied to the axillars and underwing linings. After the application, the crow is released and it flies off with loud caws and an indignant flapping of wings. These crows will contaminate others and the population will decline. It's not easy because crows are hardy, wary, and hard to capture. The next day, Gum readies the cannon, but few birds show up. He proposes another solution. Instead of poisoning the solid waste going to Eagle Mountain, he laces it with a chemical that knocks out the birds long enough for operation louse to take effect. In a matter of days, the process doubles the number of crows contaminated with the bacterial mutant. Konlon estimates that some two hundred have been treated, and all the lice in the two hundred vials are now crawling under the feathers of crows. "Will the procedure work?" asks Speer. "Time will tell," says Gum. The team disbands. Konlon wants Goodhew to be patient.

"How long?" he asks.

"Several weeks, a month, maybe more."

"I don't think the growers will be happy."

"Since when was it your job to keep the growers happy?"

"Ever since they helped elect me."

"I see," says Konlon. A wry smile lifts one corner of her mouth. "We've done all we can. If they have other solutions, let me know."

Walnuts still rain down on Loviers City with a continuous staccato tattoo. The motorized sweepers crisscross the city streets, and their revolving brushes sweep the broken shells into the refuse chamber. It's all part of the waste-recycling program. Meanwhile, the crows' voracious appetites affect the profits of the growers. They see no reduction in the number of birds. They pressure City Hall to do more. Over Konlon's objections, the mayor continues to fund the shotgun program. Konlon says that Mallophaga-infected birds will be killed, but Goodhew says he has to appease the growers.

THE RIVER BOTTOM IS not only the crows' home, it is also home to the homeless, a rag-tag group that lives in improvised shacks lined with cardboard. Blue tarps keep the rain out. A pepper tree provides shade. It's an ancient specimen, the oldest in the river bottom, and its lacy branches hang down to the ground. The canopy is so vast and so opaque that nothing grows beneath it. There, on hot days, it is always cool. The fern-like leaves of the terminal branches sprout foot-long stems, two inches apart, and each stem has narrow, elongated saw-toothed leaves. They are half an inch to three inches long. Crush them, and the sap is white and sticky. The leaves are fragrant, even pungent. In the fall, clusters of rose-colored berries hang at the ends of slender branches, and when they drop, they form a rose-and-brown carpet of peppercorns that is soft and springy.

The tree's base is deformed, and its circumference has been shaped by time and the elements. Five men holding hands can barely encircle the perforated trunk. The bark is gnarled, sinuous, convoluted, and muscular. It has grown arms and shoulders, and one bulbous protrusion resembles a head. It looks almost human. The tree belongs to the crows that nest in it and to the homeless whose hovels cluster in a nearby grove of Arundo donax, a giant cane. The shacks are situated in an opening where the cane shelters them from the chill of autumn winds. In the daytime, the crows fly off to Eagle Mountain while the homeless raid Loviers industrial dumpsters looking for food, wood, cardboard, and clothes—useful discards that sustain them. They collect empty cans and bottles and put them in borrowed carts from the supermarket. As they push the carts, the wheels clatter over the grooves in the sidewalk.

At night, the homeless listen to the sound of shotguns. Unable to sleep, they wonder how long they will have to endure this intrusion into their refuge. They gather around campfires and gripe about society's ills. They have no bone to pick with the crows. For as long as they can remember, they have shared the river bottom with the crows. Indeed, they see the birds as kindred souls wandering the skies in search of food and shelter. The crows are their sentinels and their alarm system. The intrusion of a stranger or a wild pig sets off a chain of caws that is passed on from one tree to the next. Sometimes, the police raid the river bottom. At such moments, dopers conceal joints, syringes, and plastic bags. They hide in the thickets. But now, after a dozen sleepless nights, the homeless have had enough. They abandon their shacks for the discomfort of benches in the city's parks. They lie in ragged sleeping bags, inside cardboard boxes, or under ratty blankets. They also occupy the boathouse by the lake, and their fires leave charred circles on the grass.

At first, Loviers City's residents don't know what to make of this occupation of their recreational spaces. Their interludes in the parks and on the lake are being interrupted and besmirched. The benches are taken, the lawns are charred, and the paths are littered with plastic bags. Children no longer play on the swings, slides, and jungle gyms. Visitors are accosted for handouts, and lovers are spied upon. Dismay gives way to annoyance, and annoyance turns to anger. As the anger mounts, residents send irate letters to the *Loviers City Sun*. What has happened, they ask, to Loviers quality of life? First, it was the invasion of the crows, and now, derelicts possess our parks. How much longer must the city endure the blight? What has happened, they ask, to the cleanliness campaign? Whose city is it anyway?

It's no longer Newell and Goodhew speaking; it's the people. There is a slow, rising tide of middle-class indignation. What is happening to our city? What do the colors of the dumpsters, uniforms, and flags symbolize? Are they not the signs of the new order? And isn't a new broom expected to sweep cleanly? First it was garbage, then litter, and now it's crows and bums. Earlier problems have been addressed. Excellent. But what about the winos? Are they not the leftovers, society's dregs and outcasts, no better than refuse? Why should Loviers City have to put up with the smells, the inconvenience, and the annoyance of useless people wandering the streets and infesting the alleys? If cleanliness is next to Godliness, then clearly the homeless are ungodly. They don't work, and idleness breeds trouble. Look at the parks! The people point out Goodhew's promise of baseball, but, so far, the only players are the homeless. No matter what, these people smell. They are ugly and dirty—undesirable. They are unproductive dopers. They are sinners, unlike us. They don't belong. Indeed, they are a form of social garbage, parasites. Would you entrust your child—your daughter—to one of them? If surplus is a sin, idleness a vice, and doping degenerate, then deportation may not be good enough.

Such is the tone and content of the letters to the *Loviers City Sun*. The working residents of Loviers City have come together and are now enjoying a newfound sense of identity. It's an identity based on virtue—the virtue of cleanliness and Godliness. They believe that Loviers City is theirs, and they do not want it spoiled or occupied by outsiders. Khalid says the bums are bad for business. "They keep the customers away." And the people say: "Make 'em go." *Go Away* is the new motto.

The City Council meets to discuss the crisis, and at the end of the meeting, Goodhew instructs Garcia to have his men evict the homeless from the parks. There is much grumbling on the part of the destitute, and they manifest their discontent by marching on City Hall. Rudy the Red, wearing his Grateful Dead T-shirt, leads a group of ragged protesters, some fifty strong, down the street. They wave makeshift placards outside the Council chambers. They chant their demands: "Save the crows and let us sleep!" Policemen arrive and disperse the protesters. Their presence is illegal—no marching permit. There are scuffles and the officers arrest two militants. It's an angry crowd that shuffles off into the city's streets and alleys. The group's resentment burns and smolders. Several protesters gather inside the Chinese gazebo, next to the Postmodern Library. They light cigarettes and blow smoke in nervous, frustrated puffs.

At sunset, the homeless return to their shacks in the river bottom. The crows accompany them. The homeless huddle around fires on which they cook meager meals put together from other people's leftovers. They mutter obscenities and rage at the injustice of their plight. They share five-gallon jugs of red wine and puff on joints. Outstretched hands glow in the fire's reflected light, and red faces pucker and swell with repressed anger. One woman with unruly strands of gray hair mumbles: "We won't take it anymore." An old man wearing a buffalo-plaid shirt says: "We've had enough." Others say: "How long are we going to take it? We've been pushed around for years!" A black mood, dark as the night, envelopes the outcasts. The wine and the pot soften their despair, but as the evening wears on, Rudy Squazza's resentment grows. His red beard bristles, inflamed.

The nightly shooting of crows resumes, and the men with their flashlights and guns are thrashing through the underbrush, picking off crows from the cottonwood branches on which they are roosting. The birds fall to the ground. With each thudding crow, the hearts of the homeless skip a beat in empathy. As the jug of wine circulates, feelings of thud, skip, and beat arouse the men and women. The guns are blasting, the group's blood is up, and the crows are dying. The wine, the night, and the gunshots stir outrage.

Rudy Squazza thinks of the time he dropped out. He thinks of his refusal to join the eight-to-five rat race and his unwillingness to be a part of the money making frenzy. He feels wounded in some vital core of his being—wounded by his parents, his teachers, and even his peers at the bank who have gone on to make millions and now occupy important rungs on the economic ladder. He refuses to climb and does not want to grovel. In his mind, the two are inseparable. He hates policies that export CIA violence to protect dictators and business interests abroad while mouthing civil liberties at home. He hates bigotry and ignorance. He knows he should do something about them but feels unable to organize his life. He finds its ambition disturbing. More and more, he rages at others and himself, and whenever he feels cornered by authority, the iron fist of the peremptory, something in him snaps and another self takes over. When that happens, he does things that he later regrets, such as failing to show up for work. For a time, he was a model carpenter, an exemplary mason, and a trusted painter, until his inner demons took over, souring a good work record and causing him to be fired. In the end, he decides it is easier to dumpster dive and let the devils dance.

Rudy takes another puff on his joint, inhales, and holds his breath. He exhales furiously, and his red beard glistens in the fire's light. He picks up a stick from the fire and waves it in the air, forming a circle with the burning tip. "Burn 'em," he says between clenched teeth. "Burn 'em." He jabs at the fire with the stick. "If we can't sleep, neither will they. What d' ya say?" He circles the fire, twisting his body this way and that. His knees rise to meet his chest in a frenzied dance of feet, body, and waving arms. He coaxes the group to act, cajoles and exhorts it. The fire dances in his eyes. "We can always rebuild. That's easy. But we'll make 'em take notice. For them, we're nothin' but scum, and nobody cares. Next time they'll be shootin' us. I'm tellin' ya, with people like Goodhew an' Garcia, things'll never change." Rudy's voice grows louder and his gestures more delirious. He appeals to the group's fears and pent-up resentment: the years of discomfort, the hunger, and the cold. "And now, this intrusion. When'll it end?" He looks at each man and each woman. "All we ask is to be left alone. They have taken our dignity away. City Hall has ground us down, and the mayor's heel presses our faces to the pavement."

The wine bottle is empty. Someone tosses it, and it crashes into the bushes. Rudy puts more wood on the fire and pokes the red coals with the stick. He works on the mood of the group, arousing its enmity and coaxing the embers of its discontent. He says: "Burn." The gray-haired woman says: "Yeah, burn." The old man wearing the buffalo-plaid shirt mutters: "Burn." One by one, young and old repeat the word "burn." It's on everybody's lips. The word spreads. BURN is now an angry crowd. Sparks glow and embers fly as the group explodes like a bursting star. Burning sticks fly into the thickets of Arundo. Yellow tongues of fire ignite the dry stalks and parched grass. The people pick up their belongings and in single file follow the dirt path toward the bluff. Once on top, they drop their stuff and turn around. They watch their shacks, one by one, burn and collapse.

The fire spreads. Gusts of wind whip the flames toward the southwest. The flames consume the grass, the desiccated bushes, and the parched Arundo. The blaze advances, coalesces, and ignites the dry vegetation. The fire swirls, illuminating the silhouettes of tree trunks. The fire crackles, hisses, and roars. Soon, it is a wall of red, yellow, and black. The flames climb the trunk of a tall palm, and the crown bursts brightly. Sparks and embers arc into the night. Animals ululate. Dogs bark, and the occasional squeal of a wild pig rips through every other sound. Wings of birds whir. Rudy watches a ball of fire hop toward the bluff, where it stops. He goes to inspect. The hind leg of a rabbit gives one last spasmodic kick.

The homeless hear the wail of sirens, which is soon upon them. The fire engines stop with a growl, and the firemen descend, watching the fire advance toward the bluff. The pepper tree is enveloped in flames. Its crown billows smoke like a censer, and the smell is fragrant. The branches touching the ground catch fire, and soon, the tree is a burning waterfall. The houses on the bluff are not in immediate danger. The men with the shotguns come alongside the firemen. One homeless man says: "Who done it?" Another one says: "What happened?" A woman's voice says: "It's the crow brigade that done it." More voices repeat the words: "Crow brigade!"

The accusation spreads like the fire. The words "get 'em" ignite the dry grass of homeless anger, and the homeless move as one to encircle the men of the crow brigade. A rock strikes one man on the head. His legs buckle, and his gun rattles to the pavement. A shot is heard, and the men regroup. With their guns pointing, they stand back to back, facing the homeless. The firemen focus a spotlight, point their hoses, and turn them on. The radio on the nearest rig crackles and sputters.

The following day, the *Loviers City Sun* reports the fire and the altercation. The confrontation is downplayed. No one is seriously injured. But the problem of the homeless is again urgent. They have reclaimed the parks, and the residents of Loviers City are furious. At the next meeting of the City Council, the auditorium is filled to capacity, and when the mayor brings the meeting to order, one group after another demands action. The walnut growers want faster progress on the crow front. The residents want their parks back. Rudy Squazza asks for a long-term solution to the dilemma of the homeless.

"You can burn down our shacks and force us out of the parks, but that's not a solution. What are you going to do when the county has ten thousand homeless? Shuffle us from one place to another, like a pack of cards? I may have chosen my lifestyle, but others have not. Men and women who can't take care of themselves and need medication. They can't help it. Where did you think they would end up when the governor of our state closed the mental hospitals? Disappear? It's a disgrace! We deserve social services, food, and a place to sleep."

The mayor acknowledges the legitimacy of Squazza's demands and says the Council will address them. "But it takes time," he says before describing the Mallophaga intervention and its long-term prognosis. He assures the walnut growers that everything possible is being done to protect their interests. He tells Rudy that, in the short run, the city will help rebuild the shacks in the river bottom. Until then, the homeless can use the parks. "Who knows, maybe by the time your dwellings are finished, the shooting will have stopped."

"What about a long-term solution?" says Squazza.

"We'll try to come up with one," replies Goodhew. The meeting ends, and everyone is—more or less—dissatisfied.

Halloween is in the air. The autumn wind blows yellow bands of leaves across the lawns. Pumpkins and jack-o-lanterns smile and snarl. A low-flying witch—complete with green gloves and black, pointy shoes—collides with a sycamore. Her arms and outstretched legs embrace the trunk. She sits on her broomstick, waiting for the children to notice her conical hat, long hair, and flowing cape. The children are dressed like goblins, devils, and skeletons. They ring doorbells: "Trick or treat!" They receive candy, chocolate, raisins, apples, and walnuts. They clutch bulging bags and run from one door to another.

Witchcraft animates every house. Also present are the souls of the dead and the shrill laughter of children. Loviers City swirls with give-and-take, the movements of disguise, and the fun of make-believe. Ghosts hide in the shadows, and vampires suck the blood of victims. The tricksters tingle with excitement, and their parents smile indulgently. Small groups form in the dark, burst into the light of hallways, claim their prizes, and dissolve into the night. Their amorphous bodies flow from one street to another, pause, spread, regroup, and coalesce. Scary costumes slink around corners, past bushes, and the glare of orange faces. Goblins exist, and Loviers City is alive with the spirit of Halloween.

ON NOVEMBER 1, C.G. places twenty envelopes in each of the four designated piles. She delivers them to the other three members of the jury with a note asking them to select three winners. The note says that at 4:00 p.m. on November 15 the judges will meet in her office to discuss the twelve best poems. Then she will Xerox copies for further evaluation.

After the meeting, the judges take the twelve best poems

home. They agree to rank them and meet again in three days in order to select the finalists. C.G. sits down in her favorite chair, puts on her glasses with the green rims, takes a sip of herbal tea, and begins to read. They're not bad. None of these submissions is politically incorrect; the bigotry of the earlier entries is gone, replaced by a more-or-less successful rendering of group identity. There are poems extolling African American freedom, Latino consciousness, Native American identity, LGBTQIA pride, feminism, the psychology of non-violence, the church, the homeless, an auditorium, a stadium, the soul of the Republican Party, and the unity of workers. C.G. ranks them all, one to twelve.

When the four jurors meet again, C.G. writes the titles of the poems on the blackboard and the rankings of each jurist. One is the best score and twelve the worst. The lowest cumulative score wins. After all the scores have been added, the four winners are: "Women Arise," "You the Audience," "Yankee Stadium," and "Homeless." C.G. sends copies of the four poems to Goodhew and then makes the necessary preparations for the poetry reading at the Thanksgiving festival on Saturday. Since the admission is free, she looks forward to a good turnout. Meanwhile, suspense is growing. Only the jury and Goodhew know who the finalists are. *The Sun* agrees to print the ballots. The poems will be read, and the two winners announced by popular acclaim. *The Sun*, the web, and flyers have been publicizing the event for days. There will be free food and soft drinks and a cash bar for those who want hard stuff. How can it fail?

The orange pumpkins of Halloween now color preparations for Thanksgiving, even as the witches' brooms keep Loviers City clean. Supermarkets vie for customer allegiance and advertise the saving power of spending. "Buy more ... Let's go shopping ... Everything's on sale ... Early-bird specials ... Super sale ... Two for one ... The holiday begins." Animated ads claim to have the fattest turkeys west of Plymouth Rock. Pilgrim cutouts wearing tall hats, black clothes, and white collars hold wild turkeys. Jingles—*A free bird here, another one there*—chant the freedom of the founding fathers, exhorting customers to buy chicken, ham, steak, cranberries, stuffing, nuts, yams, potatoes, gravy, butter, spices, vegetables, oranges, persimmons, pears, grapes, wine, juice, coffee, tea, mints, cake, ice cream, and pies— pumpkin, apple, pecan, peach, cherry, and mincemeat. Eat, drink, and celebrate because it's Thursday. Loviers City stuffs itself, and at the forward-looking First Unanimist Church, the homeless get a free meal with all the trimmings. On Friday, the yellow trucks roar through the neighborhoods, gather the solid waste, and race each other toward Eagle Mountain where they dump the food that feeds the crows and gulls. It's a long holiday weekend. Surfeit. Waste. American eagle. The sun shines, make hay, and throw away.

It's a clear Saturday evening. The moon is full, and several thousand people have gathered in front of the Mission Inn, waiting for Santa Claus to flip the switch that will illuminate the Festival of Lights. Four people are standing on an improvised platform. C.G., the Festival Chair, reminds the crowd that the Poetry Festival will take place at eight o'clock in the auditorium. Patrick McHugh, the owner of the Mission Inn, introduces the mayor. Goodhew takes the microphone, welcomes the crowd, and eases himself into a short speech laced with baseball, apple pie, Christmas cheer, good will, and peace. He thanks the people of Loviers City for their participation and generosity, for their patience and understanding, and for their cheerfulness that is so in keeping with the spirit of the holiday season. "You have turned this city around," says Goodhew, "and the city thanks you." He gestures toward a fat, red-clad, white-bearded Santa Claus. "Now, on with the show." Santa throws the switch, and a million lights go on. The crowd gasps, and an "awe" of admiration bonds the group together. Light cascades down six buttresses of the Inn. The tiny lights on the crowns of the trees in the courtyard and on the sidewalk next to it wink and blink. Dressed like characters in a Charles Dickens novel, animated men, women, and children move their arms and heads as though waving to the people below. Some blow horns, some play violins and cellos, while others hold packages tied with red and green ribbons. One group is singing a Christmas carol: "O Come, All Ye Faithful." They look like Victorian ghosts, ancient figures of another century gesturing to the crowd and sharing their faith in giving and celebrating the holidays. There is gladness and glee. The faces of the children are dazzled, and the adults are happy. Even the jaded teenagers respond with reluctant admiration. Everything sparkles. The lights in the trees and the eyes of the revelers reflect each other in alternating currents of wonder and joy. Thanksgiving and Christmas coalesce into one colorful, illuminated display. The crowd jubilates. It has become the god of lights, and its collective body is excited, its mind electric, and its attention convivial. The Festival of Lights warms all hearts. *Joy to the World.*

Eventually the people disperse. Peripheral entities are the first to slip into the shadows. Then, larger clusters separate and walk around the Inn, admiring the lights and the animated figures. In due course, the god of lights is composed only of fragmented units moving this way and that. They have no self-consciousness, and their existence is ephemeral. Most lack direction, except for the hungry people going home for dinner and those looking for a restaurant. There is a line of diners outside the Pepper Corn. Another line is waiting outside the door of Gloria's. Food may be uppermost in their minds, but it is not written on their faces. Many are thinking of the Poetry Festival and looking at their watches. They soon will be gathering by the auditorium plaza fountains where the tall jets glitter in the light of oval lamps. At last, the doors open, and the crowd pours into the auditorium. The ballots are handed out, and the seats are occupied. Unlike the Beethoven audience, this one is less formal, disparate, and louder. The Lost Wandering Blues and Jazz Band plays RELAXIN' AT THE CAMARILLO, and the sounds coming from the pit augment the group's contentment. In attendance are people of all ages and races: Caucasians, African Americans, and Latino Americans, plus a sprinkling of Asian Americans, a few Native Americans, and some Chinese Americans. There also is a large contingent of homeless people sporting beards and hats and wearing odd clothes: ratty shawls, leather vests, and worn-out sneakers. Several empty rows separate them from the other spectators. C.G. hopes the food will last.

The doors close, the lights dim, and RELAXIN' AT THE CAMARILLO fades. C.G. walks into the spotlight in the center of the platform, and her voice, purring, thanks the audience for the good turnout. She thanks the mayor and the *Loviers City Sun* for their support. She thanks the panel of judges, the auditorium manager, the electricians, the support staff, and last, though certainly not least, Ziad Khalid's restaurant, The Pepper Corn, for the free food and refreshments in the lobby. All present are invited to partake—loud applause, a few whistles, and many "yays." C.G. says: "The poems will be read in random order. After all four have been read, each person should mark the ballots one to four, in order of preference. The poems are printed on the ballot. Write 'one' next to the title of your first choice, 'two' opposite your second choice, and so on. After the poems have been read, while you help yourselves to food and refreshments in the lobby, the ballots will be counted, and the two winners will be announced." Cheers and whistles.

C.G. introduces the mayor, and he goes to the podium. Loviers City's blue, green, and brown flag hangs from a staff on the left side of the stage, and the state bear-flag hangs on the right side. Goodhew's cheeks glow in the spotlight, and he throws some nice and easy pitches to the crowd. He praises Loviers City's civic pride, the trash collectors, and the SS. He thanks everybody for their collaboration, interest, participation, elaboration, cohabitation, transportation, and tolerance. The crowd cheers. More whoops and whistles. The music of the jazz ensemble punctuates the mayor's pronouncements with the JELLY-ROLL BLUES. The lights dim momentarily and a puff of smoke envelopes Goodhew. When it clears, a tuxedo-clad magician and a sexy, ponytailed brunette in a bathing suit walk briskly to center stage. They do a hat-and-rabbit trick, an elaborate rope-of-many-colors-handkerchief trick, a disappearing act, and a swords-in-the-box act. The crowd roars its approval. More JELLY-ROLL BLUES, applause, and flickering strobe lights. More smoke. The suspense mounts. The mayor reappears and introduces Grace, Silber, Rissotto, and Wilson, the four readers of the poems. There are now four chairs on the platform, arranged in a crescent around the podium. The mayor walks to the blue-green-and-brown flag and unfurls it with a sweeping motion of his right arm. Long applause.

"And this," he says, "is our piece of resistance." He gestures toward the sexy brunette. She bows obligingly, flicks her ponytail, and wiggles her butt. "Seriously though," says Goodhew, "the real *pièces de resistance* are the poems, and that is why we have gathered here this evening—to honor our poets. Everything else is frosting on the cake. You are the judges, and the names of the two winners are in your hands. The poets have written their poetry for you, and you, in turn, honor them with your presence. You and they are the yin and the yang, the hand and the glove, and the ethics and aesthetics of our collaborative endeavor. Now, on with the show. May the best man or woman win." Applause and more JELLY-ROLL BLUES as Goodhew, the magician, and the ponytailed woman walk off stage. Gregor Rissotto stands and approaches the podium, shielding his eyes as he looks out into the auditorium. He wears a beige sports jacket, a light blue bow tie, and his balding head glistens in the light.

"This is a poem by Larry Foote from City College." Loud cheers. "The title is 'Yankee Stadium.'" Rissotto shuffles several pages, clears his throat, and reads the first stanza:

YANKEE STADIUM

"Play ball!" he said
   The wind-up pitch
A strike
   Soars into a sky of
Blue and white enmeshed
   In Coca-Cola red
And thirsty fans who pause
   Then leap and cheer
And roar
   In manners now refreshed.

Rissotto pauses, coughs twice, and picks up where he left off:

An oval cause
   Uplifts the stadium
And carries it beyond
   The banners
Flapping in the wind
   The yells bounce off
The Goodyear blimp
   —That floating boat—
And rise like helium
   In fervent throats.

When Rissotto reaches the third stanza, he pauses again, takes a sip of water, and wipes his glistening head with a white handkerchief:

"Home run!"
   Shouts the joyous
      Crowd as
         One
Hundred thousand lungs

Of fun
All cheering while
    The runner races
Round the summer bases.
    When the ball drops
Beyond the score board
    Yankee fans in
Unison cry out
    "Two to one."

Rissotto grins, and applause fills the hall. He bows, thanks the audience, and takes his seat. There are a few dissenting calls: "Yeah, Padres," and "Go Red Sox," and "We're for the Giants." The crowd, however, is pleased, and the jazz ensemble plays an inspired HONEYSUCKLE ROSE. The stagehands remove the chairs, and the readers go off stage. Under very low lights, the magician and his accomplice reappear and in slow motion do a fancy levitation with a hoop that threads the woman's body through, inside and out again. Oohs and aahs emanate from the audience as the stiff supine body of the draped assistant ascends and descends. More HONEYSUCKLE ROSE, followed by a flash of light, white smoke, curtain, auditorium lights, and the smiling and bowing presence of the magicians. Wild applause and the lights dim.

When the hall quiets down and the lights come back on, the four readers are again sitting on stage in a semi-circle. Nora Silber stands and walks briskly toward the podium that pops up in front of her as if by magic. She wears a black dress, a necklace of yellow amber, and amber earrings. Her black hair is streaked with golden highlights.

She says: "This poem was written by our local and highly-acclaimed poet, Pamela Ostrow. It is dedicated to the women of the world in general and to the women of Loviers City in particular, because we have nothing to lose but our shackles. Its title is 'Women Arise.'" Silber squares her shoulders, and the amber necklace sparkles. She begins:

WOMEN ARISE

Men rule the world
    They govern
The lines of their authority
    Mark the limits of our lives
And the boundaries of our
    Dependence
The subjects we are taught
    In school
Define our expectations and
    Outline opportunity
Men expect their wives to listen and
    Obey
    Have children
    Cook and clean
And when we say that's not enough
    They bray obscenities
They want us to remain
    Subservient
Imprisoned by their codes
    They preen and strut
They earn their dominance
    They say
They also say we are too lenient
    Too close to nature
    Too Emotional
    Unclean
    We cannot learn
Love us they say
Embrace us
    And we do
        But fire rages

We are mean sometimes
Despite our signature
And we burn unhappy

Knowing that
Man's geometry is false
That his squares confine our
Dignity
    Compress and corner us
    His angles violate the
        Circles
      Of our sensibilities and
    Frustrated
We sometimes scream
But men hear only
    Sentiment
        They do not tolerate the
        Curves of our
          Rebellion
They muffle desperation
With aggression
Thinking that power suffices
To restore the balance
And undo the harm
Of silence
Hail women of the world
    Unite   Rebel
Speak out
        Claim your freedom
Assert your independence
        Grasp the Holy Grail.

The women applaud enthusiastically, but the applause from others is neither wild nor subdued. It is dubious, although accepting. Silber scans the auditorium. The crowd is not homogeneous, and it lacks cohesion. The applause from a contingent of African Americans and Caucasians on the left is more vigorous than the clapping of the Latinos and the homeless on the right. She notices that the people have not seated themselves at random, as she had supposed, but rather according to clusters of ethnicity—identity. There is a sprinkling of Asian Americans. The homeless and Native Americans are oddly segregated. The applause from the Latinos is at best lukewarm but hot from a small group of white women who are now standing in order to demonstrate their support. Silber is not surprised, only disappointed that applause for the feminist cause is not more pronounced. Why don't all women want freedom? Are they happy in their bondage? Does inequality suit them? She attributes their acceptance of second-class status to ignorance and the weight of cultural baggage.

Silber's thoughts are interrupted by the receding podium and the wail of a bagpipe. She turns and walks off stage. The stagehands remove the chairs. A Scottish piper appears. He walks forward, followed by six dancers dressed in yellow-and-black plaid kilts, matching knee socks, black vests, and white blouses. They step forward nimbly, one by one, while the piper in his kilt and matching hat squeezes the leather bag under one arm, puffs out his cheeks, and blows. The girls do a lively Highland Fling with elaborate footwork, flexing knees, pointing toes, and turning bodies. Their arms form arcs above their heads. The piper's elbow presses the bag, the chanter plays its melody, the drones sound the keynote, and the fifth and the reeds wail. The dancers' teeth shine brightly and the pleated skirts twirl and flounce and bounce. When the performers finish, the audience cheers with abandon. The dancers take their bows and skip off stage in flashes of black lines and yellow checks. The applause is unanimous and the enthusiasm sincere. The hall is of one mind, and temporarily, it puts all difference aside in order to express its pleasure in the music, the dance, and the talents of the girls. There is one large manifest body of happiness. The dancers reappear, bow several times, and skip off stage.

With the clapping still vibrating in his ears, George Wilson walks on stage. He wears a broad smile framed by a massive white beard and flowing white hair. A cane accompanies his limp. The podium rises to meet him, and he hangs the cane on the rim. He adjusts his horn-rimmed glasses, raises both arms in an embrace of the audience, and says: "Welcome." The audience applauds, still held together as one by the sound of the bagpipe and the dancing steps of the highlanders. All eyes are now on Wilson's white beard and mane of white hair. Many think he is Santa Claus himself. He says: "I hope the Highland Fling has set the tone for the poem I am about to read. I hope the unanimity holds. This poem, entitled 'You the Audience,' is by Chauncey Trapp. Those of you who frequent the library know Chauncey, and he needs no introduction from me. Suffice it to say, this remarkable poem is for all of you. It is all of you." Wilson clears his throat and reads in a low, modulated voice:

YOU THE AUDIENCE

You the people in the crowd
    Today
Listen to my voice
To what I have to
    Say
You are the mass
    Assembled here
The unformed clay of
    Yesteryear
Listen to my words
    Heed
These stirrings—
Another kind of unity
    Will bind
The breath of my intent
And mold you into

> One—
> Grasp this poem
>   You are mine
>   Heel
> Feel the transformation
> Let the syllables of time
>   Reform your mind
> Your will be done
> Your spirit like a dove
>   Ascends
> You are a god
> You are in love.

Wilson finishes reading and takes off his glasses. The crowd is puzzled, uneasy, and not certain how to respond. No one in the audience has ever been addressed so directly by a poem or its author. Seldom have so many people felt violated, insulted, and coerced. Never have they been asked to desert their individualities and abandon their bodies in favor of a group entity and its collective soul. The crowd is apprehensive, unwilling to shed one identity for another, and reluctant to move toward the deification—the consciousness of itself as a larger entity—of a cellular regime. For one brief moment, selfishness, bias, and the ready-made—in concert with the SLAM SLAM BLUES—give way to the larger model, but as the sound of the modern jazz fades, the divisions in the auditorium reassert themselves. The applause is mixed. The clapping is polite and contained in the back but fairly exuberant in front. It is not regulated by divisions of color or ethnic background but by something else, something beyond race, something approaching the human.

Wilson wonders if such confrontation works. He wonders if the subliminal coercion of television commercials, much as he hates them, isn't more effective as an agent of persuasion. After all, commercials appeal to unconscious desire, to happiness, the longing to be loved, the fear of difference, and the death wish. It must work because the economy is like one big merry-go-round and all consumers love to ride the animals of the money machine. Buy, buy, buy. Shop until you drop. Instead of persuasion, this poem wants unconditional surrender, and it asserts itself brutally—almost like rape. Who wants forced submission instead of involuntary collusion? And, after compliance, then what? Are people better off? This conscious broadside is only symbolic, of course, but why would a group submit to the intrusive rhetoric of a poet and, by extension, the oratory of any politician? But then, good politicians also appear on television. Is television the only reality? Social media may well have taken over. These ideas course through Wilson's mind as he listens to the audience's fragmented applause. When do you decide that the leader's ideas are imposed, and when does the group select him or her voluntarily? How do you get things done, and what do you want? The clapping, although not truly victorious, lasts longer than Wilson had expected, and when it finally subsides, and the clown and the acrobats of the next act bound on stage, he believes that "You the Audience" might have struck a chord.

Two clowns collide, do a pratfall, and waddle about in their floppy, red-and-white polka-dotted clothes. The face of one clown is white and happy; the other face is black and sad. Their noses are round and red. The acrobats leap over the clowns, jump backward and forward, somersaulting in the air. Then they climb each other like a human ladder until two are standing on the shoulders of the man below—three in all. They brace their bodies for the fourth acrobat who, somersaulting upward from the balancing board, lands on the shoulders of the third man. The four-man unit sways momentarily from the impact, and every knee bends to absorb the shock. Balance is restored. Wild applause from the crowd and heartfelt strains of the JELLY-ROLL BLUES. The sad clown kicks the happy one, and the performers take their bows. The spirit of play envelops the hall. The audience is glad. Warm feelings circulate, and pleasure prevails.

It's time for the fourth and last poem. The readers are back on stage, sitting in their chairs. The two floodlights focus on the podium, and C.G. walks toward it. Her ringlets of red hair tremble in the light. She tugs on the jacket of her dark-green business suit, adjusts her green-rim glasses, and says: "The fourth poem you will hear this evening is by Rudy Squazza, a long-time resident of Loviers City. Its title is 'Homeless.'" Lusty cheers from the homeless in the audience. She begins:

HOMELESS

We are the homeless
We live in the park
What do you do there
After dark?

We are the wretched
We wander the streets
We push our carts
In search of treats.

We are unwanted
They say we're no good
We ransack garbage
To find our food.

We are the winos
Who lounge in the square
We sleep and brood
Nobody cares.

We are in limbo
Society's dregs
We fare badly
On our last legs.

Give us a place
To call our own
We should not beg
To find a home.

It's not too much
That's all we ask
We're all alone
Loviers City
Rise to the task.

There is a moment of silence, then vigorous applause from the homeless, followed by polite clapping from the others. Everybody remembers the park issue and how contentious it has been. Even if the audience's reaction is less than enthusiastic, C.G. welcomes it. The homeless shacks have not been rebuilt, the parks are still occupied, and the people of Loviers City still chafe. Although she understands the public's animus, C.G.'s sympathies are with the homeless. She wishes Goodhew would find a shelter for them.

IN THE BASEMENT OF the First Unanimist Church, the homeless are served a frugal meal on every Wednesday of the year. And each Thanksgiving, church volunteers cook a complete dinner for the less fortunate. C.G. helps out and has been happy doing so. But lately, help has been sporadic. Everybody is angry about the parks, and many Loviers residents think of the winos as waste. Despite *The Sun's* solicitations for food and clothes, the response has been sporadic. C.G. thinks of the cost: two hundred dollars feeds eighty people. That's not bad. She wishes the city would do more but doubts that much will happen until the unwashed get roofs over their heads. Judging from the applause, their poem will probably not win. The house lights go on. C.G. asks the audience to mark the ballots and hand them to the ushers.

As the people move en masse toward the food in the lobby, C.G. eyes the rug at her feet. Its pattern is composed of large, dark green diamonds on a beige background, and inside each diamond is the city's double-cross and bell-in-belfry logo. C.G. notices that many of the boys and girls milling about are wearing school uniforms: blue, brown, and green. C.G. oversees the counting of the ballots in the room next to the ticket office. The results are interesting, although not unexpected. Four hundred forty-three votes are cast for "Yankee Stadium," two hundred eighty-six for "You the Audience," ninety-six for "Women Arise," and sixty-two for "Homeless." C.G. writes Larry Foote's name on the winning certificate and the five hundred dollar check. She writes Chauncey Trapp's name on the second prize certificate and the three hundred dollar check. Honorable mention certificates go to Pamela Ostrow and Rudy Squazza. C.G. joins Goodhew in the lobby, where the jazz ensemble is now playing SERENADE TO A SHYLOCK. The food is going fast, and there is a line at the cash bar. Goodhew makes his way to the microphone, tests it, and says: "We are ready to announce the evening's winner and distribute the awards." With modest gestures, broad smiles, and happy handshakes, the four recipients claim their prizes. Rudy Squazza says he wishes he had a wall on which to hang his certificate. There is unanimous applause. The food, the drinks, and the modern jazz are working their magic on the crowd. The people are happy and the decibel level is high … very high. Eager fingers reach for Buffalo wings, shrimp, meatballs, cheese dips, vegetable dips, cauliflower clusters, crackers, bread, ham, salami, cold cuts, pineapple chunks, strawberries, grapes, and shelled walnuts. There is now food on paper plates, and people balance them in one hand, a beer or a coke in the other. C.G. circulates with a glass of wine in hand. Midst the happy ambiance and general hubbub, she catches a phrase here and a word there— conversational fragments, odds and ends, and snippets of this and that. She drinks the new wine and listens to the phrases hang together, like an exquisite corpse.

HAVE YOU TRIED THE SHRIMP? ... ALL I WANT IS A NIGHT IN THE BLUE ROOM WITH NICHOLE KIDMAN ... IRAQI HEAD SEEKS ARMS ... GENERAL CUSTER WAS A POMPOUS ASS ... THE TOBACCO LOBBY PAYS HOLLYWOOD TO SMOKE ... IF NIETZSCHE LIVES CAN GOD BE DEAD ... I CALLED YESTERDAY BUT NOBODY ANSWERED ... THE UNVEILING OF THE NEW MARTIN LUTHER KING STATUE ... TWO DEAD CROWS IN MY SWIMMING POOL THIS MORNING ... DRUNK GETS NINE MONTHS IN VIOLIN CASE ... RUSSIA IS IN FREE FALL ... TOO MANY WALNUTS ... I'VE ALWAYS BEEN A YANKEE FAN ... NO ONE SELLS BOOKS BETTER THAN OPRAH ... HOW WOULD YOU LIKE A TWO MILLION FATWA ON YOUR HEAD? ... BRETT ASHLEY WAS AN EMANCIPATED WOMAN ... I FELL OUT OF A DUMPSTER AND BROKE MY LEG ... HAVE YOU READ THE MANUAL OF DEIFICATION? ... NOTHING SUCKS LIKE ELECTROLUX ... SAVE SAN IGNACIO LAGOON ... MITTERRAND'S MISTRESS WAS AT HIS FUNERAL ... SHE WANTS TO BE THE BRIDE OF CHUCKY ... THE UNIFORMS STINK ... NEVER WITHHOLD HERPES INFECTION FROM LOVED ONES ... RAYMOND IS ON JURY DUTY ... YOU SHOULD TRY THE MOD ARCHIVE ... THE ROAD IS BETTER THAN THE INN ... YOU COULDN'T PAY ME ENOUGH TO SLEEP WITH MABEL ... HIGH SCHOOL DOPERS CUT IN HALF ... NEVERMORE ... SHE HAS A GREEN THUMB ... AMERICA BRINGS THE PEOPLE OF THE WORLD TOGETHER ... NINETY-FOUR ILLEGAL IMMIGRANTS DIE OF THIRST IN THE DESERT ... WHEN QUEBEC SECEDES WE CAN OCCUPY THE REST OF CANADA ... ENRAGED COW INJURES FARMER WITH AX ... I ADORE APOLLINAIRE ... BELIZE WAS A BLAST ... I WISH I COULD SWIM LIKE A POLAR BEAR ... THE HOMELESS ARE EATING ALL THE FOOD ... I BET VAN GOGH COULD RELATE TO EVANDER HOLYFIELD'S EAR ... THE HOSPITAL IS BEING

SUED BY SEVEN FOOT DOCTORS ... ONE OF MY HENS IS A ROOSTER ... SHIRLEY IS THREE MONTHS PREGNANT ... THE MAYOR IS AN S.O.B. ... GOOGLE UNANIMA ... THE KURDS DESERVE A HOMELAND ... OBESITY STUDY LOOKS FOR LARGER TEST GROUP ... WHO'S AFRAID OF JASPER JOHNS? ... THE IRAN CONTRA DEAL WAS NOTHING COMPARED TO THE CIGAR ... NEXT MONTH WE'RE GOING UP THE YANG TSE ... ROBBE-GRILLET SHOULD HAVE WON THE NOBEL PRIZE ... MINERS REFUSE TO WORK AFTER DEATH ... I WANT TO GO TO BELLAGIO ... I'LL CALL WITH THE RECIPE ... TRAVEL IN ASIA IS A BARGAIN ... THE RACCOONS SHAT ON MY ROOF ... I WROTE SIX LETTERS FOR AMNESTY INTERNATIONAL ... MY COMPUTER CRASHED ... RED TAPE HOLDING UP BRIDGES ... THE WEATHERMAN SAID WE'D GET RAIN ...

C.G. gets a refill of white wine and joins Wilson and Silber by the shrimp table. She puts four crustaceans on a paper plate, dips one in red sauce, and slips it into her mouth.

"Good show," says Wilson. He takes a sip from a plastic cup filled with bourbon and ice. Silber raises her cup of white wine.

"Cheers," she says. They touch cups.

"Where's Tony?"

"He couldn't make it. Had to grade midterms." Goodhew joins the group.

"Congratulations," he says. "It's a triumph."

"We couldn't have done it without you," says C.G.

"Nonsense. You deserve all the credit."

"If you insist." They banter back and forth, flattering each other. The shrimp on the table is all gone, and the hungry mob is now devouring the meatballs and Buffalo wings. The faces in the lobby are black, white, brown, gray, pale, and flushed. They are all talking, eating, and drinking to the sound of DARK EYES.

"How much did all this set us back?" asks Wilson, leaning on his cane.

"Thousands," says Goodhew. "But it's worth it in P.R. The

contest couldn't have come at a better time, considering our problems with the crows and the homeless."

"We were lucky with the poems," says Silber. Her amber earrings reflect the light. "But I'm disappointed the feminist one didn't do better. I thought it was the best. And the lines where the square shapes of man's authority violate the circles of a woman's sensibilities were, I thought, brilliant."

"Perhaps," says Goodhew. His cheeks are ruddier than usual. "What do you expect in a community with traditional values?"

"I understand the reasons," says Silber. "I'm just disappointed, that's all."

"Everything being equal," says Wilson, "baseball will always carry the day. Still, I was pleased 'You the Audience' did as well as it did, considering the chutzpa of the author. Not that I blame him. Chauncey is one aggressive dude." There's a spot of red sauce on Wilson's white beard. C.G. reaches with her napkin and blots it. "Thanks," he says.

"The credit is all yours," says Goodhew, smiling through his mustache, "and the poets too, of course. You folks selected winners that deify the group. That was important. That's what Loviers City is about." He lifts a bottle of Bohemia and drinks. "I'd better keep circulating. Keep the constituents happy." The three other jurors refill their drinks and shuffle toward the platters of fruit. Silber puts one strawberry and two chunks of pineapple on her plate. She spears one pineapple with a toothpick and pops it in her mouth. Out of the corner of one eye, C.G. sees a woman with gray, stringy hair. . The woman, who is wearing a faded red jacket with a tear on one elbow, looks around and surreptitiously slides a slab of Brie into a Bullock's shopping bag.

"They prefer food to poetry," says Wilson.

"The jazz helps," says C.G., chewing the strawberry.

"As for audience reception," says Silber, "the Beethoven concert was better." She fidgets with her amber necklace.

"There's a lot to be said for an evening of total music," says Wilson. Not that this evening's variety was bad. But it didn't have the same cohesion."

"Can you envision an evening of poetry only?" says C.G. "We'd be lucky to get an audience of fifty."

"Let them eat food," says Silber. Wilson chuckles. "There never was cake."

"But we do have our homeless."

The Sun's HEADLINE SAYS: MAGICAL EVENING. The reviewer gives the festival high marks and prints all four poems. He describes the enthusiasm of the crowd, the jazz, the Scottish dancers, the Chinese acrobats, the Las Vegas magicians, and the food. Goodhew is pleased that the reviewer highlights the aesthetic of the group and its point of view. He refers to "Yankee Stadium" as a living entity whose cells are the baseball fans, whose joy is delirious, and whose reactions to the home run are unanimous. The reviewer also likes "You the Crowd" for its audacity and for the way the poet forces the attention of the audience, compelling it to think of itself as a whole. "It's in the metaphorical sweep," he says, "in your willingness to accept group consciousness." He also praises "Women Arise" for its feminist sensibilities and figurative language. As for "Homeless," he says the poem calls attention to their plight in exhortations that are both appropriate and moving. The review also pats the mayor on the back for attracting such a large crowd and for bringing together the colors of the flag, the *Pluribuses* and the *Unums*, and diversity and unanimity, not to mention talent extraordinaire. He hails the beginning of a new literary movement, one that Walt Whitman had hinted at in "*Salut au Monde,*" which, with Loviers City's unusual ethnic diversity, can now embrace everybody. "The world has come to Loviers City and Loviers City is the world. We are they, and they are us." The mayor folds the morning paper, drains his coffee cup, and smiles. Things are perking. If only the crows would fly away and the homeless with them.

Goodhew peruses the morning paper, and his eye catches a headline: BODY FOUND IN WALNUT GROVE. "That's all we need," he says out loud before smacking the paper with the palm of his hand. He calls Garcia on the phone.

"Fernando? It's David. How are you?" After the preliminaries, he says: "Whose body is it in the walnut grove?"

"Some woman," says Garcia. "Strangled and dumped. It's Khalid's grove."

"Shit," says Goodhew.

"You said it."

"Any motive or suspects?"

"Not yet. But we're looking."

"Keep me informed."

"I will."

A few moments later, after Goodhew hangs up, his phone rings.

"Hello?"

"David. It's Ziad."

"What's up?"

"You know the night shooter who was injured during the river-bottom fire?"

"Yes."

"He died last night."

"No! How?"

"At home."

"I thought it wasn't serious."

"So did the hospital, when they released him."

"Jesus."

"I want those homeless prosecuted," says Ziad.

"But we don't know who threw the stone."

"Damn it, David. They're all guilty."

"I know how you feel, Ziad, but we can't prosecute everybody."

"Why not?"

"It can't be done."

"We'll see about that! Just for the record, I'm calling my lawyers."

"Don't be impulsive, Ziad. I'm looking into the shelter problem, and we have promising leads."

"Giving them shelter is not the solution, David. We need to get rid of them."

"That's easier said than done."

"For you, maybe. As far as I'm concerned, they're outta here."

There is a loud thud on Goodhew's roof. He walks across the patio onto the lawn and looks up. A crow is in the rain gutter with one black wing hanging over the side. "Jesus," says the mayor. "It's raining crows!" When he arrives at City Hall, he informs the Council that the homeless problem is the most urgent item on the agenda. "It's been one hell of a morning," says Goodhew. "Bodies everywhere."

It's a bright morning. The flag is snapping briskly in the December sunshine, and the yellow trucks are making their rounds. The mechanical arms lift the toters and dump the garbage. The city carpenters are rebuilding the river bottom shacks for the homeless. They still occupy the parks. The walnuts are being harvested, and Khalid is angry at the crows and the homeless. The crop is down forty percent. Walnut shells no longer litter city streets or clog the drains, but dead crows are everywhere: on streets, sidewalks, lawns, and the roofs of houses and buildings. The Mallophaga is working, and the birds are dropping like flies. The Brown toters are full of dead crows, and neighborhoods are beginning to smell. To cope with the overflow, Speer assigns an extra round to the truck schedule. Somebody suggests that Eagle Mountain be renamed. An irreverent person says the eagle on

Newell's bell should be a crow. The SS crew no longer tags the toters. Instead, they scour empty lots, bushes, trees, and ivy for dead birds. Garcia reassigns the work of petty criminals. Instead of the freeway detail, they now do neighborhood sweeps. The men in orange vests pick up dead birds and drop them into orange bags. The residents are edgy. Crows keep falling from the sky. The chickens are scared and have stopped laying eggs.

Every Sunday, Gladys Goodhew serves her husband breakfast on the patio, which has a nice view of the golf course. But no one is playing golf. Black carcasses litter the greens, and people in golf carts gather the dead birds. Gladys serves bacon and eggs. She sets the plate in front of her husband, and he looks at the two yolks. They are a pale yellow.

"What's wrong with the eggs?"

"They're store bought."

"Why?"

"Our hens no longer lay." She breaks off a piece of toast and dips it into the anemic yolk.

"These taste like plastic," says Goodhew.

"I know. Our yolks were orange. Not like these." Gladys Goodhew's eyes widen, and the yolk-dipped piece of toast stops short of her open mouth. The mayor follows the direction of his wife's gaze. A large rat scurries across a trellis beam.

"That's one big rat," he says, chewing on a piece of bacon. His wife shudders.

"I hate rats!"

"Which do you hate more? Crows or rats?"

"Rats, of course. In my dreams, I'm a raven."

"Have you heard of the saying: 'All we have to hate is hate itself?'"

"No."

"I invented it."

"Clever man."

"I'm saving it for when I become President."

"I see. And which war are you thinking of?" says Gladys

mockingly. "The crows or the homeless?"

"The crows. But I don't really hate them."

"Then save it for the homeless."

"No, that's Khalid's bag. My bag is to put out the trash. Isn't that why we got married? So that our gendered roles remain separate. You work, I dispose. Besides, I'm good at it. Haven't I organized Loviers City?"

The SPCA is furious. It has been writing letters to *The Sun* saying that killing crows is an unnecessary abomination, a cruel solution. Poison, Mallophaga, shooting—they all violate animal rights. Animals are entitled to live their lives, and they deserve to be treated humanely. Indian cultures venerate the crow, and its spirit is sacred. To violate its sanctity, they say, is to court adversity. Man is rapacious, indifferent to the balance of nature, heedless of the needs of other creatures, and selfish in his anthropocentrism. Man may be a wolf unto man, but with respect to other species, he is far worse. He shoots rhinos and elephants for their horns and tusks. He shoots the tiger for his penis, for the powders and soup that are alleged to restore sexual potency. Greed, lust and blood money are destroying the planet. Despite the letters to the editor and to the mayor, the extermination of the crows continues, unabated.

Early one morning, on his way to the office, Goodhew is shocked to see crow carcasses dumped on the steps of City Hall. Black wings, feathers, bodies, heads, and feet are piled on top of each other. The heap smells. Tiny white worms fleck the feathers of the crows. "Holy maggots," says Goodhew. "It must be the SPCA." He calls Speer and asks him to clean up the mess. Speer says that whoever did it dumped several toters' worth of dead birds. He thinks it's the homeless, but Goodhew reminds him that they don't have trucks. "I don't know which is worse," says Speer, "the birds or the bums. They both litter, and they smell."

"Yes," says Goodhew. "The SPCA sends letters, and it litters."

He hangs up and turns to the sports page. Big headline: GREEN LURES BROWN TO BLUE. He can't believe his eyes.

The headline seems to refer to the colors of the flag and the toters, the very symbols of Loviers City. Sportswriter: "Dodgers acquire Kevin Brown, baseball's first one hundred million dollar player—fifteen million dollars annually for seven years." "That's a lot of green for one pitcher," thinks Goodhew. Sportswriter: "Brown led the Florida Marlins to the 1997 World Series title and propelled the Padres to the 1998 World Series. His fastball has been clocked at ninety-seven miles per hour, and he was the most coveted starting pitcher in the blue-chip free-agent class." So, Brown is blue, and green made it possible. Goodhew fantasizes about Loviers City having a baseball team, a real team, not just the rhetoric he pitches from the mayor's mound to the local players. He mulls over the coincidence of colors and imagines himself the manager of a world-class team. What a trip. The Yankees better watch out. It's going to be baseball fever for a lot of fans, and they'll have to pay big bucks for the higher price of tickets. There's a monster out there driving up the competition, luring the crowds, cultivating the game, and paying the stars whatever the market will bear—mega-millions for home runs and shutouts. It's the spirit of baseball flapping in the wind: blue, brown, and green.

KHALID REMEMBERS HIS DAYS as a boy in Beirut, before the Civil War, before the opposing factions tore the city apart. He remembers Mount Saneen, the sea, the orange groves, and the olive trees. He sees their silver-green leaves, ancient gnarled trunks, and convoluted bark that once felt the hands of prophets and apostles. He remembers the goats, the camels, and his uncle's trips to Damascus. He remembers the diamonds his uncle smuggled in the sacred book. He remembers the humid summers and the rainy winters, the waves crashing against the jetty, the minarets, and the smell of jasmine and hot pita bread. He remembers his father's business and the colors of the Oriental rugs, the same colors as Loviers City: red, blue, orange, and green. It's like another time in a different galaxy. It's as though the shell that killed his father and wiped out his business never exploded, except in his memory. His mother is now blind, and she remembers nothing. His wife and two daughters don't even know what it was like. When he tells them about those days, he chooses to leave out the bad parts.

Khalid's businesses—the department store and the walnut groves—have been profitable.. Loviers City has been good to him, and he wants to keep it that way. Walnuts are his favorite. The Placentia, Franquette, Payne, and Mayette trees have glossy yellowish-green leaves and gray, fissured trunks. He has been spacing them twelve to the acre, especially for the new plantings. But problems persist. The soil is none too good. It requires a lot of fertilizer, and the irrigation system is in need of repair. After the harvest, he will head the trees low, so the crowns shade the trunks. The hulling, drying, grading, and bleaching are now in full swing, and he is happy when the stamping of the shells begins with his exclusive brand—the cedar of Lebanon.

Khalid does not speak about the hard times, but he remembers them: Ellis Island, the run-down apartment in Jersey, the trip west, and washing dishes in dirty diners. It hasn't been easy. He is proud of his success as a businessman and impatient with indolence—a form of moral laxness to be tolerated if need be but suppressed whenever possible. The habits of the homeless represent everything he has struggled to overcome. He finds their encroachments painful and disturbing. He does not understand their handicaps or their lifestyle, and their occupation of the parks is a distasteful reminder of difficult times now best forgotten.

For his business ventures, he dreams of a smartphone in every pocket and Skype linking all members of his family, from California to the Middle East. The cloud and social media have been a godsend, better than cleanliness. They have opened new markets and expanded international contacts. Khalid has money in the bank, and he adores his teenage daughters: Leila and Jasmine. He respects his wife but dislikes her creeping, middle-age spread. As for dangerous liaisons, he has had a few now and then, more or less, during a business trip here, another one there, sometimes mixed with pleasure: antidotes to domestic blandness, to the boredom of the quotidian, to age gnawing at youth and the flabbiness around his middle. Despite being in his late fifties, a night with another woman energizes him. But every time is no longer enough. He wants variety, surprise, and new settings. Ordinary sex gives way to belts, wrist-ties, and ankle-straps. He experiments with exotic positions that his parents never could have imagined. He buys transparent lingerie in black and rose for Nicole, his secretary, a pliant partner in the games he plays to rejuvenate the flesh and keep the gremlins of time at bay.

Nicole walks back and forth, almost naked in her finery. Khalid sits watching her, imagining ancient exploits and Bedouin abductions. "These garments," she says, "feel like silk and satin. And my cache-sexe speaks eloquently of what it hides and the diversions we shall now invent. *N'est ce pas, mon amour?*" Her feet are bare; her smile wide. The black bra plumps up her breasts and bares the rounded tops and buds. A red rose nestles behind one ear. Her black hair is the simoom blowing across the desert, and her pirouettes are hot columns of sand rising toward the sky. She is his Arabian mare. He mounts her, and they gallop over the dunes, the inclinations, and the valleys. The sunset and the starlit night are just beyond the horizon. Nicole is Ziad's passion, and he gives her flowers, jewelry, and exotic vacations whenever his business trips take him to Hong Kong and Singapore. A good secretary, he says, is worth her weight in diamonds.

Nicole is bright, ambitious, competent, and sensuous. She understands her boss's business and oversees the details. Ziad likes it that way, and he is excited by her beauty, her youth, and her subservience. He likes to exaggerate his dominance, and she submits to the role of victim. She plays her part, and it's a game they both enjoy. When she cries out, her plaint whips him into fierce endurance. He is young again, and his strength rides the perfume of her loins and melts into the softness of her embrace. He says the mole on her cheek is the dark hole of Calcutta. *Oh Calcutta!* Her green eyes, he says, are the jungles of Borneo. And he travels between Calcutta and Borneo, exploring the regions in between and farther south. Sometimes, he loses himself in the winding paths and lush folds. A sudden bite draws blood. She blots his earlobe with a Kleenex and says she takes no prisoners. Despite his dominance, she knows he is her slave. He is worth his weight in walnuts.

At City Hall, Khalid's weight is worth more than walnuts. He is the most influential businessman in Loviers City, and Goodhew knows he has clout. Khalid files suit against the homeless, and a date has been set for the hearing. The lawyers for both sides are preparing briefs. Khalid's suit alleges the disruption of public order and violation of the public good based on four infractions:

1. Rudy Squazza's disregard for law and order when he blocked traffic and proclaimed that cleanliness was next to Godliness;
2. The demonstration in front of City Hall without a permit;
3. The unlawful and prolonged occupation of the parks; and
4. The death of a city official on November 16, the night of the fire in the river bottom.

John Osbourne is the presiding judge. After the initial formalities, he listens to the arguments. The lawyer for the plaintiff says that the four incidents reveal a pattern of abuse, a disregard for the law, and a violation of the public good. The lawyer for the defense says that the allegations are frivolous and without merit. He asks that the suit be dismissed. The two lawyers argue back and forth. When they have finished with their opening statements, Judge Osbourne dismisses item one, on the grounds that it is irrelevant, and item four, saying that without proof of guilt against a named person, it is impossible to sue all the homeless. "Such an entity," he says, "is too amorphous and the charge too general." He says he will hear arguments on item three, the unlawful and prolonged occupation of the parks, and reserve judgment on item two, the march on City Hall. "The march," he says, "may be a tangential yet related issue."

Khalid's lawyer cites national policy governing public parks. He says that parks are a place of refreshment for the people, that they are an area designated to remain serene and tranquil. "They are a domain that must exist unimpaired, to be enjoyed by all but also passed on in their pristine state for the use of future generations. Parks," he says, "are to retain an aura of dignity. They are not places for demonstrators, and they should not be subjected to a carnival like atmosphere. The issue here, your Honor, is intent. The march on City Hall and the subsequent occupation of the parks were an expression of intent because the slogans used, and the placards displayed, were a form of speech. This speech is harmful to the public good because it violates the defined sanctity of the parks. Did the protesters not identify the nature and content of their complaint? Clearly, they wanted to change the status quo, despite the fact that parks are inviolate and are not subject to change. Furthermore, the parks should not be held hostage by the demonstrators. They must be protected for the use of future generations, and they must not suffer change at the hands of any one self appointed group." Khalid's lawyer cites the government's action against the Vietnam War protesters as precedent and, subsequently, their eviction from the park in front of the White House.

The lawyer for the homeless says that the public good is a subtle, intangible, and non quantifiable category. "Who is the public?" he asks. "And are not the homeless entitled to the same consideration as everybody else? If the parks are public land, and the homeless are members of the public, then they, too, are entitled to use the parks."

Khalid's lawyer argues that because the homeless have been demonstrating, they do not, in fact, use the parks as visitors. "The parks," he says, "are a space for peace and quiet. Because the homeless have identified the nature of their complaint, they are no longer part of the general public. Therefore, they are not entitled to occupy the parks. Furthermore, by wishing to change the status quo, their demands create unstable meanings. Instability goes against the concept of timeless serenity. Mr. Squazza's T-shirt and the skeleton on it, endorsing The Grateful Dead, are part of that provocation. Most people find the idea of gratitude in death offensive."

The lawyer for the homeless says that wearing a Grateful Dead T-shirt in no way countermands the idea of timeless serenity. "On the contrary," he says, "it enhances it. What greater serenity than in death? Besides, the people are not trying to change the parks. Their occupation is temporary, and the only status quo they want to alter is their own. Do not the mentally and physically challenged have a right to life, liberty, and the pursuit of happiness? If not, why are they being persecuted? Is society not obligated to protect those who cannot protect themselves? It's not the homeless who are harming the public good but society that has harmed the homeless by failing to take their special needs into consideration. Should the homeless be disfranchised because they are handicapped? Is not society responsible for all its citizens, particularly those who cannot care for themselves?"

Khalid's lawyer says that the homeless have chosen their lifestyle. "The city," he says, "is obligated not to interfere with their free choice. But when their freedom infringes on the freedom of the public to use the parks, then the law has to intervene. And when they endorse a morality of death, such speech is an attack on the public good."

The lawyer for the homeless says that wearing a T-shirt with somebody's logo on it is not a threat to the serenity of the parks. Khalid's lawyer says that the rhythmic beating of a bongo drum, and the display of placards, is a form of speech. "An identifiable part of that speech is the skeleton." The lawyer for the homeless says that on Halloween there are skeletons everywhere. "No one objects to them. In fact, merchants are encouraged to sell them."

"Yes," says Khalid's lawyer, "but they are not in the parks."

"How do you know they are not in the parks? Have you been there during Halloween?"

"The fact remains, Your Honor, that the demonstrators cannot enjoy protection in the parks as visitors because they are speaking for themselves. They are endorsing homelessness as a cause."

"Your Honor," says the lawyer for the homeless, "if you evict the homeless from the parks, you will, in essence, be stating that we are governed by a state aesthetic that suppresses protest. The inescapable conclusion will be that this city, the county, and the state are indifferent to the plight of the homeless."

"The plight of the homeless is not at issue," says Khalid's lawyer. "What is at issue is their speech, and it threatens the timeless serenity of the parks."

"Your Honor, what is more important? People or parks?"

The hearing ends, and Judge Osbourne closes his folder. He says he will take all arguments under advisement. When he reaches a decision, he will let them know.

Osbourne calls Goodhew to say that he has to make a decision on the homeless. He says Khalid's lawyer has precedent on his side, based on the eviction of the Vietnam War protesters from the park in Washington, D.C. Goodhew asks Osbourne to hold off on his decision, saying that he wants to talk to Khalid and, if he can, persuade him to drop the suit.

"Good luck," says Osbourne.

"Thanks, I'll need it."

Goodhew calls Khalid and asks him over for drinks. Khalid's voice sounds distraught, and Goodhew asks him what is wrong.

"It's Nicole," says Khalid, his voice catching in his throat. "She's dead."

"I'm so sorry," says Goodhew.

"One of my workmen found her body in the walnut grove."

"My deepest sympathy." Goodhew decides that the body mentioned in the newspaper must be Nicole.

"I'll kill the bastard who did it!"

"Garcia will do all he can to apprehend the perpetrator."

"I'm posting a reward."

"Listen Ziad, I know this is a bad time for you, but we need to talk—about the homeless."

"It's one of them. I know it is."

"We can talk about that, too."

"The walnut grove abuts on the river bottom."

"Can you come over to my house later this afternoon? About five? I'll mix a batch of martinis."

GOODHEW MIXES A PITCHER of dry martinis, puts one green olive in each stemmed glass, and the two men walk onto the patio. The greens on the golf course are green again, and there are golfers on the course. The crows are flying west toward the cottonwoods. They fly in irregular groups. Two birds glide sideways and downward in a playful trajectory, catch a thermal updraft, and rise swiftly. Most of the golfers have finished playing, but a few carts still move along the pathways. Goodhew offers his condolences.

"I'm sorry about Nicole," he says. "I know how good she was and how much you relied on her. Any leads?"

"No, nothing."

"If there are answers, Garcia will find them." Goodhew takes a drink, and Khalid does likewise. The martini is cold, and Goodhew curls his tongue around the familiar taste. "Perhaps you know that Nicole wasn't the first victim. Two weeks ago, Garcia's men found a body next to the downtown off-ramp. Actually, it was the clean-up crew that found her. She, too, had been strangled. And, like Nicole, she was in her early thirties and an attractive brunette. Because of the resemblance between the two women, Garcia thinks it may be the work of a serial killer."

"I still think it's the homeless."

"It's the homeless I wanted to talk about. The Council has made some decisions, and since you missed the last meeting, I need to go over some details with you.

"They're a bunch of scumbags."

"I know how you feel about them, but please, hear me out. The problem is—what to do with ten thousand homeless? Because that's the number we're talking about. We, the city, believe it's a county problem, but the county says it's ours."

"It's not my problem," says Khalid. "If it were me, I'd deport them all."

"Where to?" asks Goodhew.

"Anywhere."

"Yes, but how?"

"I'll give two hundred dollars to each of the one hundred homeless we've identified—if they'll leave town. That's twenty thousand dollars and good riddance."

"Look at it this way, Ziad. One hundred out of ten thousand is not a solution. When they leave, others will take their place. The park situation can be settled. When we do, the homeless will be out of your hair. Why not donate the twenty thousand toward the proposed shelter. The Council has approved it, and Loviers City will commit to the care of one hundred people. If other cities in the county do likewise, the problem will be solved. The homeless will be out of the parks, and they will no longer be a public nuisance. What do you say?"

Khalid takes two walnuts out of his pocket and squeezes them in the palm of his hand. The brown shells scrape and grate as he revolves one around the other.

"These are my worry beads," he says. "They help me think." Goodhew sips his martini.

"You know, Ziad, the Council has voted ninety thousand dollars for the newly-formed Reach Program. We can get fifty thousand dollars in federal emergency shelter grant funds, and we need another forty thousand dollars for support programs and counseling." Goodhew pauses while Ziad sips his drink. "If you were to donate twenty thousand dollars toward the shelter instead of wasting it on bus tickets to nowhere, we could begin right away." Goodhew looks into Khalid's brown eyes. "I can understand your anger, Ziad, but we need you on board. Besides, the Council has already voted for the shelter. You can sue the homeless out of the parks, but you can't sue them out of the shelter. Haven't you always been a strong supporter of Loviers' best interests?" Goodhew pops the olive in his mouth and chews. "We'll put a plaque up in your name. The Khalid Fund: a fund with vision. We'll launch a campaign to raise money, to supplement your contribution. I see it as a positive thing to do."

Khalid rotates the walnuts in his hand, and with each revolution, Goodhew hears the grating of the shells. The crows over the golf course continue their westward flight toward the river bottom, and the sun casts oblique rays onto the greens. "We solved the crow problem, and your walnuts are now safe. I know we can solve the homeless problem." Khalid rotates the walnuts in his right hand, thrusts them into the pocket of his gray jacket, and says: "Okay … I'll do it. I'll donate the twenty thousand to the fund. But if one of the homeless is responsible for Nicole's death, God help him."

"Thanks, Ziad. I knew we could count on you. You won't regret it."

THE SCHOOL UNIFORMS AND Konlon's talks have been a success. Shootings are less frequent, weapons on campus have been eliminated, class discipline has improved, school morale is up, the SS is popular, the football team is winning (are they not wearing the colors of the flag?), and order prevails. For filling more toters with dead crows than any other group, Sanitary Squadron #7 is awarded a brass plaque with the profile of a crow etched on the shiny surface. It is put on display in a glass case in the hallway opposite the principal's office. The award occupies a place of honor next to the athletic trophies. Student test scores are up and the debate team is on a winning streak. Loviers City High is on a roll.

To assuage the thirst generated by such achievement, The Coca-Cola Company installs vending machines at school exits and entrances. In the gym, a big red-and-white banner says: *Drink Coca-Cola.* Its subsidies pay for team uniforms and equipment. In the classrooms, smaller red-and-white banners say: *Study Refreshed.* In the gym and on the playing fields, more red-and-white banners say: *Play Refreshed.* In the hallways, red-and-white banners say: *The Real Thing.* The school dedicates itself to maximizing the potential of each student. Every one counts. Fruitopia reigns. Excellence, togetherness, unanimity, study, and play all exist refreshed.

Leila Khalid drinks her coke and drops the can in the recycling bin. The bell rings for her ten o'clock English class. She sits in row three, next to the window. She unzips her bag, removes a tube of lip balm and applies it—the upper lip first, then the lower. She puts the cap back on.

"What is that?" asks Nora Silber.

"Lip balm," says Leila.

"What kind?"

"Carmex."

"Do you have a doctor's prescription?"

"What for? It's only lip balm."

"We have a problem," says Silber.

"We do?"

"Yes, L.C. High has a policy of zero tolerance. You know that! No guns, no drugs, no medication of any kind without a doctor's prescription."

"For chapped lips?"

"For anything."

"But you don't need a prescription for Carmex. I bought it myself at CVS."

"Over the counter?"

"Yes."

"I'm going to have to ask you to report to the principal."

"Whatever." Leila puts the Carmex back in her bag, closes *The Old Man and the Sea*, the part where the fish leaps out of the water and glistens in the sunlight, gathers her books, and goes to the principal's office. She explains what happened. She and the principal exchange the same questions and the same answers. He asks to see the Carmex, inspects it, puts it down next to the phone and calls Mrs. Khalid. Leila listens while he explains the zero tolerance policy to her mother. "Your daughter will need a doctor's prescription to bring Carmex on campus." The principal confiscates the lip balm.

"When you get the doctor's prescription, go to the first-aid office. Only the nurse can apply it."

"You mean I can't put it on myself?"

"That's right."

The doctor thinks a prescription for Carmex is stupid, but he writes one nonetheless. His writing, as always, is illegible. Mother and daughter drive to the drugstore and buy another tube. The next day, Leila reports to nurse Cogg, who applies the lip balm.

The SS puts Carmex, ChapStick, Burt's Bees, and all other brands of lip balm on its list of banned substances. The Carmex Control goes into effect, and the Balm Squad patrols the halls of

Loviers High, determined to nab chapped-lip-offenders—anyone who would dare use forbidden and uncontrolled ointments, salves, unguents, pomades, cremes, or emollients. Picabo Street, please take note.

The winter viruses are spreading, flu is in the air, and colds, coughs, and chapped lips multiply. There is a long line of students outside the nurse's station waiting for their medications. The line extends the length of the hall and curls around the corner. Nurse Cogg is overwhelmed. Bottles break, germs scatter, and students are late for class, causing significant disruptions. The red-and-white banners say: *Study Refreshed*.

New vending machines appear on campus, and new school subsidies come into being. The administrators are happy. Blue and-white banners go up next to the red-and-white ones. They say: *Snickers*. Important learning is taking place at L.C. High. Nurse Cogg dispenses medications, and the Balm Squad patrols the corridors searching for "Felony Carmex," as some are now calling it.

"Hey," says Konlon."

"Hey," says Silber. "How's the environmental class going?"

"Quite well. We're into the preservation of historical sites— from Indian geoglyphs and stone mazes to Spanish missions and Victorian houses."

"Sounds interesting."

"It is, and they're everywhere. Goodhew wants the county to protect the sites and market them to potential tourists."

"He's a real promoter." Silber unwraps a Snickers and takes a bite.

"Wants to put Loviers City on the map." Konlon blows her nose and puts the Kleenex in her bag.

"He probably will. He's good at getting what he wants."

"The city could use the revenue. Goodhew is always complaining about the budget." The class bell rings and several teachers leave the faculty lounge. Konlon looks at the line of students in the hall. "What's new on 'Felony Carmex?'"

"Isn't that the dumbest thing?"

"So why did you report it?"

"Because zero tolerance is school policy."

"On lip balm?"

"It's not my decision. And I'm not going to second guess the Board." Silber chews on her last bite of Snickers.

"I would have overlooked it."

"The Board can always change its mind, considering the outcry."

"Do you think it will?" asks Konlon.

"No. The bureaucratic mind is a stubborn mule. You can pull it by the tail but nothing moves."

"There must be something."

"It would have to be dramatic," says Silber, "like shooting the principal." The football coach comes in and says: "Hi guys." He goes to the vending machine and selects a can of Fruitopia.

"Nicole's death was dramatic and unexpected. That was a week ago, and the police have no clue." Konlon blows her nose. "Do you have a take on it?"

"Ziad should have been the victim," says Silber.

"Why do you say that?"

"He's such a lech. No woman is safe. He'll paw you to death, any chance he gets."

"I wouldn't know."

"Take it from me." Silber shakes her silver-streaked black hair. "At the festival reception he slobbered all over me. And it wasn't the first time."

"Poor Nicole. That's a brutal way to go." Konlon gets up, goes to the vending machine, and inserts her Visa card. A red-and-white can of Coca-Cola Classic rolls noisily out of the slot. She opens it with a hiss and takes a drink. The imprint of her lipstick blends with the red of the can.

"You can say that again." Silber bites a hangnail on her little finger.

"Rumor has it that Ziad and Nicole were an item."

"It's more than rumor."

"Please tell."

"It's common knowledge that she accompanied him on his business trips," says Silber.

"Don't all secretaries?"

"Ha!"

"Call me old fashioned," says Konlon, "but I thought secretaries made coffee and sat on laps."

"No way. Except for Nicole. She had her perks."

"I've been wondering why a beautiful person with perks would end up dead."

"Maybe that's why," says Silber.

"Really?"

"There's always a reason."

"Are you accusing somebody?"

"Sometimes there can be a wifely reason."

"You mean Mrs. Khalid?"

"I'm not accusing anybody," says Silber, "just spinning scenarios. Pure fantasy."

"Okay, spin me a wifely scenario." Konlon takes a drink from the red-and-white can.

"This is pure conjecture, mind you, but imagine yourself in her shoes. You're fifty, plump, not getting any younger." Silber plays with a strand of hair.

"Isn't that every woman's plight? Sounds clichéd to me."

"Life is a cliché. Anyway, Nicole is young, beautiful, and Ziad spends more time with her than with his family."

"What else is new?"

"Stop interrupting," says Silber. "I'm framing my story."

"I'd say you're framing Mrs. Khalid."

"Is it that obvious?"

"I like narrators who hide their devices," says Konlon. "You know, like God: present everywhere but visible nowhere."

"I'll try to be invisible," says Silber. "Their marriage is *flat*, and their daughters are going to college. Ziad is restless and wants a divorce. There, in her old age, is Mrs. Khalid … abandoned."

"I can still see you," says Konlon. "You're describing the story, not showing it."

"Is that so?"

"Anyway, if I were her and knew about Nicole, I'd either get a divorce or I'd sit tight. Ten more years and the bloom *is* off Nicole. Besides, why would Ziad rock the boat? He has a home, a family, and a mistress."

"Yes, but suppose he told his wife he wanted a divorce."

"And Nicole ends up dead? Wouldn't that be too obvious?" Konlon is getting into the story. There is a tinge of excitement in her cheeks.

"The obvious frequently hides the truth, like Poe's purloined letter. It was there in plain view and nobody saw it." Silber smiles.

"Nicole isn't the letter," says Konlon. "She's a body, and she wasn't hidden."

"The truth is not about Nicole's body." Silber wraps a strand of hair around her index finger. "What's hidden is the 'who did it.'"

"And who is that?" says Konlon.

"His wife. Isn't it obvious?"

"If it's that obvious, why isn't she behind bars?" There is a sparkle in Konlon's pale blue eyes.

"Maybe Garcia and his men have no imagination. It takes imagination to solve crimes. Think of Maigret." Silber adjusts the pillow and leans back on the couch. "Do you have a scenario?" Konlon sets the red-and-white can down on the side table.

"Ziad did it."

"I'm listening."

"Suppose Nicole is embezzling funds from the company. Ziad finds out and threatens to expose her."

"He can't do that," says Silber. "The moment he does, Nicole goes to the wife and spills the beans."

"Ah, but wifey already knows, so there's nothing to spill."

"Yes, but Ziad and Nicole don't know she knows."

"Whose script is this?" says Konlon.

"Just pointing out possibilities." Silber leans one elbow on the arm of the couch.

"Okay. They don't know, and Ziad is furious. He's lavishing expensive presents on Nicole, and she's milking him dry." Konlon flexes one ankle back and forth.

"I don't know about that. If he likes her that much, why would he care?"

"I've got it. Nicole has another lover. Now, Ziad is both furious and jealous."

"That's good," says Silber. "That should do it."

"Ziad arranges one of their little trysts. He ties her to the bed, and after making angry love, he strangles her." Konlon flexes her other ankle.

"And how does he get her to the walnut grove?"

"In the trunk of the car, like everyone else."

"Don't you think the police will stop him?" says Silber. "In a low rider?"

"No. They either don't see him, or they think he has a load of walnuts. Besides, it's a dark and stormy night, and the wind is howling in the trees. He opens the trunk and throws the body over his shoulder."

"You've been reading too many bad novels. You can't say, 'It's a dark and stormy night.' That's a terrible cliché. It's been used."

"I can if I want to. It's my script."

"Nobody will publish it."

"I thought we were solving a crime," says Konlon.

"What's the difference? But I know one thing. You can't solve crimes with clichés. Maigret would turn over in his grave."

"Now that's a cliché," says Konlon.

"The dead women are not clichés," says Silber. "And what really bothers me is the way they were dumped, like trash."

"Yes. I keep thinking of the tinsel brightness on a Corn Nut bag … or the iridescent blue of Nestlé Pretzel Flips. You know how you slow down at an off-ramp, open the window, and throw out a wrapper?"

"Like the hooker? Ugh."

"Another scenario: Nicole has a second lover. He's jealous, wants her to leave Ziad, and she won't." The bell rings. "Time for my next class," says Konlon.

"Do you think people who litter go to heaven?" The two women look at each other and laugh. There is an uncertain mixture of mirth and discomfort. They leave the lounge and elbow their way around the line of students waiting for the ministrations of Nurse Cogg.

It's Friday, and there is an air of excitement. Loviers High has a game with Santa Mara, its archrival. The football squad, the cheerleaders, and the students are psyched for the big event. Blue, brown, and green banners say: *Beat SM* and *Whip SM*. The coaches have prepped the team for blood, and the players are eager. The whole campus is looking forward to the Saturday afternoon blitz. Confidence buoys everybody's spirits. The band is playing, the instruments shine, and the girls' pom-poms are fluffed with optimism.

In brown letters, the cheerleaders wear LOV on the front of their green sweaters. Beneath short brown skirts, their bare thighs flick their blue pom-poms up and down. They cheer vigorously, and the fans applaud the blue circles, green jumps, and brown kicks. The girls prance, leap, and twirl. The home crowd yells: *Kill SM*. In the opposing bleachers, the SM fans shout: *Kill LOV.* The LOV's players are wearing blue helmets, green jerseys, and brown pants. Big red banners say: *Play Refreshed.* SM's team is wearing yellow helmets, yellow jerseys, and black pants. The teams square off, the whistle blows, and the lines of players collide. There is a blur of shapes, colors, and sounds. Play evolves on green grass under a blue sky. There are runs, passes, pileups, lineups, and first downs, second downs, third downs, and punts. The players run, clash, fall, get up, and march down the field. Touchdown! The fans yell, the band plays, and the cheerleaders cheer. The blue, brown, and green fans jump up and down. The player who scored wiggles his ass and raises an index finger. Leila shouts loudly for her boyfriend. She adores him. They will party tonight. No one notices the tube of Carmex.

KHALID MAKES ARRANGEMENTS AT the Three Lambs Mortuary for Nicole's funeral. On the lawn in front of the two-story brick building is a life-sized marble statue of Christ holding a shepherd's crook. Jesus is looking at three lambs. Khalid turns his black Mercedes into the circular driveway, drives past the statue and the lambs, and stops under the porte-cochère. Bart Holcomb greets him at the door.

"I'm so sorry for your loss," he says, shaking hands and ushering Khalid into the room of last decisions. The walls are honey-combed with niches containing cremation urns and paper flowers: red tulips and yellow chrysanthemums. There are cardboard receptacles, polished veneer boxes, brass octagons, huddled ceramic angels, and Doric columns with a spread eagle on top. The two men sit down at a long, mahogany table, and Holcomb shoves some papers across its shiny surface. "If you would please sign. It's just a formality. My deepest sympathy. We're here to help in any way we can." Holcomb hands Khalid a pen. "Let me tell you from the outset that we do not recommend the Neptune Society. They are not reliable, and we have had too many complaints." Holcomb's expression is both stern and earnest.

"I had something else in mind."

"Good, because we do no business with Neptune." Khalid peruses the papers. "What kind of a funeral did you have in mind? Cremation or burial?"

"A dignified burial."

"Good. That's the best kind. Gives the family a chance to say goodbye. Pay its last respects. View the beloved. Achieve closure.

A dignified burial is what we do best." Holcomb's gravelly voice is serious, comforting, and reassuring. "I'm sorry about the papers. You understand, we have to do this." Khalid signs. "You will like our service. Our embalming is state of the art. We are here to help." Holcomb clips the pen to his shirt pocket. "When you're ready, we can go to the casket room." Khalid follows the mortician into a vast room with coffins everywhere. "Did you have a particular one in mind?"

"Yes," says Khalid. "In fact, I did. I'd like walnut. The best you have." Holcomb rubs his hands together and directs Khalid toward an aisle. There are caskets on both sides. They walk past wooden coffins, mahogany coffins, metal coffins, large ones, small ones, cheap ones, and expensive ones.

"Here's our top of the line," says Holcomb. "Look at the grain of the wood. See how it shines?" Holcomb rubs it with the palm of his hand. "It has been treated to withstand time and the elements. The handles are polished brass, and the inside is lead-lined. When closed, it seals out the moisture. We think that's important. It gives the family peace of mind." Khalid examines the quilting and runs several fingers over the smooth cream-colored surface. "Silk and satin," says Holcomb. "Very comfortable. The beloved can rest in peace."

"This one it is," says Khalid. He touches the stitching of the padded material and thinks of Nicole—the last time they were together, the last time they made love, the last time her soft skin touched his. He misses her. Her eyes were almost golden, like ripe almonds. Nicole was his passport to youth, and now she has gone to another country. Khalid misses her laughter, her mischievous games, and her playful abandon. He thinks that he will never be able to replace her. He would fill the casket with diamonds—if that could bring her back. It's a ransom fit for a mistress—a now dead mistress, a forever dead Nicole. He feels a wave of anger rise from deep within him—anger against the man who killed her, anger at the injustice of it, and anger at the waste, the terrible waste of a life that has been taken too soon.

"You have made the right decision," says Holcomb. "It's the Cadillac of caskets. Excuse me, you drive a Mercedes. It's the Mercedes of caskets. Your loved one will ride to heaven in comfort. We can guarantee that."

"I'm glad to hear it," says Khalid. "What would I do without you?"

"I appreciate that," says Holcomb. "I truly appreciate what you just said. We're here to serve, and if there is anything more we can do, please don't hesitate to ask. We know how difficult your loss can be." Khalid is taken aback by the other man's effusiveness, not sure if he is being one-upped because of an ironic comment, or if, under the circumstances, this is true comfort sincerely dispensed.

"You're too kind," says Khalid. "The family is grateful."

"Don't mention it," says Holcomb. "Some people don't value our work. Many take it for granted. But it is true. What would happen without us? Are we not the terminal of last resorts? Do we not fly the flag of Loviers City? Are we not the place of transition between life and death, between the now and the hereafter? Our sanitation is exemplary, and our procedures impeccable. We even provide long-term cryogenic solutions. Not many places are equipped for that. If you want the head of your loved one— or your own—frozen for future regeneration, we can arrange it. We can even arrange to have you placed head-to-head in the cryogenic chamber. Think of that!" Holcomb is dancing back and forth, and Khalid thinks that he is remarkably nimble for so portly a man.

"That must be very expensive."

"It's not cheap, but when you think of the possibilities— waking up three hundred years from now and looking into the eyes of your beloved. Wouldn't that be worth it?"

"What happens to the body?"

"By then, science will regenerate it from the head. Think of the recent research on stem cells and nanotechnology. It's the head and brain that are critical." Holcomb does a quick step forward, a two-step to his left, and back again. "We could regenerate all of Loviers City—you, the mayor, Newell, his congregation, and everybody else. God's chosen few. The ultimate resurrection. A cryogenic solution. Our town, preserved for posterity, but without the homeless, the tutes, the criminals, and the dopers. Only the best. The one percent. The crème de la crème ... skimmed off the top to protect the integrity of the future. Then, we can have unanimity."

"That is truly visionary," says Khalid. "Have you talked to Newell or Goodhew?"

"No, I haven't. Do you think I should?"

"Of course. I think you should leave no head unturned. You could advertise something like *Death and Resurrection*, or *Freeze with Ease*, or *Die Refreshed*.

"That's good. I like that!" Holcomb dances back and forth. "Mr. Khalid, it's been a pleasure doing business with you. I look forward to seeing you again."

The day of the funeral is chilly and overcast. The trunks and fronds of the tall palms stand motionless against a flat, gray sky. Nicole's parents fly in from Wisconsin. They are staying at the Mission Inn. They admire the bells and the architecture. All they have to do is walk across the street to the First Unanimist Church where Nicole is lying in front of the altar in her walnut casket. The casket floats in a sea of flowers: red roses, white lilies, and yellow chrysanthemums. A burnished copper shaft of divine light shines, cascading from the glass window above the cross. Nicole looks like sleeping beauty waiting for the kiss of her prince. Khalid, his wife, and two daughters sit in the front pew on the left. Nicole's parents sit stiffly on the right. Fellow-workers, friends, and neighbors walk down the aisle and distribute themselves to the left and to the right.

The organ stops playing, and there is a moment of silence. Newell stands to welcome the assembled mourners. Accompanied by the sounds of the organ, the group sings "Our God, Our Help in Ages Past." Newell reads the Twenty-third Psalm:

The LORD *is* my shepherd; I shall not want.
He maketh me to lie down in green pastures:
He leadeth me beside the still waters.
He restoreth my soul ...
and I will dwell in the house of the LORD for ever.

Newell speaks of the dedication of the deceased, of her past and future life, of mortality and resurrection, of the now and the hereafter, of loss and hope, and of faith and love. Mr. Sebastian stands and, says, in a voice choked with emotion, that Nicole will always be his little daughter. Mrs. Sebastian is unable to stand. She dabs at tears on her cheeks with a white handkerchief. Khalid stands and eulogizes Nicole's work and loyalty. A friend speaks of her wonderful sense of humor. Another lauds her generosity. A neighbor says that Nicole always removed her toters from the curb on time. When the sharing is over, Newell recites the Lord's Prayer. The voices of the mourners accompany him. Everybody sings "Amazing Grace," the organ plays the exodus, and the people mill around the lobby. They go to their cars. Three motorcycle policemen accompany the cars going to Walnut Hill. A homeless person reclining in the Chinese gazebo next to the Postmodern Library looks across the street at the long black hearse emerging from the driveway of the First Unanimist Church. He wonders who has died. He reflects briefly on mortality and the human condition, gets up, and walks across the street toward a man standing in the church door.

"Who died?"

"Nicole Sebastian," says the church attendant.

"Was she an important person?"

"Important enough."

Rudy Squazza walks down the alley behind Denny's, hoists his body over the side of a big, blue dumpster, and lowers himself into it. His head casts a round shadow on the yellow wall inside. He wades through piles of newspapers toward an opening in the rubbish, picks through cardboard, and begins diving. Aha! A mangled box with three doughnuts inside, reasonably fresh, and no ants. He picks up a red apple, dented, but not spoiled. Rudy rubs the Macintosh on his left sleeve and peels the bruised part with his Swiss army knife—a dumpster trophy from another scavenge. Apple and doughnuts for breakfast. Not too bad. Further down in the rubbish he finds a pair of used Nikes, tied together with their laces. They are newer than his. He sits down on a box and tries on the right one. It fits. He puts on the left shoe, ties his old pair together, and leaves them on the box. At the bottom of the dumpster, he finds a quarter, a dime, and two pennies. He moves more cardboard aside, and his hand hits something hard: a paper bag, and inside it, a bottle, a hip flask of Jim Beam, opened but almost full. He unscrews the cap and drinks. Good stuff. He screws the top back on and puts the flask in his hip pocket. He discards a smelly box of tomatoes, another box with a moldy cherry pie inside, kicks two empty wine bottles, and decides to call it quits. He hoists himself back over the top of the dumpster, lowers himself to the pavement, and sits down. He leans against the side of the dumpster and lifts his face toward the sun. He drinks.

Rudy Squazza is now zonked out of his mind. Above his head, a white graffito says: *Fuck Refreshed.* Rudy is listening to KLCR on his transistor radio. He raises Jim Beam to his lips and takes another drink. The bourbon tickles his windpipe, heats his esophagus, and blazes into his stomach. He wipes his mouth and beard with the back of his hand, belches, and tastes apple and doughnut. The voice on the radio says that at the stroke of midnight all twenty-dollar bills will turn into worthless paper. "The treasury," says the voice with an oozing reassurance, "is replacing old Jackson. You know what that means? Obsolete, man, obsolete."

Rudy reaches into the pocket of his leather vest. He pulls out four dollar-bills, one ten, and one twenty. He studies the green, white, and gray shades of the twenty-dollar bill. *20* is printed in each of the four corners. A somber, bespectacled Jackson occupies the medallion in the center. *Twenty Dollars* is printed under Jackson between two 20s. *United States of America* occupies a slender scroll above Jackson's head, between two other 20s. Next to each 20, inside a large banner-like scroll, is the number *12*. The signature of the Treasurer of the United States is to the right of the 12, on the left side. The signature of the Secretary of the Treasury appears to the left of the 12, on the right side. To the left of Jackson's bust is a small round stamp with a black *L* in the center. On Jackson's right is another green stamp that says: *Department of the Treasury*. The word *Twenty*, in gray, is superimposed on it. In its center, a white shield displays a pair of scales. An old-fashioned key is visible below them. "For justice and opportunity?" says Rudy to himself. He mutters: "What justice and what opportunity?" Printed above the L stamp, it says: *This Note is Legal Tender For all Debts Legal and Private*. "I'd better tender this before it's too late," says Rudy to himself. He turns the bill over. There is a picture of the White House and the number *20* printed on each corner of the bill. *The United States of America* is printed above the White House. *In God We Trust* is printed between the White House and The United States of America. "No trust after midnight," says Rudy at the top of his voice. He tilts his head back, lifts the flask, and drains it. "Time to find some trust." He staggers to his feet, tosses the bottle into the dumpster, and walks down the alley with an unsteady gait.

On the street, Rudy loses his balance and steadies himself against a lamppost. He shields his eyes and looks up at the double-cross bell-in-belfry logo etched against the morning sky. A black-and-white car cruises down College Avenue. The cruiser stops, and a voice says, "Look who's here. How're ya doin' Rudy?" Another voice says, "Is cleanliness still next to Godliness?" Rudy walks toward the curb, ignoring the voices. But his shoe catches on the uneven paving, and he falls, sprawling onto the sidewalk. Strong arms lift him by the armpits. The two officers walk him to the squad car and insert him into the back seat.

"It's against the law to be drunk in public," says the officer in the passenger's seat. The blond hairs on the back of his red neck fold into two deep creases.

"Do you have change for a twenty?" says Rudy.

"Why's that?" says the neck with the creases.

"Because, at midnight, it'll be worthless paper."

"Sure it will," says the driver. He looks at the other officer, and they both laugh. "What are we gonna do?" says the driver as he turns right on Main Street. He has big hands with black hairs on the knuckles.

"Teach him a lesson," says the neck with the creases.

"He needs a lesson," says knuckles.

"A sober lesson," says the neck.

"Down by the lake," says knuckles. The cruiser accelerates past the Postmodern Library, past the Fake Mission Inn, turns left on Market, and heads toward the park. It circles the lake and stops at a remote spot near two sycamores.

"Okay, Rudy," says the neck, "time for your lesson." He opens the rear door and pulls Rudy out. A crow caws at the intruders. A hand pushes Rudy's head down, and he falls to one knee. The neck with the blond hairs kicks him in the stomach. Rudy gasps. Knuckles kicks him in the butt. Rudy groans. A truncheon hits him on the arm and shoulder. Another blow stings his back. He protects his head, and the blows hurt his hands. The crow caws loudly. The sun glints through the leaves in the trees. The dirt in Rudy's mouth feels gritty, wet, and warm. It tastes like copper pennies. Coppers—hitting, kicking, and teaching him a lesson. Their voices sound like a broken record. He feels the heels of his shoes dragging on the gravel—a moment of weightlessness and then … splash. The water on his head and neck feels cold. He sinks. His feet touch bottom. He stands, gasps for air, and opens his eyes. They smart. Through a blur, he sees two blue uniforms.

"You failed that lesson," says one uniform.

"Maybe next time," says the other. Rudy rubs his eyes. The men say: "See you around, Rudy." The uniforms sheathe their truncheons, get in the police car, and drive away. Rudy walks toward the bank, staggers up, and collapses. There is a sharp pain in his chest, and his right arm hurts. The blood from the cut on his head mixes with the water running into his eyes.

He regains consciousness in a makeshift lean-to. Pinholes of light are visible through the tarp. Someone has taken off Rudy's clothes, and he is now between two blankets. His body aches, and there is a bandage on his head. He touches it gingerly.

"Them pigs worked you over good, man." Rudy moans. The voice says: "I thought they was gonna drown you."

Rudy slips in and out of consciousness, and when he comes to again, he is in a bed with sheets. On the wall there is a television screen. A woman in green comes into the room and says, "My name is Ramona."

"Where am I?" asks Rudy.

"In the hospital," says the woman in green. Rudy fingers the cast on his right arm, then the bandage around his head. He shifts his body and feels a cutting pain in his chest.

"What happened?"

"A broken arm, two ribs, one concussion, and many stitches."

"Is that right?"

"How did it happen?"

"Justice worked me over."

"Justice?"

"No, maybe it was trust. Can't remember."

"Take these. It'll ease the pain." The nurse raises the head of the bed, and Rudy feels another sharp pain in his chest.

❖

EVERYTHING ON SALE! THE holidays have a focused energy. Christmas is in the air—lights, ribbons, paper, boxes, presents, and trees. Real trees, fake trees, they're all green, like the greenbacks. Loviers City prepares for its annual extravaganza, a time when Baby Jesus presides over the buying power of the faithful. People go to the malls, the stores, and the shops, but no one will drop until after the New Year's sales. They announce the season's final spending spree. Meanwhile, "Adeste Fideles" is in the air. Red-and-white banners say: *Shop Refresshed.* And high-schoolers wonder where they have seen that sign before. Jovial Santas—dressed in red and wearing white beards—ring bells. Coins slip through slots and clink into cans. *Jingle Bells.* The music of angels and drummer boys encourage the buying mood. Hands reach for merchandise, pack it, wrap it, and carry it home, where it is unwrapped, wrapped again in Christmas paper, and stowed under the tree. Soon, other hands will rip off the ribbons and the paper.

Presents galore. Nothing mars the exuberance. For Khalid, it is the promise of profit. During the holydays, people buy, give, take, and bake. Eat, drink, and be Mary's child in the manger— or the Wise Men following the star of Bethlehem and bearing gifts. This is Loviers City, and in every neighborhood, there's a crèche—illuminated plywood cutouts of the holy family looking at the newborn.

The shoppers go to the malls where they hear "O Holy Night" at every entrance. They charge their purchases and pay on the installment plan, or they buy with coupons and discounts. Peace on earth among men of good will is also a piece of the financial pie. And the star on the tree in the store says: *Buy, Buy, Buy.* Consume despite obsolescence, quality discards, and technical failures. You can bank on it with the usual incentives: pre-season sales, post-season sales, and all-season sales. The economy sails on the winds of profit, and the sloop of indulgence tacks with optimism. In the air, planes bring passengers from distant corners of the land, and as they look down upon the city, they see luminous grids. They see ribbons of light. The freeways are illuminated arteries, and the cars' headlights are yellow corpuscles.

The spirit of Christmas spreads across the valley in checkered patterns and winking bulbs. Suburbia's houses glitter with blue, red, green, and white lights. Wreaths of holly deck the doors. Jingles jangle, liquor pours, and eggnog quenches. Chimney's smoke, sleighs fly, and reindeer prance over homes in which an occasional mouse still stirs. Newell is preparing a Christmas sermon. Goodhew is orchestrating the downtown Festival of Lights. C.G. has bought and wrapped Tony's presents. And although Khalid is mourning Nicole, he is filling his daughters' stockings with presents. He thinks of cache-sexe, but each daughter gets only a tube of Carmex. Garcia is prepping his men to patrol the streets, the homeless are huddled in the river bottom, and Squazza is lying in a hospital bed.

Yes, Loviers City is a town with a mission. It has a soul. It knows that heaven is for brethren, that haste makes waste, that you'll do time if you do crime. The people love their city. They want it to thrive, be clean, and beautiful. The toters also serve. Don't delay, obey. Do three Cs and you will get the Rs. Ring the bell of Pluribus, and if you drop, be sure to pause and shop refreshed. God bless you gentlemen and women on your merry rounds, and when you pay the bills, remember, need is not greed, whereas cleanliness is next to … On the days you throw away, think of the *Blue, Brown,* and *Green.* It pays.

"Did you hear about Nicole?" C.G. stirs her cappuccino.

"Yes, Ziad is devastated." Wilson takes a sip of black coffee from a beige cup with a green bell on the side.

"I hope they catch whoever did it," says C. G. as she continues stirring.

"All they have to go on are several footprints in the irrigation ditch." There is a drop of coffee on Wilson's beard.

"Don't you think it's odd that Nicole would end up in the walnut grove?" The espresso machine behind C.G. hisses loudly, and she looks up, startled.

"Do you think that means something?"

"I'm not sure. I just think it's odd."

"You don't think Ziad had anything to do with it?"

"They were very close."

"Or his wife?"

"It has happened before." Wilson raises his eyebrows and frowns. C.G. bites into a glazed doughnut.

"Do you know any hit men in Loviers City?"

"No, but that doesn't mean there aren't any."

"You should write a whodunit," says Wilson.

"Maybe I will … if you'll have a book signing at Moby Dickens."

"Hey, guys, mind if I join you?" Rissotto looks relaxed in his brown polo shirt. C.G. wonders how a bow tie would look on the open collar.

"Have you heard the latest?" He continues talking, not waiting for an answer. "Another body. This time in the canal. One breast missing." Rissotto pauses, waiting for the effect of his statement to sink in.

"Is that so?" says Wilson, looking around Zeno's to see who else might have come in. "Don't you see? That means Ziad is off the hook."

"Who said he was on?" says Wilson with a slight edge to his voice.

"Because somebody walked into police headquarters with the missing part." Rissotto leans back in his chair with a satisfied look on his face. C.G. shudders and says: "That's horrible."

"Who is it then?" says Wilson.

"The body or the man?" Wilson harrumphs, and C.G. thinks that Rissotto is enjoying the suspense. Rissotto gets up and goes to the coffee bar. Zeno's is filling up with Sunday morning aficionados. "Gregor can be infuriating," says Wilson.

"That's how he is," says C.G. "You mustn't let him get to you." She blots the corners of her mouth with a paper napkin. "Infuriating or not, he was good at helping us select winners for the poetry contest."

"Except for that poem about the mind of the Republican Party."

"You were eloquent in quashing that one." Rissotto returns with a double crème espresso and a brownie topped with almond slivers.

"Where was I?" says Rissotto. "Oh, yes. The body was a tute, and the man was a trucker." He sips his espresso and smiles. "Never hook up with a trucker." Wilson winces.

"How do you know all this?" asks C.G.

"My friend on the force," says Rissotto.

"Is he always handy with hot tips like this?" says Wilson.

"Who said it was a he."

"Excuse me?"

"I didn't know you had a friend on the force."

"Well, now you do," says Rissotto, peeved.

"I'm glad you have a friend on the force," says C.G. "Please go on."

"What's to go on … Hooker woman, trucker man."

"Is that all?"

"You want more?"

"You're the one who started it," says Wilson. There is a moment of silence, and they each sip their coffee. Finally, Rissotto says: "The truck driver walked into the station, confessed, and displayed the breast."

"Just like that?" asks Wilson.

"Just like that. In a Ziploc. He took it out of his pocket, looked at the deputies, and confessed."

"Why would anyone confess to something like that?" says C.G.

"My friend says he had a guilty conscience."

"Freud would have a lot to say about that," says Wilson.

"The missing breast," says C.G., "of course. What every man wants!"

"His mother," says Wilson.

"You guys are morbid," says Rissotto.

"It's your story," says Wilson.

"Please go on," says C.G.

"Anyway, the hooker's name was Melinda Boyer. She was a drifter who hung out at gas-station coffee shops and discount motels. Liked to sing at the top of her voice, in public. That way she wouldn't miss a trick." Wilson winces again. "Been arrested for drugs and petty theft."

"And the trucker?" asks C.G.

"Name of Chip Berger. Liked rough sex. Tied his victims up with a rope before strangling them. Said he put Melinda's body in the cab of the tractor-trailer rig before dumping her in the canal. Drove around with it in the back for two days."

"Your friend is sharp on detail," says Wilson. "Was she there when this man, what's his name, Chipped Beef, displayed the breast?"

"I don't know."

"Come on, Gregor. You're holding out on us."

"Okay, she was there. He sliced it off with a razor. Are you satisfied?"

"It's not for me to decide," says Wilson. "I imagine that was up to Chip."

"At least she'll never need a mastectomy," says Rissotto.

"Now who's being morbid," says C.G.

"Sorry."

"I wonder if they gave it a biopsy?" says Wilson.

"You boys are terrible," says C.G. "I don't think I want to have coffee with you any more."

"Sorry, C.G. Sometimes black humor gets the upper hand. Seriously, though, Gregor, what about Nicole and the other woman? Did our man Humburger say anything about them?"

"He did. He confessed to them also."

"Other hookers, I can understand," says C.G. "But Nicole? How could she ever get involved with someone like that?"

"Beats me," says Rissotto.

"Maybe we should ask Ziad," says C.G.

"Remember me?" says a man in a black suit, blue-and-red paisley tie, white shirt, and gold cuff links. He looks around the hospital room. His chestnut hair is combed and parted on the left.

"Tyrus Ullman, of course," says Rudy Squazza. "Our lawyer for the homeless. An unexpected pleasure."

"I've been looking for you everywhere. Your people said you'd been hurt."

"Trust and justice worked me over."

"That's what I wanted to talk to you about. Mind if I sit down?"

"Please." Ullman eases himself onto a chair.

"First, you need to know that Khalid's suit against the homeless has been dropped."

"Good news," says Rudy. "Does that mean we can stay in the parks?"

"For now, yes. But the best part is that the city is working on plans for a shelter."

"It gets better all the time. I'm glad you dropped in. Can the nurse offer you a glass of water?"

"No thanks. Now that the parks issue is a non-issue, I wanted to ask you how this happened." Rudy recounts the lake incident. When he finishes, Ullman asks him to describe the officers.

"One had short blond hair and a red neck. The other one had long dark hairs on his knuckles." Rudy moves his body to look at

Ullman. He feels the sharp pain in his chest.

"Is that all?" says Ullman.

"That's all I remember."

"It's not much to go on … Do you remember what day it was?"

"The day that all twenty-dollar bills turned to worthless paper." Ullman looks nonplussed, and Rudy repeats the statement he heard on the radio.

"Must have been a hoax. My twenties are still good."

"Hot dog," says Rudy. "That means mine is too." Ullman repeats his question and asks Rudy how long he has been in the hospital. Rudy says he doesn't know. Ullman excuses himself and goes to the nurse's station. When he returns, he says, "It's been four days. If we count back from today, that means it must have happened on Monday. Does that sound right?"

"Yeah … Monday was the last day of my weekend binge." Rudy grimaces.

"If we can identify the officers, we have a lawsuit that's worth a lot of money." Ullman opens his attaché case and takes out a yellow pad and a silver ballpoint pen. "Monday, the eighteenth," he says out loud while writing on the pad. "Can you come up with something better than hairy knuckles and a blond cut?"

"One was called Trust and the other one Justice." Rudy rubs his red mustache with his thumb. Again, Ullman looks nonplussed, and Rudy says: "I guess they were both about five-ten or five-eleven." Ullman's pen scratches across the yellow pad.

"Anything else?"

"I don't know. It wasn't my best day." Ullman looks up from his pad. "Wait a minute." Rudy pulls on his beard, trying to recollect. "Gary … one of them said, 'Gary.'"

"Which one?" Rudy fingers the bandage on his head.

"It was Knuckles. Knuckles called the blond one Gary." Rudy's beard quivers with satisfaction.

"Were they young or old?"

"Maybe late thirties. Perhaps early forties."

"Okay, Rudy. We've got something to go on. A blond officer

in his early forties, named Gary. He has a short haircut and a partner with black hair. We're in business."

"And this is worth money?"

"You bet. It works this way: we file a lawsuit against the city seeking damages. We'll go for five million, for unprofessional conduct and dereliction of duty. The officers should have taken you to the station and booked you. Instead … well … I don't need to tell you what you know already. But in a court of law, your arm, the ribs, the concussion, and the rest amount to a lot of pain. There will be physical damages and punitive damages. Much depends on the final medical report. But first, I've got to find the officers." Ullman puts the pad and pen back in the attaché case and snaps the shiny brass lock. "Do you know when you'll be discharged?"

"No."

"I'll ask on my way out. Well, Mr. Squazza, it's been good talking with you. And I'm sorry for your pain. I'll be seeing you again."

"Alfredo, how are you? Please have a seat." Garcia sits down in the stiff armchair opposite the mayor's desk—a big walnut desk with a glass top. Goodhew's back is to the window and his face is in shadow. Garcia adjusts his eyes to the glare. "Alfredo, we have a problem—big lawsuit. And I need you to tell me what happened." Garcia shifts nervously in his chair and says that two of his officers helped a homeless person who had fallen into the lake. "That's not what I heard," says Goodhew.

"You can't trust the homeless," says Garcia.

"There were witnesses," says Goodhew.

"They're all liars."

"Broken bones and a concussion don't lie, Alfredo." Goodhew

drums the top of his desk with the fingers of his right hand. "Our notorious Rudy Squazza was in the hospital for almost a week, and there's a detailed medical report on his injuries."

"He fell out of a dumpster." Garcia casts his eyes wildly around the mayor's office, from bear flag to city flag.

"I thought he fell in the lake?"

"He did. I mean, before the lake."

"I don't want a cover-up on this one, Alfredo." Goodhew's voice is cold and clipped. "Your men acted unprofessionally, and you've got to deal with it. There's too much at stake." Garcia is about to say something, but Goodhew interrupts him. "I mean it, Alfredo. There are rogue elements on the force, and you've got to cull them out." Garcia pinches his lips and folds his arms across his blue chest. "This lake episode is the last straw. The case is going to trial, and the city is being sued for three and a half million dollars. Do you think we have that kind of money to cover your ass with?" Garcia crosses and uncrosses his blue-trouser legs. "The Council won't stand for it … and neither will I." Garcia tries to say something, but Goodhew interrupts. "If you can't do something about the problem, we'll have to find someone who will." Garcia acknowledges that he gets the message. "Good," says Goodhew. "I want names, layoffs, resignations, firings. Whatever it takes. Do I make myself clear?" Garcia says he understands. "And I want it done now. With a full report from you by next Tuesday."

After Garcia leaves, Goodhew asks his secretary to get Khalid on the phone.

"Ziad? Hi, this is David Goodhew."

"Hello, David, how are you?"

"My condolences again, Ziad, for Nicole."

"Thanks, David. I appreciate that."

"I have the police report."

"I'm listening."

"She was one of three local victims of a big-rig trucker by the name of Chip Berger."

"Are they sure he's the one?"

"They're sure. He turned himself in with a body part from the last victim and eventually confessed to all three murders."

"So it wasn't one of the homeless."

"No."

"What does it say about Nicole?"

"You mean how it happened?"

"Yes."

"Her car was spotted on Weir Road between the freeway and Loviers City. It had a flat tire. The theory is the trucker stopped to help and abducted her."

"Shit and fuck!"

"Yes, it's terrible. I'm so sorry."

"Fucking asshole. I hope she didn't suffer."

"I hope not."

GOODHEW POURS HIMSELF A cup of coffee. He likes it black. He helps himself to a Danish and a paper napkin. Konlon pours cream into her cup and stirs it with a wooden mixer. Ohr is chewing on a doughnut. Khalid is sitting to one side with a sad look on his face. He takes a sip of coffee from his preferred cedar cup. Speer comes in and greets the Council members with his customary "good morning everybody."

Goodhew hears a *pop*. Something hits his right shoulder. More *pops*. A coffee mug shatters, and Goodhew dives under a table. Konlon is on the floor next to him. From the corner of his eye, he sees Ohr go out the back door. More shots. The sound of breaking glass. Goodhew feels a hot trickle on the back of his head. A door slams. Silence. Footsteps. Then metal clicking against metal. Konlon and Goodhew look at each other. Goodhew closes his eyes and lies motionless. His shoulder hurts. There is banging on the door. A crash. A splintering of wood. *Pop, pop, pop.* A voice says, "Freeze." More shots. Silence. Goodhew opens his eyes. There's a red stain on the rug next to Konlon's hip. Footsteps. Somebody says, "It's safe. Are you okay?" Goodhew gets up on one knee and then stands. The blue, brown, and green flag is lying crumpled on the rug.

Men wearing swat-team paraphernalia swarm into the room. Shouts. Confusion. A wail of sirens. "In here … Everybody out … Make way." Men dressed in white appear. They carry stretchers. Goodhew holds his right shoulder with his left hand. Khalid pokes his head up from behind a desk. Speer and Konlon are lying on the floor. The men in white are leaning over them. Ohr, talking on his phone, walks through the splintered door.

"Am I glad to see you!" says Goodhew. "Are you okay?"

"Yes. I jumped from the balcony and landed in a bush. A few scratches … nothing serious. Then I called for help. How are you?"

"A nick on the shoulder." Goodhew looks at his red fingers. "But I'm worried about Speer and Konlon." Garcia appears.

"What happened?"

"You tell me."

"Do you know the man?"

"I didn't see him."

"He's shot."

"Will he live?"

"Too soon to tell."

"Anyone else?"

"One of my men."

"We'd better get you to the hospital," says Ohr. "You are bleeding." The two men step over the flag, the broken coffee cups, the red stain, and an overturned chair. They cross the lobby, the glass doors open, and they go out. The police are cordoning the area with yellow-ribbon tape, and on both sides of the steps, people lean in behind it, craning their necks. Goodhew wonders how so many men and women could gather in one place so quickly. The flashing red lights on the vans and police cars are blinding. A television announcer speaks into a microphone: "This is LCRW. It's been an eventful morning. The mayor and two members of the City Council have been shot by an unknown assailant."

The following day, *The Sun* headline says: MAYOR SHOT. A sub-heading reads: "Two Council members, one officer, and the attacker wounded." There is a front-page full-color photo of the mayor being interviewed by the media. His walrus mustache envelops the microphone. Newsmen surround him, and cameras click. Goodhew's right arm is in a sling. C.G. thinks there is nothing like a good shooting to catch the interest of the public—instant news for millions of viewers and social media. Loviers City is now the navel of America. Everybody wants to know who the shooter is.

The mayor talks about the man with the handgun and how, after entering the Council chambers, he locked the door from the inside and started firing. How, wounded on the shoulder, he himself feigned death. The newscaster says that the man also shot Albert Speer and Kathy Konlon and that Thomas Jefferson Ohr—as bullets lodged in the wood paneling—escaped through a back door, jumped from a balcony, and called for help on his cell phone. One policeman is in serious condition, and the intruder is in critical condition, shot after the police broke down the door. All the wounded are being treated at Community Hospital. The mayor, having escaped with a superficial shoulder wound, does not know who the intruder is or the reasons for the attack. The incident is under investigation by local authorities.

C.G. zaps the screen, and it goes black. But she imagines talking heads on millions of sets in rooms in city apartments, suburban homes, and rural houses all across America. News entertains the nation and feeds its curiosity. News blurs the lines between the real and the unreal, between tragedy and fantasy. *The Sun* adds nothing to the discourse, except for interviews with Council members and witnesses who give detailed accounts of the shooting. No motive emerges, and no one knows who the attacker is. C.G. wonders if it's a homeless person or someone from the SPCA. There's no reason for disaffection by the homeless. They're getting a shelter and all kinds of new services. Squazza's beef is legitimate beef, and he's suing the city. There's no point in shooting a cash cow. Besides, he's just out of the hospital and in no condition to hurt anyone. The SPCA? After dumping the truckload of rotting crows? It's plausible, and they have attacked animal research facilities in the past. But they always strike clandestinely, free the animals, fade away, and then take responsibility. Did they not claim the truckload of crows? Or did somebody else claim it for them? It's hard to know. But why do it if you don't claim the deed? C.G. is puzzled.

Tony calls from Texas. "Honey, are you all right?" C.G. says she is, and Tony says the shooting has been all over the news. "Is Loviers City safe? Are you?" She reassures her husband, and he says he misses her. She says she's looking forward to more time with him after Christmas. Tony says there's always so much going on in Loviers City; C.G. feigns surprise.

"Do you mean to say nothing happens in Austin?"

"Nothing like this!"

"What about the officers who were shot recently? And that poor black man who was dragged to death behind the pickup. What's his name? James Byrd?"

"That was Jasper, not Austin!"

"Yes, but it was Texas, and it was infinitely worse. Besides, we don't have hate crimes in Loviers City, just an occasional deranged trucker who strangles women. And he doesn't even live here."

"That's what I'm worried about."

"Don't worry, darling. The chief of police is a friend."

"That worries me more."

"You have no respect for the law."

"That's right."

"They catch criminals."

"Only when they turn themselves in."

"Anyway, now that Chip Berger is behind bars, you have nothing to worry about."

"I hope not."

"You don't. Really."

"California is a crazy place. I worry about you and cults like Heaven's Gate."

"As though you didn't have Waco."

"That was different."

"It certainly was. They didn't kill themselves. The FBI did it for them. It knows nothing about the religious fringe."

"Sure it does."

"Not then, it didn't. And your escapee from death row?"

"You mean Martin Gurule? He's not *my* escapee."

"I worry about you, darling. Your lunatic fringe is much more violent than ours. California may be crazy, but Texas is demented."

"At least we don't have child molesters."

"Have you looked under every stone?"

"I wouldn't throw stones if I were you."

"At least I don't live in a glass house!"

"Not to worry about glass houses. It's grass huts that are dangerous."

"How so?"

"There was once a village chieftain who liked to stow thrones. Year after year, he stowed them in a grass hut until, one day, a throne fell on his head."

"Oh, my."

"The moral is, if you live in a grass hut, you should not stow thrones."

"Ha, ha … very funny."

"I thought so. Anyway, be careful, think of me, and sell the grass hut."

"I think of you all the time. I love you."

"Hugs and kisses."

"Kisses to you too. Bye."

Everybody in Loviers City is talking about the shooting, and because nobody knows the attacker, everybody has a theory. High on the blame list are the homeless and the SPCA. They are the two groups most frequently cited. Some people blame abortion activists, and every now and then, when someone mentions Roswell and New Mexico, they say it must have been an alien. A young man wearing a Uranus T-shirt claims to have seen a flying saucer hovering over City Hall. One thing is certain: Loviers City is alive, although perhaps not well. It's as though someone has kicked a hornet's nest. A middle-aged father in a brown suit, a white shirt, and striped tie says the shooter is a deranged faggot. He stations himself in front of the First Unanimist Church and waives a sign that says: *God Hates Faggots*. His blond, sixteen-year-old daughter spells him from time to time. She stands in front of the Postmodern Library, holding the sign. A reporter from *The Sun* asks why. She says: "God is perfect hate."

"What is perfect hate?" asks the reporter.

"It's God's condemnation of faggots."

"But the church tells us that God is love."

"Not when faggots are involved. For them, God is hate."

"How do you know that?"

"He talks to my daddy."

There was a time, not long ago, when Loviers City was united and happy, unanimous in its pursuit of Godliness. Recently, however, splinter groups have surfaced, and they disrupt the purpose of the *Blue*, *Brown*, and *Green*. There have been beatings, shootings, and strangulations. Where once order prevailed, disorder, like the Gorgon's head, threatens to turn all hearts to stone. C.G. is beginning to think that Newell's power of positive thinking—the very force that animated Speer's yellow trucks, colorful dumpsters, and the people's pooper scoopers—has given way to the lure of bigotry; that the hate she saw in the early poetry submissions has not disappeared, but has in fact surfaced with a vengeance; and that Satan himself is stalking the good will of Loviers City. She thinks that the cold wind of the Santa Ana threatens its warm unanimity and that self-serving ignorance is subverting the efforts of those who would mold the city into a harmonious whole. C.G. shares her concern with Goodhew, and he expresses his own unease at the turn of events. They are having lunch at the Loviers Flag Café. C.G. orders a chef's salad, and Goodhew orders soup and a turkey sandwich.

"What was it like, lying there on the rug? Waiting for the assailant to finish you off?"

"Scary as hell, like all eternity … until the swat team yelled 'freeze' and the shootout started. When the assailant locked the door, I thought I was a goner."

"I would have been petrified."

"Time stopped. And it didn't start again until after I got up off the floor."

"I can't imagine anything worse."

"It felt like I was in two simultaneous zones: one horizontal and the other vertical, like dream and reality. Except that this nightmare was real, and when it was over, everything … the confusion and chaos … still seemed unreal. Then, suddenly time resumed, after its earlier suspended state." The waitress brings their food.

"Anything to drink?" C.G. orders ice tea, and Goodhew asks for coffee, black.

"That's a story for your grandchildren."

"No doubt. For a moment, I thought I'd been shot in the head. Then I realized that the hot trickle down my neck was coffee."

"Thank God for coffee."

"What would we do without it!" Goodhew laughs, and C.G. nods her head. "What I can't figure out is the shooter's motive."

"Is he still in intensive care?"

"Yes."

"How are Albert and Kathy?" C.G. spears pieces of ham and lettuce with her fork.

"Improving. And the officer will live."

"Who do you think did it?"

"We have no idea. I called the SPCA, but they said they had nothing to do with it. And I asked Squazza to look at a picture of the attacker. He said he had never seen him before."

"Where does that leave us?"

"Nowhere." Goodhew bites into his sandwich.

"I'm sorry to hear that."

"I could strangle the two officers who beat up Squazza! Do you know that we have a three-and-a-half-million dollar suit on our hands? Just when our finances were in good order and we were ready to help the homeless."

"It must be frustrating."

"You can say that again. All the churches have offered to help, not just First Unanimist. The City Council voted to allot two hundred thousand dollars for converting the empty Goodyear warehouse into a shelter. And Reach will provide daytime social services through June thirtieth. And we'll get matching federal funds for both. Don't you think that's a big step forward?"

"I do."

"The key is to provide job training, mental health, and substance abuse treatment so we can move the homeless into self-sufficiency. And the Department of Public Social Services will coordinate it. We're the first to put it all together."

"You deserve a lot of credit for keeping the issue alive."

"I can't believe Khalid wanted to deport them."

"He did?"

"Yes. He was going to buy them a one-way bus ticket to nowhere." Goodhew sips on his coffee. Two drops cling to his mustache.

"The crows did a lot of damage to his walnut crop. I imagine he took his frustrations out on the homeless."

"That's no excuse."

"Maybe not, but he feels threatened. He came up the hard way."

"Didn't we all? It's a good thing the person who strangled

Nicole was employed … and the shooter too. There would have been hell to pay had the homeless been involved."

"I'm so relieved no one was killed." C.G. sips her tea. There is a smudge of red lipstick on the straw.

"Once he recovers, the shooter will face plenty of charges."

"How's your shoulder?"

"Feels pretty good. The stitches come out tomorrow. Gladys says they are as neat as the quill of a crow."

"Neat?"

"Neat is good. She believes in the mystical power of crows."

"The Homeless" is one of Nora Silber's class assignments, and Jasmine Khalid has chosen it as her topic. She thinks it will be more interesting than "Violence on Television," "Home Safety," "Roe vs Wade," "Corporate Mergers," "Renewal of the Inner City," or "Vouchers and Public Education." Jasmine is aware of her father's dislike for the homeless, and her choice reflects no small measure of teenage rebellion. She and her sister knew about Nicole, but their disapproval showed itself only in hostility and alienation, although Jasmine feigns a loving attitude in order to exploit her father's guilt and generosity.

Ziad is opposed to the idea that a daughter of his would ride a motorcycle, but, in time, he succumbs to her pleas. She says she will be ultra-safety-conscious and never do anything stupid, like going too fast or taking chances. She claims that motorcycles, when handled correctly, are safe. She says: "I will drive defensively and never drink at the bars, that is, the handle bars." She smiles demurely and curls her father's objections around her little finger. He is not impervious to his daughter's charms. Jasmine is more beautiful than his former mistress and wears a teenage blush. There is no worm in the rose of her cheeks, and her scent insinuates itself into the crevices of his resistance. Dorothy Khalid, her mother, is uneasy about motorcycles, but the husband's will prevails. For Christmas, and after an appropriate period of driver education, Jasmine gets a red Ducati Supersport 750, a black leather jacket, leather pants, and a helmet. She, or rather she and the Ducati, are sex on wheels—an erotic dream machine. She feels a boost of holiday octane: a desire to blast out of convention, a foretaste of what she's been missing. She says none of this to her parents, only a blushing "Thank you" as she throws her arms around her father's neck and plants a daughterly kiss on his left cheek. The small lights on the Christmas tree wink from one branch to another as father, mother, and the two daughters open presents wrapped in red, green, and gold.

That afternoon, Jasmine takes her new 750 for a spin. In her black helmet, black leather jacket, leather pants, black gloves, and boots, she and the machine are one. Her black hair hangs in ringlets around the collar of her jacket. She listens to the growl of the Ducati Supersport and the whistling of the wind around her visor. She feels free and in control when she squeezes her thighs against the red fuel tank, shifts gears, and accelerates. Bushes, trees, and houses slip by as she leans into the curves. Soon, Loviers City is behind her, and the desert unfolds. Joshua trees, saguaro, and yucca go by in a blur. Jasmine listens to the throaty purr of the engine. The acceleration thrills her. She is flying. She feels a high beyond pot and speed. Body and mind together ride on the afternoon currents of air and light. Her senses are attuned to the vibrations of the machine and the eternal rumblings of infinite space. She is not afraid.

Ziad asks if she had a good ride. She presses a cold cheek against his and says, "Oh, Daddy, I've never been happier." Ziad is happy too. He has never seen his daughter so excited. He tells Dorothy that the Ducati was a good choice and not to worry.

Christmas comes and goes, but the winter rains remain. The crow population returns to normal—that is to say they still fly the skies of Loviers City but in reduced numbers. They no longer rain walnuts from on high, nor do they themselves drop like flies. They no longer afflict people's daily lives. The dogs howl less frequently, the cats are less skittish, and the hens, once again, are laying eggs. Gladys Goodhew stops buying anemic eggs from the supermarket. The eggs with plastic-tasting yolks are a thing of the past. She and her husband, David, enjoy the rich, orange-colored flavor of their Araucana eggs. Goodhew still believes that haste makes waste.

Despite the desolate look of the charred river bottom, the homeless return to their newly-built shacks in anticipation of more comfortable digs at the renovated Goodyear warehouse. The social service programs kick in, and the homeless now live with higher purpose. They feel less abandoned. Squazza's ribs no longer hurt, but he has headaches that could split the world. Khalid's new secretary, unlike Nicole, has no surplus virtues, and he, therefore, is more attentive to his wife and daughters.

The SS combs the neighborhoods, the yellow trucks resume their roar, and the trash from the toters pours into their gaping maws. Sanitation squads check the swirls before the smells unfurl. Next to the freeways, the dopers and petty criminals wear their orange vests, pick up the weekly quota of litter, and drop it in the orange bags. Loviers City inches ever closer toward Godliness. At the downtown bus terminal, above a urinal in the men's room, a black graffito on white tile says: *Pee Refreshed*. Outside, the hookers display long, bare legs and wear flimsy iridescent blue and yellow dresses. They ply their wares up and down the street of arrival and departure. Garcia and Khalid want to hustle them out of town, but Goodhew is thankful that Chip Berger is behind bars and no one else has been strangled. Newell refers to birds' nests in your hair, and the congregation thinks of crows flying westward into the sunset. The ancient pepper tree stands scarred but alive.

Wilson sells books at Moby Dickens, Rissotto and Silber teach their classes, Ohr keeps a lid on disagreements, and Konlon—now recovered from her thigh wound—pursues new environmental venues. Speer undergoes facial surgery for the bullet that fractured his jaw. Tony calls C.G. from Austin, and she talks to him about the new art show she is organizing at the museum. The shooter regains consciousness but is still in the hospital and not talking. Garcia fires Knuckles and Creases, and Ullman is suing them and the city. The basketball season is in full swing, and Loviers High is winning for the *Blue, Brown,* and *Green.* Coca-Cola and Snickers pay for equipment and uniforms, and their vending machines snap and rattle. Cogg applies Carmex to Leila's chapped lips.

It's the year of the millennium, the year of the anticipated worldwide computer meltdown, the year that will revert to 1900 in the flash of a second. In one brief moment, one century will disappear with an electronic crash—total collapse ... chaos. People are edgy and nervous. Paranoid pundits warn of reverse cash flows, stock fluctuations, global recession, and negative returns—universal symptoms of a world economy gone sour. Prepare. Do not dally. Sell. With currency devaluations, buy gold. The market, as it lives and breathes, is a monster without mercy.

Citizens stockpile food and cash. In California, they say the crash may be worse than the big one—the earthquake that will bless Las Vegas with views of the Pacific Ocean. Fearful people buy pistols, guns and, rifles to ward off looters. Mine is mine, they say. They are the survivalists who, when the ocean liner sank, chopped off, with an axe, the fingers of those drowning and clinging to the sides of the lifeboat. Doomsday cults, clones of Heaven's Gate, proliferate. Hysteria grows with every passing day. 2000. The end of the world. Face your maker. Repent now. Crucify the faggots. Hang the harlots. Dismember the homeless. Eradicate sin. Divest yourselves of evil. Know the devil. Hate. Pull the teeth of temptation. Be prepared. Scout the opposition. Join forces. There is strength in numbers. March united toward the celestial launching pads for embarkation into eternity—the eternity of bliss. Meanwhile, beware of the Y2K millennium bug.

For some time now, Loviers City has been developing a

consciousness of itself, cultivating self-awareness, an identity that assimilates the individual into the group without submerging idiosyncrasies. Differences are encouraged, provided they do no damage to the group. Despite Khalid's efforts to ban the homeless, his initiatives have been rejected by the City Council, and ironically, he now has a plaque honoring his twenty-thousand-dollar-contribution to the shelter. Loviers City has been highlighting its social responsibilities, and thanks to Goodhew's and Newell's efforts, its social services are beginning to make a difference.

Although the homeless can still be seen on the streets, they spend the night in the newly renovated shelter where, now that it is winter, they find warmth. They are grateful. In their own way, the homeless also make a contribution to Loviers sense of order. They pick up bottles and cans and the litter missed by the motorized sweepers. Khalid calls them vultures, but Goodhew, with Konlon's prompting, points out that vultures are an important link in the natural order of things. Goodhew reminds Khalid that even if they are ugly and eat rotting flesh, they perform an essential function. They eat leftovers. The mayor urges the residents of Loviers City to think of the homeless as important scavengers who save the city money—money it would have to spend to hire additional garbage collectors. "It's a quid pro quo," says Goodhew. "We provide the shelter; they help keep the city clean. Does that not merit God's blessing?"

GREGOR RISSOTTO WALKS INTO Moby Dickens and spies George Wilson peering into a computer screen from behind the desk.

"Happy New Year!" Gregor removes his khaki golf hat and rubs his balding pate with an affectionate palm.

"And the best of cheer." Wilson punches a few keys and looks up. "What can I do you for?"

"I'm looking for a first edition of *In Our Time*."

"Let's see what's available." Wilson punches keys and fidgets with his left hand as titles and information etch themselves across the screen. "I can get you a signed first edition—Boni and Liveright, 1925, without a dust jacket, in so-so condition—for about fourteen thousand. A first edition, unsigned, in better condition, again without a dust jacket, is around five thousand."

Gregor strokes his chin, looks at the shelves of books and says: "Fourteen thousand is a bit steep. I'll go for the unsigned. This way, in my time, I'll be able to afford a first edition of *Sanctuary*." He hands a Visa card across the desk.

"I should have it by next Friday."

"Excellent … How's business?"

"Not bad … Christmas is always good." Wilson hands back the card. "How's the new semester?"

"It's a so-so class. A couple of students are talented. But most of them want to write best sellers and make lots of money, like Sheldon and Steele."

"Everybody wants to make money."

"But only a few are chosen." Gregor returns the Visa to his wallet. "I tell my students that S & S write trash. You know, like the stuff we dump on Eagle Mountain."

"What do they say?"

"Never mind the trash, as long as it sells. If it sells, they say, fame will come."

"Dubious fame. In time it smells."

"You know what my class said last semester, while we were reading *Moby Dick*? You'll appreciate this … Why does Melville use so many words?" Wilson leans back in his chair, opens his mouth, and laughs silently into his white beard. "So, this semester I'm using short contemporary stuff, like *Spanking the Maid* and *The Dead Father*. We buried the *Father* and now we're spanking the *Maid*."

"Is it working?"

"Too soon to tell. They like the shorter length, but most don't know what to do with metafiction." Gregor twists his hat in both hands. "'If the father is dead,' they say, 'How can he be alive?' As for the maid, they don't like the way her many entrances contradict each other."

"Have you tried more traditional fiction?"

"Yes. I had them read "Hills Like White Elephants," and you know what they said? 'It's too hard. We don't understand what Hemingway is getting at.'"

"Maybe students don't know how to read?"

"You may be right. Between television, video games, and virtual reality, books may become obsolete."

"And I'll go out of business."

"Not as long as I'm alive."

"It's five o'clock. Can I buy you a drink?"

"Sure." Wilson closes shop, locks up, and the two men walk down the street toward the Mission Inn, past the pool, the tall palms, the big bell, the archway, and into The Blue Parrot. Gregor sees his reflection in the illuminated mirror, and his gaze scans the labels on the bottles. He eases himself into a padded chair near the bar and Wilson does likewise. A waitress wearing a dark blue décolletage and a short blue-feathered skirt takes their orders. The two men visit the hors-d'oeuvre bar and return with little meatballs, cheese, crackers, salsa, and Fritos. The waitress brings the martinis, each one with a pickled onion on a toothpick.

"Cheers."

"It's not only that students don't know how to read any more," says Gregor. "They don't like what we read. We used to read Thackeray, Eliot, Dickens, Swift, Milton, you know, the canon. Nobody's interested in the canon any more. Like dress codes, now it's race, class, and gender ... queer attitudes and ethnic stereotypes. My colleagues in English have become anthropologists and sociologists. They want to deconstruct our culture's encoded values, improve society. Even Shakespeare is suspect. They say we fought the Revolution but remain colonized by English literature."

"There's a red herring," says Wilson. "If we dismiss Shakespeare, what happens to the pleasure of the text? Besides, delight in language is not confined to English. It could be Montaigne or Dostoevsky. Does reading them mean we're the vassals of France and Russia?" Wilson sips his martini. "Or Kafka and Borges? Are we then subservient to languages such as German and Spanish?" A blue parrots squawks in its jungle cage of tropical plants.

"Literature has been displaced." Gregor impales a meatball on a toothpick and opens his mouth. "People prefer entertainment news, the talk shows, funny videos, scary police chases, sex on the Internet, web sites, you name it. Letter writing was once an art form. Now, it's texting and tweets. We want instant communication, contact without substance." He drains his martini, signals to the waitress, and orders another. "We've been desensitized and isolated. Alone. It's just you and your screen. There's no room and no time to talk about love or death or feel anything that hasn't been prepackaged." Wilson finishes his martini, and when the waitress returns, he, too, orders another.

"I love books," says Wilson. "That's why I started Moby Dickens." He chews on a cracker and a cheese cube and sips on the fresh martini. "You open a book and there's the wonderful feel of the cover, the look of good print, and the touch of paper. Then there's the pleasure of reading and re-reading, of leafing forward and backward. You generate meaning. You experience the rush of the writer's creative spark ... and your own. You grasp the muzzle of language. You feel it breathing. You're in tune; you're part of a process. Words and sounds have an orgasmic pull, an internal rhythm, and a symbiosis. While it lasts, death has no dominion over time." Wilson pauses, looks at Gregor, and says: "Wow. Listen to the martinis talking."

"Let them talk," says Gregor. "It's a pleasure, a real pleasure."

Rissotto says, "I've been teaching a course in Creative Writing that features fiction by Barthelme, Calvino, Coover, Federman, and Robbe-Grillet. After reading *The Dead Father*, the students do a three-page imitation of Barthelme. When they finish *Spanking the Maid*, they will imitate Coover. After Jealousy, they will try their hand at a three-page Robbe-Grillet, and so on.

The two friends talk books and ideas. They order a third martini and talk to the waitress. When finished, they leave a substantial tip. The Blue Parrot does not squawk.

THE STUDENTS ARE SEATED around the table, the bell rings, and Paul Moser enters, late as usual. He says: "Mr. Rissotto, my computer crashed. I lost the story."

"You don't say." Gregor has heard that excuse so often; his answer is ironic. "You can't trust these modern machines."

"I'll have it for you on Monday. I swear." Moser, wearing Levis, seems contrite. Gregor smells cigarette smoke.

"I'm sorry, but I'll still have to mark you down for lateness."

"But my computer crashed."

"Seems unfair, I know. But next time, you can plan ahead. I'm sure you'll write a better story." Paul Moser takes his seat at the far end of the rectangular table. Two more stragglers come in, and Gregor checks their names on the class roster. Three absent. He looks into the faces of seven boys and five girls, reviews the material of the previous class session, and then launches into the topic for the day—metafiction. How it differs from classic realism. How it doesn't try to tell a story but is instead the story of telling. "What does it mean to say that fiction is the story of telling?" Gregor looks at the students.

Jasmine answers: "It's about the writing process." Jasmine's friends call her Jazz. She's a bright high school senior taking an advanced-standing course at City College. Gregor thinks she's the best in the class.

"And the writing process is?"

"The narrative of the writer's coming to grips with his material."

"Excellent. And the writer's material is?"

"Language."

"Language it is," says Rissotto. Painters have paint, musicians have notes, and writers have words." He pauses. "But don't traditional writers use language?"

"Yeah, but they use it the old-fashioned way," says Moser.

"How's that?" says Rissotto.

"You know. To tell a story."

"You mean, to tell a story the old-fashioned way?"

"Yeah, with characters, plot, suspense. To give a snapshot of reality."

"And metafiction isn't that?" Rissotto leans back in his chair, hoping for, and somehow expecting, an intelligent answer.

"No way, man. It's too implausible. Take the dead father. He's still alive, and his children are dragging his giant body across the country. That's no snapshot. That's fantasy."

"And fantasy isn't reality?" says Rissotto.

"You may be bigger than life, but you're no dead father. Not yet, says Jasmine." The class laughs.

"Thank you," says Gregor. "I appreciate that." He looks at Cheryl Igo, hoping to expand the conversation. "What about the other novels? Like *Spanking the Maid*? Are the maid's many entrances realistic?"

"No," says Cheryl.

"How many times does the maid come into the master's bedroom?" says Jasmine.

"You tell me," says Gregor.

Cheryl says: "At least a dozen. And each time is different … as though the author couldn't make up his mind."

"He gives us many beginnings," says Moser. "And each one contradicts the other."

"How would classic realism do it?" Gregor leans forward, his elbows on the table.

"The maid gets one entrance," says Jasmine. "That's it. No

fooling around."

"Then, why so many entrances? Doesn't that make it a bad story?"

"That depends on where you want it to go," says Cheryl confidently.

"Is it supposed to go somewhere?" says Gregor.

"Well, yeah," says Don Parker. "I kept hoping for more. Nothing happens."

"A lot happens," says Jasmine. "The maid has her pail, the sponge, the mop. And she finds strange things in the master's bed, like his erection, a fetus, and a bull's pizzle. You want more?"

"Yeah, I want more."

"That's because you're reading it the old-fashioned way." Jasmine's eyes dart from Parker to Rissotto and back. "If you read it the way Coover wrote it, you would read it metaphorically. The master is the writer, and the maid is language. The narrative is the master's struggle to impose order on the maid's disorder."

"He has a higher purpose," says Moser smiling, "like her bare ass. That's why he keeps spanking her." Laughter.

"It's the drama of the creative process," says Jasmine.

"Good," says Gregor. "I like that. It brings us back to the story of telling." He likes the way the discussion is evolving, and he himself wants to make the point. "The story in this story is not about something else. It's about itself. Metafiction is self-reflexive, and the characters in the narrative are not really people but language itself. It's about the writer's struggle to organize a coherent whole out of the imaginative process."

The class discusses the other novels, with Jasmine, Paul, and Cheryl doing most of the talking. They're the only ones who like metafiction. Don Parker and the others prefer a traditional storyline and real flesh-and-blood characters. They don't like to read metaphorically. And *Moby Dick* will always be too long. Even with short stuff like *Jealousy*, they want characters with names, not a nameless husband who is jealous of his wife and is never described. And they wish the boy and the girl in Federman's *Smiles on Washington Square* had met. Their romantic expectations are frustrated. And the aborted beginnings of ten novels in *If On a Winter's Night a Traveler* are like being left with ten dead fetuses. What's Calvino up to?

Gregor thinks that the success of each student's pastiche is linked to his or her talent and reading preferences. At the end of the semester, he adds up their cumulative grades and gives Jasmin, Paul, and Cheryl an A for the course. The others get an assortment of *Bs* and two *Cs*, mainly for late papers and absences. Gregor thinks that grade inflation is here to stay.

RISSOTTO IS MAKING NOTES for a novel. With a blue ballpoint, he jots down ideas in a red spiral notebook. He likes the intimacy of the handwritten, the heartbeat of a script that is part of the arm, the eye, and the mind. Later, he will revise on his computer, but he thinks that the machine distorts the flow of a first draft, notes particularly. He doesn't know yet what to call the novel, but he wants it to be about Loviers City, something like Sherwood Anderson's *Winesburg, Ohio* but different. Not what goes on behind closed doors and window blinds, but something that is group oriented. He wants to dramatize the life of a town in intricate detail and broad complexity, to paint the whole as a living thing, a place that is both flesh and soul. Not the psychology of the individual, although his or her needs and fears will be part of it, but the psychology of a city: how it works, what it wants, and where it is going. Not whodunits, embezzlement, sex, power, greed, jealousy, love and loss—all of it embellished with chainsaws, espionage, murder, fast cars, faster women, and powerful men. He wants some of these shenanigans squished into a novel but only if they contribute to the body of the text—a text with bone, nerves, blood vessels, connective tissue, skin, complexion, and, yes, even hair, particularly hair, since Rissotto has so little of it.

Rissotto wants to write the novel of recent events: murder, sex, poison, and all the rest. He wants to describe people, animals, sanitation, and cleanliness—all the happenings and relationships that define a town. Can he write such a novel using the old conventions? Linear plot, detailed descriptions of characters, interactive motivation, suspense, and the familiar stuff of classic realism. Of course he can. Why not? But there are other options. On the one hand, Loviers City exists, so he can't undercut its presence with metafiction. He can't pretend it isn't there. On the other hand, he himself names the people in it. Who kills crows? Who plants an ancient pepper tree? Who flips the switch for the Festival of Lights? Who rides through the desert with Jasmine on her red Ducati Supersport 750? How does he reconcile the two?

Rissotto wants to create a ring of counterfeiters run by the chief of police. He wants a whole network of corrupt citizens to produce and distribute the bills: 100s, 50s and 20s. Rissotto is fascinated by the real and the false, the authentic and the unauthentic. Does it matter if a false bill can't be distinguished from a true one? Is the counterfeit a threat to society and, if so, who will mediate between the legitimate and the illegitimate? The FBI? If Garcia, the representative of law and order, is subverting the order he is paid to protect, where is the line between good money and bad? Besides, he'll have to rename Garcia, because that is his real name, and he can't use a real name in fiction. He will have to change it to something else, perhaps Gomez. Yes, Adolfo Gomez. So, Garcia, alias Gomez, will be the bad policeman who corrupts the system. But once the system has been subverted, corruption becomes the norm, and that standard establishes its own legitimacy. Who decides what is true and what is false?

He will also have to rename Newell, Goodhew, Grace, Squazza, and the rest. That'll be fun. Rissotto goes to the telephone directory and flips the pages from G to N to S. But how does he take a whole town, nevermind the people in it, and organize differences in a way that make sense? How does he give it cohesion and consciousness? Not an easy task, but an interesting one. Whether it's worthy remains to be seen. The proof of the pudding, as they say, is in the … Rissotto thinks back to the beginning, to Goodhew's campaign to beautify Loviers City, to Newell's conviction that cleanliness is next to Godliness, to the crows, the walnuts, the homeless, the fire, and the shooting, and to the events in a town imbued with the spirit of positive thinking—its consciousness of self, woven into the buying mood of holiday fever. Will it be able to sustain the momentum, or will Gomez's counterfeit bills subvert the town's good will?

Garcia believes in law and order, and he is not corrupt. That's why his name needs to be changed. That's the difference between fiction and reality. Reality can be bland or tragic, but in fiction you always need conflict. Think of it—Gomez versus Loviers City! The bad versus the good. The unauthentic versus the authentic. Or is it the other way around? Can the values be reversed? He'll also have to change the name of Loviers City— to protect the innocent. How about Lordsboro? Or Amityville, Eden Hill, Walnut Grove, or Santa Bara? Rissotto leafs through the atlas looking at county maps and state roads. He writes down names. He lists three columns for an imaginary town signifying Loviers City—the real place. Rissotto's favorite names are Buford, Americus, and Winsted. Each name relates to what is going on in Loviers City.

Meanwhile, thinks Rissotto, a lot has happened, but you can't just describe raw events, like the shooting in the City Council chambers. And what do you do with the homeless, the serial killer, and the explosion of crows? Maybe the trick is to take one thing at a time—use the newspapers, book reviews, and television as generative sources, weaving them together and seeing what happens. Maybe something will emerge from the collective fabric of daily events—the whole cloth of chaos. Not that you can juxtapose random happenings. Or can you? There's got to be more. That's why you want a ring of counterfeiters, so you can distinguish between the real and the false, the good and the bad, fact and fiction. Rissotto thinks of the radio hoax, when the announcer learns of the Mafia's plan to flood Loviers City with counterfeit twenties. The announcer tells the residents that after midnight all the bills will be worthless paper. Rissotto wonders how many people actually went to the bank, and if any of the twenties were fake, not that it matters. He's free to improvise any way he wants to. In fact, he floods Americus with counterfeit money because Americus is what Gregor has decided to name Loviers City.

MEANWHILE, JASMINE CRUISES AROUND town on her new wheels in search of homeless people to interview for her school paper. She is wearing faded Levis and a heavy black sweater, not the outrageous leather of Christmas. She sees no homeless people in front of the Bank of America or the Fake Mission Inn but spies one in the Chinese gazebo. She parks her machine at the curb and saunters across the grass. One look at the man's drunken leer changes her mind. She continues her search around the supermarket, the park, the bus station, and the recycling area. A homeless person is pushing a shopping cart full of empty bottles. Another is pushing a cart full of cans. They join a line of people next to the large bins. The Ducati growls to a stop, and Jasmine gets off. She leans the machine onto its kickstand and, with a five-dollar bill in her hand, approaches a woman with long gray hair that hangs down over the collar of her stained blue jacket.

"Hi. My name's Jazz. Did you get a good price for your cans?"

"What's it to you?"

"Nothing, really. I thought you might like to earn five dollars."

"How's that?" The woman looks at her suspiciously.

"I'm doing a school project, and if you'll answer some

questions, I'll pay you." The woman agrees, and Jasmine turns on her hand-held recorder. "Start with your name and say whatever you want. You know, how long you've been homeless, what it's like, stuff like that. Okay?" The woman clears her throat and says: "My name's Alice. Been on the street for maybe nine years. Um-m-m, ever since the company laid me off. Tried to get another job, you know, but couldn't. I used up my savings, couldn't pay the rent, and got evicted. You know how it is. Slept in my car, but I couldn't afford to pay for gas. So, I sold it. Had to eat. Ended up in the river bottom. Later, after they started shooting the crows, I slept in the park, along with the others. Now, I'm in the shelter. Thank God. The folks at Social Services are good. Maybe now I'll get a job."

"Thanks, Alice. You're my first interviewee. You'll bring me luck, and I wish you the best." Jasmine gives her the five dollars.

"God bless you." Alice raises her hand in a gesture of farewell, and Jasmine turns toward an African-American man wearing a red cap. He has a scruffy beard that looks like gray wool.

"Do you mind if I ask you some questions?" The man says he is not opposed to earning five dollars.

"What d' yuh wanna know?" He leans on the metal cart.

"Same stuff I asked Alice. You know, what it's like on the street?"

"It's no picnic, if that's what yuh mean."

"I don't mean anything in particular," says Jasmine. "It's a school project."

"Well, see, it's like this … hustle all day for a few bucks, eat what yuh can, an' sleep outside. Sometimes it's a party. But most a' the time it ain't. See. Maybe once a year. Only when we torch the shacks." The man scratches his wooly beard.

"You set fire to the shacks?"

"Well, things sorta got outta hand. For normal, it's just a party. Yuh know, wine an' stuff."

"Can you tell me about it?"

"Sure." The man describes the drinking around the fire,

Squazza's dance, the shooting of the crows, the sleepless nights, and the spontaneous combustion of group anger that ignited the brush, the bamboo, the makeshift dwellings, and the trees. He speaks with awe about the spectacle of the burning pepper tree. "Should'a seen it. It was like, what d'yuh call them things in church? Over the saints' heads?"

"A halo?"

"Yeah, a halo. That's what it was like. It was cosmic. But we shouldn't 'a listened to Squazza."

"Why not?" Jasmine holds the recorder closer to the man.

"He's what got us into trouble with City Hall. Afta we started sleepin' in the parks. Yuh know, the demonstration an' all. Then the po-leece beat 'im up and threw 'im in the lake. Now he hangs out in the boathouse. They messed up his head." The man talks some more about dumpster diving, hidden treasures, and all the things you can find if you know where to look. "Fill your cart with stuff. Even get a good lunch." He trails off. Jasmine thanks him and gives him a five-dollar bill. He smiles and says: "Any time, Missie Jazz. If yuh wan' more information, jez ask fo' Walter. Got it? Walter."

"Okay, Walter. Thanks. Tell me, what does Squazza look like?"

"Got a red beard. Longer 'an mine. Can't miss it."

"Thanks, Walter." Jasmine walks to her Ducati, gets on, rides it home, transcribes her interviews into the computer, and makes plans to visit the boathouse. The next day, after school, she cruises around the lake. A man with a red beard is sitting on a bench next to the wooden jetty, not far from the moored canoes. She turns the engine off and parks the machine. The man tosses a piece of bread into the water. Ducks paddle toward it. A white duck snatches it with its yellow bill, swallows, and looks around. The man tosses more pieces of bread, and the ducks gobble them.

"Are you Rudy Squazza?" asks Jasmine. The man looks at her faded Levis and black sweater.

"That's me. Who are you?"

"I'm Jasmine. My friends call me Jazz." Rudy's beard is redder and bushier than she had imagined. "Friendly ducks."

"Pretty friendly … if you have food." Rudy tosses two more pieces at the ducks, and they paddle toward them.

"It's a nice spot. I wish I'd brought some bread."

"Have some of mine." Rudy hands her an old crust. She breaks it in two and throws one into the water, away from the birds. Several flap brown wings, skimming the surface.

"Thanks." She tosses the other piece, and the ducks go after it. "You come here often?" Jasmine sits down on the bench beside Rudy.

"Pretty often. I like to feed the birds. Sometimes the swans come around, but today they're on the other side."

"I like swans."

"Yeah. They're graceful."

"Very graceful."

"So what brings you here?"

"Nothing, really. I was trying out my new wheels. My old man gave 'em to me for Christmas."

"Great wheels. I could go for wheels like that." Rudy approaches the Ducati and examines it. "What's the engine?"

"A four stroke 90° L-Twin. 9,000 RPM."

"Nice."

"Would you like a ride?"

"Sure."

Jasmine straddles the motorcycle and starts the engine. Rudy gets on the back. She tells him to hold on, and he puts his arms around her waist. The Ducati rumbles forward, Jasmine shifts, and the machine accelerates following the narrow road around the lake. It's not a big lake but big enough for one green canoe, two paddlers, five white swans, and several fishermen holding long rods. At the far end, there is a thicket of trees. A murder of crows flies out of the branches. Jasmine makes one slow loop around the lake and then a second fast loop hugging the curves. She stops at the jetty.

"Thanks, Jazz. I enjoyed that." Jasmine revs the engine. "Cool machine."

"Maybe someday, when I've got more time, we can take a longer ride."

"I'd like that."

"Bye for now."

"See you around." The motorcycle leaps forward with a roar, and Jasmine, not looking back, disappears around a bend in the road.

It's a pleasant Sunday in January, and the temperature is in the high seventies. Garcia is clipping privet in his back yard. The blades of the trimmer hum. He shapes the top of the hedge horizontally and then the sides, vertically. His eyes smart from sweat and sunscreen. He sets the trimmer down, removes his leather gloves, and wipes his face with a red bandanna. He looks up at the shrill kee-e-e-ah of a red-tailed hawk. In the western sky, crows are flying toward the river bottom.

Garcia, the police chief, feels frustrated. There has been no answer to the identity of the City Hall shooter, and he has had to fire the two officers who beat up Squazza. He is unhappy about the direction the city is going in and uneasy about the mayor's approach. Clearly, there is good, and there is bad. And there is a line to be drawn between them, but the mayor sees everything in shades of gray. Garcia would rather cut to the chase instead of going around in circles. Like Khalid, he wants the homeless deported, and he does not approve of Goodhew's social programs. He thinks the mayor is soft on crime, and he fears that this attitude spells trouble for his men on the force. They're the ones who have to cope with violence in the streets. It's wrong to second-guess instant life-and-death decisions. He thinks that a shelter and social services for the homeless are not the right solution. Were it not for Goodhew, the homeless would be long gone, and his police force intact. His men have been grumbling about leniency in high places. At the moment, however, he does not have the clout to oppose the mayor, but one of these days, he thinks, there's bound to be a showdown.

Several crows pursue the hawk. It flips over on its back and extends its legs. The crows glide away from the exposed talons. The raptor resumes its circling, wings outspread. Garcia puts his gloves back on and restarts the trimmer. The engine sputters, coming alive with a puff of blue smoke. His house is set on two acres of land near the river bottom, and the bushes growing in the southwest corner of his lot are thick and overgrown. The branches hang down over a stacked pile of firewood. The clippers are noisy, and Garcia angles the blades around the bush. He feels a sharp sting on his right forearm, another on his left, and, in quick succession, stings on his neck, ear, and cheek. Bees fly around his head and arms. He drops the trimmer and runs toward the house. The bees buzz around him in erratic trajectories, stinging him again on his face and arms. They stay with him, stinging, despite his efforts to evade them. When he reaches the sliding glass door on the patio, he opens it, squeezes through, and closes it behind him. Hard. Bees cling to his T-shirt. He smacks one on his arm and another on his cheek. He steps on them on the tiled floor. The bees outside are bouncing off the glass door. He yells to his son: "Killer bees! Close all doors and windows!" Ruben comes into the kitchen and sees bees in his father's hair. He swats them with the Sunday paper. "Ow!"

"Sorry, Dad." Garcia hands his son an American Express card.

"Use this." While Ruben scrapes stingers from the back of his father's neck, Garcia picks at the ones between the hairs on his arms. When he and his son have removed the stingers, he calls the fire department.

"Bob, it's me, Alfredo. Killer bees at my house. Get here as soon as you can. Alert the men and be careful. There are thousands." His face is swelling, and the pain is intense. Garcia goes to the medicine cabinet in the bathroom, takes a can of Bactine off the shelf, closes his eyes, and sprays his face and neck. He reaches for a towel and wipes his eyes and mustache. Then he sprays both arms. That feels better. He takes a Benadryl and washes the tablet down with a glass of water. Then he takes two aspirin. He hears the fire engine coming down the street, and with Bactine in hand, returns to the kitchen. Outside, the bees are crawling over the patio chairs, the table, and up and down the windows. The air is dense with flying insects.

Two firemen, wearing yellow suits, gloves and facemasks, walk around the house. They have metal cylinders strapped to their backs. Father and son watch as the bees attack the men. The nozzles emit a fine mist, and the bees begin to drop. The flagstones are now black with crawling insects, and the men's protective gear is covered with them. Through the glass door, Garcia yells at the men: "The hive is in the woodpile at the far end of the yard." When the men return, most of the bees on the patio are no longer moving. An occasional insect flies back and forth. The men circle the house spraying the gutters and the eaves. When finished, they return to the driveway, unstrap the cylinders, and remove their helmets.

"Thanks a lot," says Garcia. The firemen look at his swollen face and half-closed eyes.

One says, "They sure did a number on you."

"Must hurt," says the other.

"You can say that again," says Garcia.

"Do you need anything?"

"I'll be okay. What is that stuff?"

"Brent water and detergent. Clogs their breathing system." The firemen put away their gear, say goodbye, and drive off. Garcia hoses down the patio and sweeps the dead bees onto the grass. He hears the kee-e-e-e-ah of the hawk and looks up. The bird circles slowly in a blue sky. Another murder of crows flies toward the cottonwoods in the river bottom. Garcia returns to the kitchen, picks up the Bactine, and again sprays his arms and face. The medication helps, but the pain is intense. It throbs. He sits down, feeling faint, gets up, goes to the cabinet, and takes two more aspirin. Ruben is watching a football game, and through half-closed eyes, Garcia sees moving images on the screen.

Africanized bees. They're in Loviers City. Garcia knows they have crossed the Colorado River and colonized Indio; he had read, in the paper, about the field worker who was stung to death and the tethered pit bull that couldn't run away and died after being attacked. Clearly, the bees have crossed the mountain passes earlier than expected, moving west and north. Garcia feels lucky, despite the pain in his arms and head. It could have been worse. Grudgingly, he admires the insects' organization, aggression, and collective action—their single-minded purpose. Protect the hive, and when it's disturbed, attack like selfless kamikazes. One sting and you die. For the safety of the queen, guard the Mother-bee and future generations. All for one, and one for all. Just like Loviers City. No, the mayor doesn't have the killer instinct. It'll never be an All-America town with Goodhew in charge. He's too soft. You need to attack crime head on. Fry the killers, put away the dopers, shut down the pimps, arrest the hookers, and banish the homeless. They're a cancer on Loviers City, and here's the mayor, feeding these people and helping cancerous cells grow and spread. It's token cleanliness. That's all. Household trash is bad enough, but human trash is worse.

Garcia thinks about the bees' distribution of labor and purpose. Workers gather nectar and pollen, construct combs, make honey, ventilate the hive, and protect it. The Queen, fertilized by one drone and one drone only, lays eggs. The larvae are fed, and the young bees, in time, replace the caretakers who have died. The surplus drones are tolerated, but when food is in short supply, they are expelled from the hive and die of starvation. Garcia compares the homeless to the drones, and he sees no reason why hard-working residents of Loviers City should feed or house the good-for-nothing. They're a drain on the community, and they do not earn their keep. The chief of police thinks of his hard-working grandfather. He, like the Africanized bees, migrated north from Mexico to Brownsville, Texas and then west to California. Garcia admires the bees' efficient organization, and he thinks that people should be more like them—stick together and protect your own. The afternoon attack has been a wake-up call, and a painful one, but "Hey," says Garcia, "no pain no gain."

Jasmine cruises around town on her Ducati Supersport 750, looking for homeless people. She has interviewed six so far, and has good, first-hand information for her project. She rides toward the river bottom. Some of the derelicts prefer the shacks to the new shelter. Jasmine feels a sharp sting on her neck, on the exposed skin between the leather collar of her jacket and the helmet. Several insects bounce off the Ducati's visor. She accelerates toward a red car coming down the road. On the door, in gold letters, it says: *Fire Department*. She stops and removes her helmet. A bee drops onto the fuel tank and slides off. She removes her left glove, runs her hand over the back of her neck, pulls out the stinger, and looks at it. "Bummer."

Jasmine turns her wheels onto the dirt road that winds toward the river bottom. It's rough and bumpy, and she notices that the burned bushes are showing signs of green. She sees fresh plywood ahead and eases her machine to a stop in a clearing between the shacks. Two women and three men are sitting on lounge chairs, their faces turned toward the sun. One of them is holding a half-empty jug of red wine. Jasmine kills the motor. The men and women look at this apparition in black leather that looks like an angel but is dressed like the devil.

"Who sent *you*?" says the man with the jug. "Gabriel or Lucifer?" They laugh.

Jasmine removes her helmet and says: "Take your pick."

"Take your pick, she says," proclaims the man holding the jug. "Isn't that something? Who-ee-e-e-e. An' she's on her own! Are you lookin' for someone, or would you like to join us?"

"A little of both." She runs her fingers through locks of her own black hair.

"A little of both! You don't say? Our Belle from Hell wants a little of both. Well, Belle, you've come to the right place. We're someone, and you can join us, any time."

"Thanks." Jasmine kicks a stone with her boot and looks at the group. She's not sure how to manage the man's flippant tone. Maybe it's the wine.

"Today's our special day," says a much younger man. He grabs the jug and takes a drink. "It's our day of Revelation. One apparition after another. First it's the Virgin, now you."

"How do you know it's not two virgins?" says the older man, laughing.

"They say things happen in pairs," says Jasmine, repeating something Rissotto once said in class.

"You don't say? Hey, how about that? In pairs no less." The younger man takes another drink from the jug and wipes his mouth with the back of his hand. "One more happenin' an' it'll make a trinity. Then you talkin' miracle, man. Wow, woman, it's the real thing."

"Like manna from heaven," says the older man. He takes the jug back. "Or the burnin' bush. Here, have some manna." He hands the wine jug to Jasmine. She crooks an index finger through the round hole on the glass neck, tilts the jug onto her shoulder, and takes a drink. "Who-ee-e-e-e," says the man. "Just like a pro." She hands the jug back. He says: "That's some machine."

"I like it."

"How fast will it go?"

"One-sixty."

"Which is faster? You or the machine?"

"The machine." The conversation is getting out of hand, and Jasmine tries to get it back under control. "Tell me about the Revelation." The people look at each other, uncertain how to proceed. Finally, the woman wearing an orange tank top points toward the pepper tree. The skin on here arms glows in the sunlight, almost the color of her body shirt.

"The tree?"

"Look at the trunk." Jasmine approaches the tree and examines the bark's charred and gnarled bulges and fissures. She walks around the base, examining the deep cracks. Her boots kick puffs of ash from the carpet of burned leaves and peppercorns. Half way around the trunk, she sees the image. It's the head of a woman, and the perforations in the bark look like arms. The woman seems to be holding a child, or something that looks like a child. The woman in the orange tank top joins her. "What d'ya think?" The trunk's bulges and fluted crevices have fused together into a human figure. The fire has burned the low branches and suckers, leaving blackened stems. Beneath the stems, in the cracks, where the tree has been scorched, sap has congealed. "Doesn't it look like a Madonna and Child?"

"It does." Jasmine sees the weeping head of a woman holding an infant. "It's surreal!" She walks back and forth examining the figures from different angles. The best spot is head-on from about ten feet. At that distance, the imperfections blend into an eerie realism that belies the illusion.

"Forget nature," says the woman. "You're in the presence of the supernatural." There's a gust of wind. The sun shifts in its orbit, and the Virgin's lips move imperceptibly. A coyote howls from somewhere, and a crow caws volubly. Jasmine is transfixed, and her body tingles. She thinks the Mother's tears are beginning to glisten.

"What did I tell you?" says the woman. Her voice brings Jasmine back to herself, and as the sun is setting, shadows obscure the image. Gradually, the trunk's sinews, once again, look like a tree.

"It's uncanny," says Jasmine.

"Yeah," says the woman. "The best time is in the morning, when the sun warms it and the sap flows. Then you see the tears." Transfixed, Jasmine walks back to the Ducati, slides onto the seat, starts the engine, and waves goodbye. The homeless group stares at the receding apparition in red-and-black.

The next day, Jasmine goes to Rissotto's office to talk about her fiction. His desk is covered with papers, and the shelves behind it are full of books. Some of the names are familiar: Coover, Calvino, Robbe-Grillet. Others less so: Eco, Kristeva, Foucault.

"I don't know whether to write it straight or not." Jasmine fidgets with a golden locket on a chain around her neck. "I could write it the way it happened, but I'd like to do something different."

"Have you chosen a point of view?" Rissotto leans back in his chair.

"That's the problem. It's my point of view, but I can't decide how to use it." Jasmine looks out the window at the bell tower. "I could write it in the first person, but it would be more interesting, I think, in the third. I would feel less involved."

"Is that bad? Being involved."

"It's hard to explain. I know it's just a tree, but the figures that materialized were so weird. And I felt strange. It's that strangeness I want to communicate." She crosses her bare legs, and Rissotto admires her red sneakers. "Doing it in the first person somehow doesn't give me enough distance. I'm afraid I'll get bogged down in clichés." Rissotto nods.

"It sounds to me as though the third person might be more objective."

"But I don't want to write it as straight realism because, at the time, something else was going on." Jasmine uncrosses her legs and tucks them under her chair.

"What else?"

"That's what I'm trying to figure out. Writing it as metafiction won't do. That undercuts the realism."

"Metafiction does more than that."

"Yes, I know. It deconstructs encoded values, but that's not what I want to do with the story. I want to capture the feeling."

"Which is?"

"What I felt was definitely uncanny."

"And it's the uncanny part you want to communicate?"

"Right. It wasn't exactly real, but it wasn't unreal."

"Are you saying that you couldn't decide between one and the other?"

"Exactly. I know the Madonna isn't real, but it felt as though she was. And I know the tears were sap, but the effect was … well … disturbing." Rissotto smiles.

"What do you want the reader to feel? The realism of the tree or the mystery of the Virgin?"

"The Virgin," says Jasmine tugging on her locket.

"There's your answer."

"Yes, but how do I do it?" Jasmine looks into Rissotto's brown eyes, and he looks into hers.

"You'll find a way."

"I was hoping you would tell me." Jasmine curls one finger around the golden chain.

"Mother and child. That's the fantastic. When your reader accepts their mystery as real, you've got it. It's the moment of hesitation between the two that gives you the edge. A small leap of faith, and you're into the supernatural."

"I'm not sure I believe all of that."

"You don't have to. Let the reader decide. He or she will anyway. Your job is to use the words that will convey the experience."

"Won't you give me a hint?" Jasmine rubs the locket on her lower lip.

"Cultivate the uncanny, slide into the fantastic, and, when you do it right, the reader will feel it."

"That's easy for you to say."

"Why do you think they pay me?"

"I'm beginning to wonder."

"Are you asking me to write your story for you?"

"Why does it have to be so hard?"

"Because when you get it right, it's the most exciting thing there is."

"Better than sex?" Jasmine looks at him through lowered lashes.

"Aren't you too young to know about such things?"

"Why does everybody treat me like a child?" She stamps the floor with one red sneaker.

"I'm sorry. You're not a child. You're a very intelligent woman."

"Too young to be taken seriously."

"Who's putting words in whose mouth?"

"Adults never take me seriously."

"We're having an adult conversation."

"But it isn't going anywhere."

"That's because we're dealing with metafiction. It's like dancing. You go around in circles. If you want to go somewhere, you use good old-fashioned realism."

"And that's not allowed?"

"Not in this course."

"Suppose I wanted to do both."

"You could."

"So why do you keep putting me off?"

"Is that what I'm doing?"

"Yes. And you know it."

"Jazz. You're beautiful. And I'm enjoying our flirtation. I even wish it could be more, because you're bright, precocious, energetic, and talented. Anything more would be unprofessional."

"But I don't want a professional relationship." Jasmine screws her face into a pout.

"Do you always get what you want?"

"Pretty much. My old man is a pussycat. You know what he gave me for Christmas?"

"What?"

"A Ducati Supersport 750. You know what that is?"

"I can guess."

"It's performance."

"I suppose that makes you hell on wheels."

"That's what the homeless said. The day I saw the Virgin."

JASMINE LIKES THE RIVER bottom. On Friday, after school, she rides the Ducati to the shacks by the pepper tree, Rudy jumps on the back, and they follow the winding dirt road downstream through the giant cane and tall grasses to another large pepper tree—this one spared by the fire. They park the machine under its cascading branches, Jasmine unstraps a six pack of Dos Equis, and Rudy spreads a brown army blanket on the soft carpet of dry leaves and peppercorns. They sit down, and Rudy opens two bottles with his Swiss army knife.

"Cheers," says Jasmine. They drink. "How's the head?"

"Better. I'm pretty much over the headaches."

"That's great."

"The lawyer wants me to say they're still intense."

"Are they?"

"No, but I'll get a better settlement if they are."

"What are you going to say?"

"I don't know." They both take a drink. The afternoon sunshine filters through the branches casting oblique rays. "I'm reading Homer. I didn't realize what a great book the *Odyssey* is … unlike Virgil. I can't stand Virgil's convoluted style. Maybe it's the difference between the Greeks and the Romans … and their gods. The Greek gods are separate and distant, whereas the Roman ones are more like people. Things get complicated. Maybe that's why I don't like Virgil." Rudy takes a long drink and the beer foams in the bottle.

"How old are you?"

"Thirty-six. And you?"

"Eighteen. How long have you been living like this?"

"I don't know. Maybe ten years."

"Don't you get bored?"

"Not really. Where I was bored, was at the job. Eight to five. Every day. Working for corporate America. That's boring. Making money for a corporation that sells a product you care nothing about!" A crow caws in the distance.

"Even if people buy it?"

"People will buy anything if you appeal to their vanity or self-interest." Rudy finishes the beer, tosses it, and opens another one.

"What do you do all day?" Jasmine looks at him with wonder in her eyes.

"I organize my time. It's nice, organizing time." Rudy pokes his finger into a ray of sunshine. He plays with the suspended motes of dust. I once wanted to be important. But that's meaningless. All that matters is the present. Ten years ago, I was living only for the future. Now, I feel free."

"But ten years from now it will still be the present." Jasmine tosses her empty bottle, and it clinks against the other empty one. Rudy opens a fresh beer.

"Aren't you the wise one." He eyes her quizzically.

"Just trying to figure you out."

"What's to figure?"

"You're bright, well read, and you organize time."

"It suits me."

"Wouldn't something else be more interesting?"

"Like what?"

"I don't know. It's not for me to decide."

"You think I'm a bum."

"I didn't say that."

"But that's what you're thinking. Rich girl slumming in the river bottom."

"I didn't mean to offend you. I just wanted to get a handle on what you do."

"Is something else more interesting? The answer is no. If I scavenge after sunrise and before dark, I find enough to eat. Scavenging at night is a waste of time, and you get all mucked up. Dumpster diving is an occupation in itself. I find clothes and occasional change. This polo shirt was almost new." Rudy fingers the yellow collar. "So was this jacket. City College discards. Rich students always throw stuff away. Good stuff they no longer want. That's how I found my Walkman." He raises the bottle to his lips and tilts it. "I haven't dropped out. I'm exploring the underbelly of the American Dream."

"Don't you ever need money for necessities?" Jasmine is fascinated by the color contrast between the green beer bottle and Rudy's red beard.

"I do, but not as much as you might think. In August, I look for a sleeping bag to replace my old one because in November and December there won't be any. I hoard vitamins and antibiotics for the days I'll be sick and Kaopectate for the inevitable diarrhea. You even find toilet paper and toothpaste. So yes, I need money for an occasional toothbrush, but everything else I might want, people throw away, even underwear. All you have to do is wash it. I do need change for the laundromat." Rudy moves his index finger counter-clockwise in the sunbeam, and the motes of dust follow the disturbance. "I can always scavenge empty cans but that takes too long … and you only get a couple of bucks. Cans and bottles aren't on my organizational chart."

"What do you do when you're not scavenging?"

"I see you."

"No, seriously."

"I read. I meditate. I barter things I've accumulated and don't want. There's a lot of good stuff in dumpsters, but most of the time, if you don't need it, it's better to leave it. There's no way for me to own things and drag stuff around, except for items I use, like a chair, a typewriter, or a boom box. I leave the television sets for others. Besides, people steal. If you own too much, someone takes it."

"Do people really throw away so many good items?"

"Of course. Isn't Loviers City's motto: *When you pay, you throw away*? It's not just Loviers. It's the great American passion. And I'm the beneficiary. There's a bumper sticker that says, *Where there's a will, I want to be in it*. My motto is: *Where there's a dumpster, I want to be near it*."

"Is dumpster diving that much fun?" Jasmine crushes several pepper leaves between her fingers and inhales the fragrance.

"You betcha. An endless supply of Americana. All you have to do is organize time." Jasmine holds the leaves under Rudy's nose. "Nice." He examines the crushed remnants. "Objects in space. That's what they are. When you play with time, you organize space, and rearranging things is a way of marking time … How about you? What do you want to be?"

"A writer."

"A writer?"

"Not any old writer." Jasmine's voice quickens. "I'd like to leave a mark. You know, like Flaubert, Kafka, or Beckett."

"And Homer?"

"Yes, Homer, too."

"That's a tall order."

"But I may have to settle for being a woman, someone like Virginia Woolf or Toni Morrison."

"Never compromise your sex!"

"Okay. A Nobel Prize would be nice, but there are plenty of laureates whose work is ordinary. I'm looking for something unique, something in me that I can express in a way that is different."

"You must know there's nothing new under the sun."

"You're so jaded."

"And you're very young."

"At least I haven't given up."

"Suppose you're an ant minding your own business, gathering food, protecting the tribe, getting drunk on aphids, fighting when the occasion demands it, and along comes a big shovel that tears the anthill apart. Each spadeful slices through tunnels and chambers, disrupting the calm of an afternoon and the rhythm of work, and the ants try to save thousands of little white eggs—the next generation. What's an insect to think? Is it an act of God? Providence? Retribution for some unknown transgression? What? Does the ant know why this is happening? Does it know how to ask the right questions? What are the answers? It's all absurd." Rudy holds the beer bottle over an ant hole and pours some of the amber liquid into it. Ants emerge, darting this way and that. "Do they think it's the flood or manna from heaven? Will they make an entry in their ant book of wisdom?"

There are now four empty bottles next to the tree trunk. Several crows settle in the branches, and one of them caws, flexing its neck and head. Jasmine looks up. Rudy opens the last two bottles. He and she sit, not speaking, listening to the vague noises of the afternoon: the crows, an occasional mocking bird, a feral pig rooting in the tall cane, and the steady hum of distant traffic.

Jasmine says: "I need to get back. My parents expect me for dinner. I'd invite you, but my father would have a fit."

"No problemo. I'll hit the Pizza Hut on College Avenue, if you'll drop me off. If I time it right, I can snag a bogus order. Late in the day, the dumpster in the back always has warm boxes."

"I have two tickets for the Rolling Bones concert next Saturday. How about it?"

"That would be great. After The Grateful Dead, the Rolling Bones are the best."

"I'll pick you up?"

"At the shacks."

"Four o'clock?"

"Four o'clock."

"Cool."

THE RED DUCATI SUPERSPORT 750 weaves through freeway traffic. It passes between cars, pickups, and SUVS, turning here, angling there, past doors—white, green, blue, red, or silver—and between mirrors, fenders, and bumpers. It moves onto an adjoining lane, accelerates, slows down, and accelerates again. One Silverado bumper says: *Where there's a will, I want to be in it.* The driver at the handlebars of the red machine is wearing black leather. The man behind has a red beard. The two riders are at odds with the crush of automobiles, and the stop-and-go of the vehicles contrasts with the forward motion of the motorcycle.

The region's workforce is leaving the megalopolis. It is going home to suburbia. Ribbons of cement connect rows of identical houses to the big city. Every morning, millions of commuters rise, drive to work, punch in, work, climb, claw, grasp, talk, eat, pee, and shit; and when all is said and done, they return to their bedroom communities where sleep recharges the batteries. Commuters commute every day, every week, and every month of every year until accident, disease, and death claim their due. These workers, unlike the random death of bees, go to their graves in well-kept cemeteries accompanied by pomp, circumstance, and tears.

The traffic into Irwin Meadows is heavy, and the cycle, like the cars, negotiates the slow entrance of the vast parking lot. The two riders park near the amphitheater gate, insert the krypton lock into the seat brace, and secure the helmets. They join the crowd on the curving roadway flanked by grass, trees, and vendor stalls selling T-shirts, hats, tie-dyed banners, brightly-colored pants, pins, piles of CDs—enough Bones memorabilia to fill a museum. Jasmine buys two beers in plastic cups, hands one to Rudy, and takes a long drink. She wipes the foam from her upper lip with the back of her hand. The crowd is electric, and the air has the smell of grass. From a crowded rack at one of the stands, Jasmine selects a T-shirt. Above the skeleton's head, in black letters, it says: *Rolling*. And under the yellow skateboard, it says: *Bones*. Rudy takes his brown jacket off and puts on the shirt: crossed bones inside a blue oval. "Perfect," says Jasmine. Rudy finishes the beer and tosses the cup into a trashcan. Jasmine buys another one. The change goes into the zippered pocket of her leather jacket. They approach a hat stand: hundreds of red, white, and blue hats. On one hat, a lightning bolt splits a skull, and the whiteness of the skull matches the upper row of white teeth. It says: *Peel Your Face*. Jasmine finds her size, and Rudy does likewise. She pays.

Rudy walks toward a red banner with blue borders and white lettering. He reads out loud: *Rolling Bones Gather No Sauce.*

"I like that. Says it all." Jasmine buys the banner, and Rudy drapes it over one shoulder. The red of his beard is of a different color. The lights dim and go back on. Rudy and Jasmine make their way toward the terrace and sit down in the front row over the hallway. The people below them are filling the loge and orchestra seats while the fans in general admission behind them form shadowed clusters on the steep and grassy slope. The lights go out, and the crowd screams. People yell and shout. They are ready.

The stage lights come on, and the band members saunter into view. Loud, fervent yells from the audience. The red, yellow and white lights sparkle on the guitars, the drums, the keyboards, and the emulator. The players pick up their instruments and tune them. The crowd, as though with one throat and twenty thousand lungs, roars. The earth-tone colors of the electric guitars are studded with bright metallic shapes. They play BONES IN A BUCKET, and the audience is immersed in a fast swirling ocean of rock & roll. Larry Maria is on the lead guitar, Bill Mesh on bass, Rob Ear on rhythm, Wickey Bart and Phil Krickman on drums, and Kent Ryland on the keyboard.

The arms of the audience are silhouetted against the stage lights, and the arms sway back and forth with the beat of the music. Many spectators leave their seats and dance in the isles. Sounds bounce off walls, amplified. The long, flowing skirts of the women swirl in the light and the shadows, and their funky movements are late twentieth-century tribal. Behind the stage, three giant Uncle Sams, wearing top hats and dressed in red-white-and-blue, point fingers at the crowd. Their faces are skeletal. The next number is PYRE ON THE MOUND, followed by DADA TRIED and MOMMY B. GOODE. The audience is happy, fluid, evolving. Yellow balloons fly up and down in the air, bouncing from terrace to loge to orchestra. Revolving lights sweep over the heads and faces, illuminating eyes, open mouths, and wild hair. There is constant movement and compelling cadence. The vocals are low-keyed, direct, real, and sometimes tender, even as the tiger on Larry Maria's guitar growls the party stripe and the Bones' anti-capitalist lyrics. The musicians wear no ties or jackets, T-shirts only. And Maria's beard and hair are full and scruffy. Rob Ear's long hair is blond and silky, and the others keep their hair in vague control with blue and red bandannas. After a convincing PEEL YOUR FACE, with stage lightning and thunder, fans wave glow sticks, and the green phosphorescence swirls in circles. Intermission follows. The spectators stand screaming the finale, and the crowd surges into the hallways. Security guards in yellow jackets regulate the flow. The smell of grass wafts through the air. Jazz and Rudy watch the women and the flying beach balls. The women skip about, waving their tie-dyed banners.

When intermission ends, the Bones play their second set, and the audience screams for Wickey Bart's and Phil Krickman's drum solos. After Rob Ear sings YOUR BLIND ZOO, the crowd chants: "We want Phil." More chants after CHINA SPYDER and again after ANIMATED PROPHET. Finally, midst great and general satisfaction, Bart begins his solo, and the crowd's restlessness subsides. His arms move effortlessly back and forth, from the drums and brasses next to him, upward and out. He is now striking the assorted shapes of the percussion instruments that hang from a rack above his head. Eventually, Krickman joins in, and the two together generate a variety of sounds. It is their space, and it reverberates from high pitch to low, the sounds echoing each other with great skill and improvisatorial zeal. Gradually, they slip into the band's syncopated rhythms, followed again by Larry Maria on the lead guitar singing BLACK AND BLUE. Yellow balloons bounce back and forth in the air. A man leaps forward from a loge, clasps one balloon to his chest, and lands in the orchestra. Play continues, and the mood of the crowd soars with the balloons.

It's a joyous festival. The fans lend their bodies and their expanding minds to the show. They harmonize hotly with the sounds that envelop them—sounds that embed feelings in flesh and bone, penetrate cells, and lodge in synapses and semicircular canals. Sound occupies all zones, taking no prisoners. It surrounds. The vanquished are zonked into nirvana—a communal realm of aural oneness—where immersion in time accelerates in slow motion, suspended, orbiting in revolutions that seem cosmic. The three Uncle Sams are pointing, the currents are flowing, and the energy is electrifying. Jazz and Rudy meld with the crowd, intoxicated by the music. They believe in *ROLLING BONES*.

Rudy says, "What a trip." Jazz agrees. Rudy adds: "Hey, man, it's like travel. Better than LSD. You start here and end up elsewhere. I feel older by several days. And it's good, man. You know what I mean? You feel good. You can do things."

"I feel changed," says Jazz. "I really do."

The security guards coax the crowd toward the exits. Pockets of stragglers form logjams in the aisles. The flow forward is stymied, and the fans are impatient—impatient, but good-natured.

"Mr. Rissotto … Ms. Silber!" Jazz tugs on Rudy's sleeve.

"Look who's here," says Gregor. Nora also shows surprise.

"Small world."

"Did you enjoy the concert?" says Jazz.

"Very much. We're dyed-in-the-wool Bones fans," says Nora. "And you?"

"It was awesome." Jazz introduces Rudy, and after some chit-chat, the crowd pushes forward, spilling into the walkways and the parking lot. Gregor and Nora locate his tan Lexus SUV and head for the exit. They follow a line of cars into a side street, jet onto the freeway, and the Lexus blends into the illuminated hum of late-evening traffic. Overhead signs and arrows in green and white say Loviers City.

"Wasn't that the infamous Rudy Squazza?" says Nora.

"I believe it was."

"Of City Hall fame?"

"You don't mean the shooting," says Gregor.

"No, the trial that got the homeless their shelter."

"That's the one. But I wonder how he and Jazz connected."

"She's doing a project for me on the homeless," says Nora.

"What kind of a project?"

"Life on the street. That's probably how they met. She's an unusual student."

"That she is. But life with her is hardly life on the street," says Gregor.

"Why do you say that?"

"Either she goes down with him, which I don't see happening, or he rises with her."

"Looks to me as though he's risen," says Nora.

"We'll see what happens. Squazza rising!"

"That we will. Whatever happens to them, it was a great concert. Larry Maria will always have me as a fan."

"Yes," says Gregor. "There's a sweetness in his voice that belies the subversion of his lyrics." He inserts a CD of PYRE ON THE MOUND and turns up the volume.

"Sweet subversion," says Nora, in a loud voice. Gregor lowers the volume.

"Good crowd."

"It was so responsive. Some fans travel around the country, following the Bones from one concert to another."

"That's loyalty for you," says Gregor.

"It's total allegiance."

"Our poetry festival could have used some of that."

"It worked pretty well though, considering the disparities," says Nora.

"But it lacked fire."

"Can't fault Goodhew for trying."

"Newell can talk about the festivals of Dionysus and the French Revolution, but the true outpourings of our time are the rock concerts. Worldwide," says Gregor.

"It's a phenomenon."

"Frenzied fans and spontaneous combustion. The only group that can match them is the World Cup, with an audience in the billions."

"Unbridled enthusiasm," says Nora.

"Yes. So unbridled that a Bolivian fan shot a defender who inadvertently scored a goal against his own team."

"That's fanaticism," says Nora. "Or drug money. What do you expect when you have competing teams and the compulsion to win?"

"It's the nature of the beast. Do you remember when the Brits clashed with their Italian rivals? That was ugly, and many ended in the hospital."

"What I like about the Bones, in addition to the music, is the crowd. It's so good-natured. Its response may be wild, but it's as warm and loving as the songs.

"You said it," says Gregor. "And you know why? The antagonist is absent. Or, if present, there only in effigy. The three Uncle Sams … plywood tigers."

"All the emotion can focus on the lyrics and the sound," says Nora.

"Well, maybe also the enemy … at least subliminally. But you don't have to fight him in the aisles."

"And the bleachers don't collapse, as they did when the soccer fans attacked each other."

"Did you know that for international matches in South America the referees need a police escort? How's that for security?"

"That's what I mean," says Nora. "We didn't even need security guards. Although, I suppose, it helps if they wear yellow jackets. Their mood matches the balloons." When the Lexus exits the freeway and stops in front of Nora's house, she says: "Nightcap?"

"I was hoping you'd ask."

"I'll show you my tattoo."

Jasmine is writing a story about the sighting of the Virgin. Gregor's novel is progressing, even as Gomez and company print counterfeit money. Gregor wants to incorporate the Virgin into his fiction, but he's waiting first to read Jasmine's story so that he can plagiarize it. He has no qualms about borrowing from other people. Hasn't everything already been said? Why get hung up on originality? People think their ideas are special, but everybody, in fact, lives in a prepackaged world. It's not just merchandise but also thoughts and feelings, how to love, whom to hate, and what to think. Gregor thinks that if God didn't exist, man would have to invent Him. Most bikers, for example, already know that God rides a Harley-Davidson ... and so does Elvis. Isn't that why he still lives? Gregor likes to play—play with words and language. He likes to borrow and invent. He thinks reality is up for grabs. Like a house that you construct, it feels natural when you live in it long enough. Then Gomez comes along, like termites, and subverts it. If he can manufacture counterfeit bills, so can the novelist. Doesn't every wordsmith ride a Harley? Jasmine may have her Ducati, but the only true bikers are HOGs. That's why Gregor wants to subvert the house of God. Once upon a time, there were two popes: one in Rome and the other in Avignon. Surely, one of them was an impostor. But which one? How do you know that Pope John Paul II's lineage didn't suppress the authentic one?

And now, the Mother of God has come to Loviers City. Or is it Americus? One city is real, and the other is imaginary. Gregor knows that when he finishes his novel, *Americus*—like Jacob and Esau, not to mention Cain and Abel—will supplant Loviers City. Wherever you look there's a supplanter. Gregor hopes to see Gomez triumph—if only to prove, once again, that it can be done. Meanwhile, people are talking about the Virgin. There is a rumor of a sighting in the river bottom, and the curious are going there to check it out. The sceptics at City College and elsewhere, the Unitarians, and the First Unanimists scoff at the idea, but there are enough believers to keep it alive. It grows and spreads, like the fire that once burned the shacks. As for Jasmine, she doesn't know what to believe. Half of her dismisses the rumor, whereas the other half can't help itself because she knows she saw the image. Whenever she mounts the Ducati, and her hands grasp the handlebars, she advances on the horns of a dilemma, a quandary. And now the boys at school call her "Angel." *Angel from Hell*. Although she resents the cliché, she is caught up in its predicament: to believe or not to believe? That is the question. She knows she exists because whenever she rides the Ducati she feels alive. The machine gives her the power and freedom she craves. At one hundred and ten, she feels sublime. Her leathers are like a second skin, and the wind lends wings to flight. *Red and Black*. A vision from somewhere. Pedestrians turn whenever she leans into a fast curve, defying gravity. She is a dream machine, and she knows it. She flaunts her goods at men, who stare with wonder and desire. She thinks of Patty-Greer Roche and ROARING THUNDER:

> Riding Women On The Hot Machines.
> Say The Best Things They Ever Seen.
> Big V-Twin, Honey Back It On In.
> Let Me Feel It Running Up And Down MY Skin ...
> Then Rev It Up Again!!!

Jasmine rides the road to the river bottom and is surprised to see people clustered at the base of the pepper tree. There is a priest in black robes, a photographer, a film crew, a woman writing on a note pad, and several homeless onlookers. It's a clear morning, and the sun is shining on the head of the Virgin. Her face is illuminated, and the tears on her cheeks glisten. The camera clicks, and Father Ortiz talks about Our Lady of Guadalupe, whose image, he says, miraculously appeared in 1531 on the cloak worn by an Aztec peasant. Ortiz says that Pope John Paul II should declare Juan Diego a saint, now that he has been beatified. "Remember, that after the Pope's visit to Guadalupe's

Mexico City shrine in 1979, he dedicated a chapel in her honor in St. Peter's. And in 1992, he placed her image next to the tomb of the first pope. That's a good sign. A sign of sainthood." The note-taker scribbles furiously. "And, during his fourth visit to Mexico, he again honored 'La Virgincita'—'The Little Virgin'—by celebrating mass in the church where her image is housed." Cameras click.

"We should not forget that the olive-skinned Virgin Mary spoke to Juan Diego in his native Nahuatl language, saying that Mexico's Indians were among her children and her chosen messenger." Ortiz looks at the film crew and raises his voice. "It was a miracle. And she turned millions of unbelieving Indians into Roman Catholics. What a legacy. In 1810, Miguel Hidalgo, the priest who sparked Mexico's break from Spain, carried her into battle. And now, for many, she embodies Mexico's faith and national identity." More camera clicks and more note-taking. A crow caws from a nearby tree. "It's strong medicine. I have a niece in Mexico named Guadalupe. Born on December 12. As for this tree, in front of us? The vision may indeed be miraculous. Steps will be taken. I will notify church authorities: the Bishops and Cardinals. We shall name her Our Lady of Loviers City. Think of it. Think what that would mean!" Ortiz clasps the palms of his hands and says a prayer. Jasmine looks at the face of the Virgin, and it seems to her that tears—tears of joy, wonder, and compassion—are flowing down her cheeks.

Meanwhile, the city hall shooter has recovered from his wounds and is in a jail cell. He sits there waiting for a sign. He believes that his attack on the Councilors, like the dumping of the crows' carcasses in front of City Hall, was God's will. He listens to the voices of conscience and is convinced that he can be an agent for change. He believes that the extermination of the birds was a sacrilege, the most egregious of many perpetrated by Loviers City. He believes that the marriage between industry and technology is poisoning the planet. He does not think of himself as a holy warrior, but the logic of conscience tells him that he must act. He thinks of himself as a humble soldier who has been chosen to play a part. He is a Protestant—that is, someone who protests. He thinks of God as immanent and Nature as the house of the Lord. He believes that all creatures, large and small, are sacred and must be protected. This is why he joined the SPCA, why he lent his hand to its militant wing—to save animals from cruelty and human predation. Animals have a right to happiness. They, too, have feelings, and their lives must be protected.

The shooter believes that slaughterhouses are a disgrace and animal experiments an abomination. He is convinced that human greed knows no bounds and that man's assault on Nature will, in time, destroy the planet. He wants to be a martyr to the animal cause, the cause of life. He thinks that dramatic action is necessary, that it is not too late to arouse public indignation. If only people could see the folly of their ways, wake up to the consequences of indifference and ignorance, and become vegetarians. If only they would see the light.

The shooter reads *The Sun's* account about Father Ortiz's visit to the river bottom. He looks at the picture of the Virgin on page one, and he thinks that her sighting is the sign he has been waiting for. He may not be a Catholic, but he believes in divine intervention. He sees the picture of the Virgin as a happy collusion between his conscience and the dictates of the Vatican. This will be his chance to repair centuries of damage—damage done by the Reformation and the misguided efforts of Martin Luther. He knows he can bring the two Churches back together, that he will go down in the history books as the savior of animals and of mankind. He will be the Noah for the next millennium, a new-age saint greater than Juan Diego. The Virgin of Guadalupe may be venerated in Mexico and Juan Diego may have been her messenger, but the Virgin of Loviers City will make him, Bernard Mingus, her messenger. Think of it … Saint Mingus! He will advocate an alliance between the Virgin Mary and the sacred crow. He sees smoke rising from the Indian campfires of the Dakotas and smoke rising on the wings of divine intervention.

The compact made in heaven will be glorious. The glory will be his.

Mingus thinks that Native Americans have it right: respect for the animals they kill and respect for the rivers and forests that sustain them. It's a stark contrast, a sacrilege even, to the technology of plunder and Loviers City's poisoning of the crows, which has destroyed the spirit of a bird venerated by Indians in Asia and the Americas. Their demise demands retribution, and the attack on City Hall is a justified response. Bernard Mingus writes a letter to the mayor justifying his attack. He signs it … "The Shooter." And he says he will reveal his identity on two conditions: one, that he be allowed to see the pepper tree where the sighting took place, and two, that his letter be published.

After reading it, Goodhew decides that he has nothing to lose. He sends the letter to the editor of *The Sun*, requesting that the paper publish it. He also asks Garcia to escort the shooter to the river bottom. Mingus's letter appears on the front page of *The Sun*. Mingus reads it with satisfaction. After the trip to the river bottom, and having seen the Virgin, he charts his strategy. First, he will write a letter to *The Sun* describing his vision of planetary collapse, and second, he will push for animal protection and the salvation of mankind. He will describe the interdependence of all living things—animal and vegetable—stressing the unity of all creation, including the unity of Christians—Catholics and Protestants. Animals, he says, have souls, and unless Loviers City repents, the spirit of the crow will return to haunt its leaders. Mingus thinks that unless men and women abandon their sinful ways, Gaia, the earth goddess, will rise in righteous indignation. He knows she can mend the ravages of exploitation and the effects of toxic waste. But first, mendacious tycoons and enemies of Nature must stop polluting the planet. He says: "The vision of the Virgin is a sign. She and Jesus, together, will reconcile Protestants and Catholics, Nature and humankind. The fact that the pepper tree survived the fire … the fact that the Virgin is the tree … the tree of life, a symbol of the power of survival and renewal. We have one more year to the millennium. One year in which to alter the scenario of doom. Which will it be … life or death? Change, rise, believe! If you don't, Y2K spells APOCALYPSE."

The responses to Mingus's letter are swift and varied. *The Sun* receives many letters to the editor, both pro and con. While all but a few condemn the shooting, the reactions to his reasons for doing so are mixed. One woman writes: "Who is this nut who thinks he can save the world by defending the crows?" In his letter, Albert Speer says: "The crows were a plague, and the city is well-served to be rid of them. Sacred or not, the only good crow is a dead crow." In his letter, Newell says: "Animals do not have souls and neither do crows." Khalid writes a letter in defense of jobs and business. He says: "The crows were lowering profits and causing layoffs. It was them or us." He agrees with Newell that "man" was placed on earth to dominate the beasts of the field, the birds in the air, and the fishes of the deep and that man's purpose is to profit from nature and to multiply. Even Goodhew feels compelled to defend the city's decision to kill the crows. His letter focuses on disease and the need for sanitation. Once more, he praises the work of the SS and the garbage collectors.

Konlon's letter is ambivalent. Although she condemns the shooting as the act of an extremist, she sees merit in Mingus's views about pollution and conservation. She says: "Mr. Mingus may be a misguided zealot, but his concern for the welfare of the planet makes sense. Global warming, the death of coral reefs, and the rising sees should be of concern to us all. Remember the canary in the mine! The ripple effect is already in full swing. Skin cancer, the collapse of the fishing industry, and the decline of reproductive sperm cells in men are all symptomatic of planetary distress." Garcia figures that, as chief of police, it would be inappropriate for him to write a letter. He asks one of his officers to do it for him. The officer writes: "Mingus is scum. The sooner we rid Loviers City of trash like him, the better. He, like the crows, is blight. He broke the law, and now he thinks he can get away with it by accusing the system. He should be ashamed of himself."

Except for what he calls "religious mumbo-jumbo," Squazza agrees with Mingus. In his own letter to *The Sun*, he accuses the military-industrial complex of a conspiracy to destroy the planet. "The rich are getting richer and the poor are getting poorer. Nobody is doing anything about it." In answer to Squazza's letter, Goodhew writes another one in which he defends his programs. He points to the opening of the new shelter for the homeless. Jasmine agrees with Rudy but is caught between sympathy for him and allegiance to her father. She knows her father hates the homeless and the crows. Good thing he knows nothing about her school project or her friendship with Rudy. He'd blow his top. These are her thoughts—the horns of her dilemma—while cruising around town with her right hand on the gearshift and her left hand on the accelerator.

In his letter to *The Sun*, Father Ortiz says that the sighting of the Virgin proves the vibrancy of the Catholic Church. He cites Pope John Paul's words urging Catholics in the Americas to resist Protestant evangelism. "If the two churches are to merge, it will only come about when Protestants recognize the error of their ways and submit to the authority of the Vatican." After reading this letter, an incensed Newell answers Ortiz by referring to the pride of the Catholic Church—pride in arrogating to itself the power to interpret God's will. "That is why we Protestants rebelled in the first place!" Newell reminds Ortiz that pride always goes before a fall, that Lucifer's pride explains his demise, and Adam's fall makes sinners of us all. "Protestants could never submit to the Pope's authority."

Mingus, in his jail cell, is delighted, yet saddened, by the spat between the two church leaders. Delighted that he could have sparked such a confrontation, yet saddened to realize that his vision of a united global Christianity may be a chimera. He writes a response in which he chides Newell and Ortiz for their pettiness, closed-mindedness, and short-sightedness. "Isn't the destruction of the planet of greater urgency than doctrinal differences? If both Churches believe in ameliorating the living conditions of the downtrodden, shouldn't Protestants and Catholics unite in order to fight their common enemy: disease, hunger and homelessness? Why dissipate your energies with internecine strife?"

Rissotto reads these letters with amusement. He is indifferent to the theological issues, and he views the excitement generated by the sighting of the Virgin as so much globaloney—Mingus's global zeal and the Churches' baloney. Rissotto is proud of his neologism, and he plans to incorporate it into *Americus*. He also thinks the letters to the editor will be useful but doesn't yet know how to use them.

Hazel Broom, editor of *The Sun*, is proud of the selected letters she has been publishing. She is pleased that, in addition to its news-gathering services, the paper can mediate the exchange of ideas between all residents of Loviers City. She is proud that *The Sun's* pages are a forum for the expression of different opinions. She tells her staff that that is what democracy is all about. Privately, she has been uneasy about the monolithic image of harmony that Goodhew, Newell, and Garcia have been projecting. She also thinks that the link between cleanliness and Godliness is tenuous, although she herself has refrained from saying so. Still, beautifying the city, solving the trash problem, and addressing the needs of the homeless are laudable enterprises. While not convinced that cleanliness is the handmaiden of salvation, objecting to such ventures would seem premature, if not ill-conceived.

Broom thinks that the sighting of the Virgin has been a Godsend. Not only has it improved circulation, she also welcomes it as an opportunity to dramatize diversity through dialogue. She thinks that the consciousness of Loviers City need not be exclusively Unanimist, and she resists Newell's and Goodhew's efforts to impose uniformity. She fears that the suppression of dissent will have negative long-term effects. After reading the letter of Garcia's surrogate and Khalid's predictable pro-business epistle, she is more convinced than ever that encouraging opposing views on current issues is the right thing to do. She does not believe that group consciousness can exist without nooks, cracks, and crannies. She also believes in the airing of differences. As editor of the paper, she is wedded to fair exchange. Indeed, she is committed to printing as many letters as she can on issues of public concern, and she is happy to publish Mingus's letter. Not only has the shooting at City Hall attracted national attention, but his wounding and subsequent silence has raised the level of suspense as well as everybody's expectations.

The content of his letter is extreme, and, to be sure, a complete surprise, but it is literate and logical. Broom doesn't agree with the policies of the SPCA or with Mingus's actions, but she feels that the controversy generated by them will increase the circulation of *The Sun*. After all, she's in the business of selling papers. There is value, she thinks, in a heightened awareness of issues and in a community's willingness to think about them. Inadvertently, Mingus has become the lightning rod for all the contention, of late, swirling in, over, and around Loviers City— or Eagle Mountain, the trash, the crows, and the homeless.

Out of nowhere—when at last Mingus reveals his identity and says he is from San Francisco—comes a zealot who brings a city together, not in like-minded obedience but in explosive confrontation. Broom, unlike Goodhew, thinks that thoughtful opposition is healthier than conditioned unanimity, better than various forms of bland agreement. She also wants to publish as many letters as she can because they all heighten Loviers City's consciousness of self. But the elements of awareness differ. Goodhew wants a fraternal consciousness based on common cause and the symbolic colors of the flag, whereas Broom wants an awareness of issues. Plus, she thinks total unanimity is impossible.

The next letter Broom publishes is from an anonymous person who believes that life—all life—is sacred. "Killing is sinful," says anonymous, denouncing euthanasia, Dr. Death, abortion clinics, and capital punishment. "But," says the writer, "sometimes, in order to make their point, in order to dramatize the issue, defenders of life must take the law into their own hands." The writer thinks the shooter has acted honorably. "From zero to hero. From no one to someone. An authentic American. A man, acting on principle. Someone who thinks before he shoots."

Rissotto is fascinated by the letter's deranged logic. Killing to protect life? He is also intrigued by the definition of authentic. Is an authentic person someone who chooses, shoots, and goes to jail with no regrets? Is it someone who, like Kirilov in *The Possessed*, pursues his ideas to the end? What does that say about Gomez, who has no convictions, and whose counterfeit money only serves to devalue real currency? Would he go to jail? And the Pope? What happened to the Pope of Avignon? Sidelined, of course. The *real* Papacy is still in the Vatican.

C.G. watches televised reports of the Pope's visit to Mexico City. What an outpouring of the faithful! What a demonstration of enthusiasm! One hundred thousand people have lined the streets and climbed the trees. Another hundred and twenty thousand cheer, stomp, and sway as the Popemobile enters Aztec Stadium. Hundreds of doves are released into the sky as a mechanical arm lifts the Pope onto a rotating red podium. He sits down on a slowly turning white chair. His address is broadcast via satellite to crowds of cheering millions across the Americas, from Los Angeles to Buenos Aires and beyond.

That's group consciousness, thinks C.G. to herself, all of it focused on the Pope. She wonders if the crowd is conscious of itself, if it knows it has an identity, if it's aware of its power. Perhaps. But only if the Pope is there. When he says that the Virgin Mary is queen of all the Americas, they cheer. When he asks them to reject the social sins of violence and injustice, they approve. He says: "The time has come to banish once and for all every attack on human life. There must be no more terrorism, torture, and drug trafficking. There must be an end to the death penalty. No more exploitation of the weak, no more racial injustice, or ghettos of poverty. Never again." The seventy-eight-year-old pontiff hunches forward in his seat. He holds onto his text with a shaking right hand, and energized by the crowd, he says: "These are intolerable evils that cry out to heaven and call Christians to a different way of living."

The Pope calls on the five hundred million baptized Catholics in the Western Hemisphere to engage in intense prayer and have a personal encounter with Christ. "The church needs new ardor, new methods, and new expression for the evangelization of America." He calls on the faithful to reject a purely economic conception of man. He wants them to create an authentic globalized culture of Catholic solidarity. "Respond to the Master who calls. Follow Him to become, like the apostles, fishers of men." Thunderous applause.

Eat your heart out, Newell, says C.G. to herself. This is crowd control. She thinks of eight hundred million Catholics worldwide—so many of them poor. What a force! They may be pious, but is cleanliness high on their priority list? Let them come to Loviers City. Goodhew will teach them a thing or two. They want bread? Give them toters and the rest—truck control and color-coded trash containers—will follow. As for the Virgin of Guadalupe, that was almost five hundred years ago. We need a new sighting to re-energize the Americas for the twenty-first century. Why not the Virgin of Loviers City? C.G. thinks about the sighting in the river-bottom. Everybody is talking about it, and now that the Pope has flown back to Rome, the media can focus on matters close to home.

And it does. News of the Virgin of Loviers City is spreading like the river-bottom fire. *The Sun* carries a banner headline: VIRGIN SIGHTED. Father Ortiz is quoted saying that the Virgin of Guadalupe and the Virgin of Loviers City—one at the time of the Renaissance and the other one now, for the new millennium—are helping to re-evangelize the Americas. Ortiz is hopeful that, despite his age and frailty, the Pope will make another trip to this hemisphere, this time to the city of angels: Los Angeles.

In a matter of weeks, the trickle of visitors becomes a torrent, then a river, and, by Easter Sunday, a flood. Loviers City is submerged. The influx of people is staggering, if not miraculous. The young, old, and middle-aged come on foot, by motorcycle, by car, by bus, and by plane. There are charter buses from Los Angeles and San Francisco. International air charters arrive from Paris, Rome, and Madrid. All the hotels are full. There is no more room at the Mission Inn. Motels for miles around are booked weeks in advance. People camp in the river bottom and in the walnut groves, under the trees. Like colored mushrooms, blue, green, and yellow tents appear, even in the parks. The homeless have been displaced. ATM machines are humming, and the Bank of America is thriving. Newell and the First Unanimist Church, however, have been caught off-guard. The concept of cleanliness is under siege.

Paper and rancid edibles litter streets and lawns. The crows have discovered a new food source, and they no longer fly to Eagle Mountain. Argentinean ants multiply by the millions, and rivulets of tiny black bodies zigzag up around curbs and sidewalks. At night, raccoons, possums, rats, coyotes, and feral dogs from the river bottom scavenge the neighborhoods. On doormats, they leave their droppings: brown, curled doo-doos with bits of hair in the seams and undigested berries.

In the daytime, the streets are lined with buses and cars. The congestion is severe. Car exhausts and diesel fumes irritate the eyes. Parking is a problem. Waves of visitors descend on the river bottom. Residents complain of blocked driveways. Garcia assigns a police detail to control the flow of traffic, but the bottlenecks are so frequent that the City Council designates one-way streets. That solves the logjams but not the parking problem. With all deliberate speed, Speer and the Council design and then approve a new parking lot to be landscaped by Khalid Construction. A vast area of giant cane is staked, bulldozed, and paved. The dirt path is now gone, and asphalt covers what was once sand, stones, and tall grasses. The shacks of the homeless are relocated to a suitable area one mile downstream. The day the lot opens, it fills to capacity with one thousand cars and fifty buses. The residents along the side streets sigh in relief. Speer sends trash collectors to clean the paper, Styrofoam, diapers, cans, and bottles. Goodhew is determined, despite the odds, to maintain the city's policy of cleanliness. A path, two hundred yards long, snakes through the cane toward the sacred tree.

The influx of outsiders is a mixed blessing. The hotels, motels, restaurants, and shops are making money. Khalid is happy. With his parking franchise and sanitation facilities, he charges an eight-dollar fee. He also controls the hot dog and soda pop stands and, in due course, sets up stalls and booths that sell souvenirs and trinkets: large and small pendants of the Virgin; gold, silver, and brass chains with crosses and rosaries; beads, necklaces, bracelets, and amulets; statuettes and pictures of the Virgin; plaster facsimiles of the Mother and Child in different sizes and colors; small replicas of the pepper tree carved in walnut; ashtrays, candles, T-shirts, banners, shawls, jackets, and hats with the image of the Virgin; bird baths, fountains, holy water, keychains, flashlights, ballpoint pens, postcards, catechisms, and abbreviated histories of Loviers City—from the time of the early settlers up to the days of the first sighting on Groundhog Day in 1999.

No one is sure who first saw the Virgin. Two homeless people step forward to claim the honor, but Father Ortiz says it won't be official until the Church designates the site as a holy shrine. This is perhaps Ortiz's way of saying that the Church will arrogate the first sighting to itself. Rudy Squazza says he was the first person to see the Virgin, but Jasmine says that she is the one. She says she has a short story to prove it. Rissotto decides not to incorporate the sighting into his novel because he thinks it's too overpowering, too disruptive, and not in keeping with the theme of the counterfeit—the fakery that holds his work together. He believes the presence of the Virgin will overshadow Gomez's efforts to subvert authority. What irony, the chief of police working to undermine centralized power! Especially when you consider the fact that, after the Civil War, Abraham Lincoln created the Secret Service to fight counterfeiters because phoney money was a threat to the unity of the nation. Think of it: unanimity threatened by the unauthentic! Also, how do you harmonize the idea of a false pope in Avignon with the zeal of new vision? It just won't work. Rissotto decides there's no longer any point in stealing Jasmine's story. She has managed to imbue it with the spirit of the uncanny, and her fiction is a gem. He gives her an *A-plus* and urges her to send it to *The Atlantic*. He has no doubt it will get published.

Meanwhile, Bernard Mingus writes another letter to *The Sun*, saying that it was his proclamation of reconciliation between Protestants and Catholics that has made everything possible and that he is the essential mediator between the image of the Virgin and the millennium. Mingus insists that symbolically She appeared to him first and that he is the only one capable of interpreting the meaning of Her revelation. Father Ortiz says that the Virgin belongs to the Catholic Church, and Reverend Newell says that's okay with him. He says that Protestants will stick with Jesus. Mingus reiterates the fact that the Virgin and Jesus belong to all of Christendom and that no one has a monopoly on either one—no one, that is, except Khalid, the city, and Coca-Cola.

Father Ortiz leads a procession of the faithful from the steps of Our Lady of Loviers City to the river bottom. Hundreds of pilgrims, carrying palm branches of every size and shape, walk past the Postmodern Library and the Mission Inn. A bearded man in a white robe rides a white donkey; its hooves go click-click on the pavement. Teenage boys and girls wave palm fronds. Thousands of onlookers point cameras and wave banners to commemorate Christ's entry into Jerusalem. At the river bottom, Cardinal Maloney, in town for Palm Sunday, is dressed in resplendent red robes, wears a red hat, and carries a long shepherd's crook. He joins Father Ortiz at the head of the procession. They follow the path toward the sacred tree where the crowd spreads out to form a semicircle. Christ dismounts and tethers a donkey to the trunk of a small tree where ribbons of cloth match the animal's short white hairs. The donkey brays three times, and the pale stripes on its withers quiver. Palm fronds wave in the sunlight, Father Ortiz unlocks the gate, and several attendants set up a makeshift altar. The faithful cross themselves, Cardinal Maloney says mass, and the Virgin behind him seems to smile on the people assembled before Her.

The Cardinal's red robes, the green leaves of the tree, and the white cloth on the altar remind many onlookers of Mexico and the colors of its flag. Some say the mass should have been in Spanish, not English, but on the whole, they are content to be in the presence of the Virgin. Faith has brought the crowd together, and their hope and expectation is the glue that binds them. They wear the face of happiness and look forward to the resurrection.

Khalid is incensed that the faithful are trashing his walnut groves, building campfires, and shitting in the irrigation furrows. The grove in which Nicole was murdered bears the brunt of the assault. The garbage the campers leave behind is harder to clean up than the refuse of the homeless. Khalid is unaware of the irony. After pondering how to cope with the problem, he cuts down the trees in one grove and sells the branches for firewood and the trunks for lumber. He imports artisans from Lebanon—artisans who once carved olive wood camels—to mass-produce effigies of the Virgin with modern tools. Smoothed and polished, the dark-grained wood has great appeal. Walnut statuettes are among the hottest sellers. In the Loviers' Virgin, many see a resemblance to Cuba's Virgin of Cobre and the Black Virgin of Concarneau. Soon, Khalid's shops occupy several street corners by the parking lot—areas that only recently have been rezoned for commercial purposes. The Coca-Cola vending machines say: *Adore Refreshed*. But the holy water, although just as expensive, is more popular. The company sends shiploads of Dasani to the

Vatican to be blessed, but despite such efforts, the Loviers City bottles, with their image of the Virgin, are the libation of choice. The Dasani bottles, now sporting labels that say *Blessed by the Pope*, are also doing well, but the majority prefers the local brand.

Khalid builds a two-story U-shaped motel with a swimming pool and a two-acre desert garden that has tall, transplanted palms. He names it Virgin Acres, and it reminds him of Nicole. But he's not quite sure why. He misses her terribly. The gift shop in the lobby of Virgin Acres sells mementos at high prices, and the new enterprises employ hundreds of people. Jars of Aloe vera sell like hot cakes. Khalid's staff of experts trains clerks in the fine arts of courtesy, friendliness, service, and sales. After the Mission Inn, the visitors from Europe, particularly the French, prefer to stay at Virgin Acres. They like what they call exotic plants, and the variety of cacti in the desert garden appeals to their sense of distance from home and displacement from the familiar. A pebble path meanders through the garden, and each species—saguaro, ocotillo. golden barrel cactus, yucca, Joshua tree, rosette succulents, aloe, heart of flame, euphorbia, columnar cactus, epiphytic cactus, living rock cactus, and prickly pear—is identified with a small marker in black and white. In the distance, the sacred tree, with its crown of fern-like leaves, is also exotic, and the uncanny image of the Virgin embedded in the trunk contributes to the overall sense of the unusual, a defamiliarization enhanced by the awesome presence of the supernatural. New shoots have replaced the charred branches. Spring has sprung, and it now covers the burned areas of the river bottom with overlapping shades of green: grasses, mesquite, and Arundo.

Visitors who are unable to find rooms in town, or can't afford Khalid's high prices, camp in the river bottom. Their litter resembles a garbage dump. Khalid complains, and Speer sends a clean-up crew. The city builds a chain-link fence around the walnut groves. To cope with the overflow, Khalid converts another ten acres into an RV campsite with full hook-ups, showers, chapel, and restaurant, not to mention the ubiquitous shops, bowling alley, basketball court, volleyball nets, and miniature golf course with castles, windmills, and streams.

There is a nasty confrontation between Khalid and the Council over the eight-dollar admission fee. Khalid says his franchise agreement and expenses authorize him to keep the proceeds, but the Council says that the tree and the lot are on city land and that a portion of the fee should go to Loviers. Goodhew says that unless Khalid agrees to share the fees, he will revoke the franchise when it expires in two years. Khalid balks at the proposal, but Goodhew threatens to sue. Money disrupts the harmony of the Council, and even Ohr's ombudsman-like skills are not enough to soothe the rift. After several stormy sessions, Khalid agrees to a compromise: admission to the parking lot and the tree will be set at ten dollars, six of which will go to Khalid and four to the City. That's a two-dollar cut from the current rate, but Khalid figures, it's better than losing the franchise.

Word of the sighting spreads south of the border, even to the smallest hamlets and mountain villages. The Mexicans are ambivalent. The Virgin of Guadalupe is part of their identity. She belongs to them, and they don't want to share the glory of evangelizing the Americas with another Virgin from the north, particularly one from the United States. Church authorities in Mexico City suggest that the Virgin of Loviers City is an impostor. They write letters to the Vatican denouncing the new sighting as unauthentic, urging the Pope to withhold approval of sanctification, and arguing that the Virgin of Guadalupe can be the only true presence in the Western Hemisphere. It is She who belongs to the poor. They say that the one in Loviers City, even if authentic, is a Virgin for the rich, that She can only redeem sins engendered by Las Vegas, Viagra, cocaine, and handguns. Unlike the Virgin of Guadalupe, who belongs to the poor, the Virgin of Loviers City belongs only to those who can afford her. However, the Church's revenues from blessing Dasani water are substantial. The Vatican ignores the requests.

Rissotto reads about the controversy and is delighted. He concludes that it will be possible to incorporate the sighting into his novel after all. The Virgin of Americus will be the fake Virgin, and her counterfeit presence will serve to undermine the authority of Guadalupe and of the Church. Despite Rissotto's glee and the fuss generated by Mexico's cardinals and bishops, the poor are happy that another Virgin has entered their pantheon. The magnetic pull of the North intensifies, and the new Virgin adds her attraction to their dream of a better life. The sucking sound that Ross Perot once used to describe the flow of American businesses into Mexico, after NAFTA and the lifting of the trade embargo, is now audible but in reverse. Despite the reinforced walls and fences, the Border Patrol, from Tijuana to Nogales, is overwhelmed. The coyotes are doing a thriving business. Their fees are outrageous: one thousand dollars and up per person, depending on the package. Despite the dangers, illegal immigrants keep rolling in. They cross by the thousands. Many are stopped and repatriated. But they try again, three or four times if necessary, knowing that eventually they will get through, unless they die in the desert.

All the gardeners and part-time workers in Loviers City are now illegal immigrants. They know nothing of the city's link between cleanliness and Godliness. Soon, the pristine suburbs are littered with wadded napkins, plastic cups, cans, beer bottles, stale tacos, salsa wrappers, a condom or two, and an occasional pile of shit and toilet paper blowing in the wind. The SS work overtime but they can barely stay ahead of all the discards. The litter overcomes the letter of the law.

The residents are angry at the trashing of suburbia but happy to hire undocumented workers who do yardwork at below minimum wage. Young men from Guatemala, Honduras, and Nicaragua, wearing faded baseball caps and old jackets, circle the neighborhoods on bicycles looking for work. They ring doorbells, clip hedges, and weed the flowerbeds with perpetual good humor and unquenchable optimism. For years, Khalid has been hiring illegals to pick walnuts and care for the trees. At peak season, from the Imperial Valley to the Central Valley, the produce—be it citrus, lettuce, tomatoes, or nuts—is harvested by illegal migrant workers. They are the unseen and unsung workers of an economy that hires them despite the law. Khalid admires their tenacity, resilience, and hard work, which is so unlike the lifestyle of the homeless.

The Virgin of Loviers City is a magnet for migrants who see the territory north of the Mexican border as a pasture of opportunity. On their way to work in the Central Valley, they visit her shrine, genuflect in front of her image, and say a prayer of thanks for crossing into the United States unapprehended. They are the ones who can't afford Khalid's prices at Virgin Acres and end up sleeping in the river bottom. At the crack of dawn, before the guards appear, they climb over the chain-link fence, skirt the admission booth, and make a clandestine approach to the tree, where they cross themselves and, with misty eyes, thank the Virgin for Her protection. The devout, particularly women of middle age, some with arms outstretched in the sign of the cross, advance on their knees, slowly and painfully. In the morning, sunshine tears, like the tears of the Virgin, stream down their cheeks. By the time the booths open and the guards appear, the migrant workers have moved on, secure in the knowledge that their hopes for a better life have been blessed by the Mother of God.

In the beginning, the tree had no protective barriers around it, but too many fingers are defacing the image and too many hands are taking bits of bark as souvenirs. The city decides to install a razor-wire atop the chain-link fence. The protective measures are designed to prevent the Virgin from disappearing, to prevent the revenues from drying up. Like the good old days, the City Council, once again, is unanimous. Immediate steps are taken to safeguard the treasure. The sick and infirm are being cured.

The abandoned wheel chairs, crutches, and walkers are fastened to the fence with stainless steel clips. They are testimonials to miraculous interventions and the Virgin's benevolence. Even skeptics admit that the cure of hysterical paralysis bespeaks the power of positive thinking. Newell is impressed, and in a vigorous sermon, he summons the faithful to a renewed demonstration of faith. He rings the bell of the eagle, and its mellifluous, high-pitched tones resonate again on thousands of television screens, encouraging donations of augmented and unanimous generosity. Unanimism lives, but the Virgin is taking her toll on Godliness. She is a Belle beyond compare, and cleanliness is not on her agenda. From the looks of the streets near the shrine and the parking lots, an immaculate neighborhood is no longer possible. The faithful—who come and go, usually in a matter of hours, and who, at the most, spend only several days visiting Loviers City—are unaware of the meaning of color-coded toters, yellow trucks, school uniforms, or the town flag. They have no time or interest in tapping into the soul of the city or experiencing the mystic union of its residents. Instead, the Virgin reigns resplendent and transcendent. Slowly and inexorably, she corrupts the unanimity that Newell, Goodhew, and others have striven to build with such diligence.

Of all the visitors, only the Japanese tourists, with their clicking cameras and smiles, understand the concept of unanimity and cleanliness. It is not by accident that Lagasaki is Loviers sister city, and the governing councils of both municipalities regularly exchange ideas and delegations. Goodhew is in frequent touch with the mayor of Lagasaki who, longer than Goodhew, has had to solve problems of overpopulation and sanitation. The two cities are on excellent terms, and there is a steady exchange of visitors. The Pacific Rim, despite the movement of tectonic plates and earthquakes, offers unusual business opportunities, and Khalid's walnuts are a popular item with Japanese consumers in general and the residents of Lagasaki in particular. The shrine of the Virgin is now a designated tourist site, and due to its religious nature, it garners special consideration. A pepper tree outside the protective fence is covered with white ribbons and bits of white cloth that Japanese visitors have tied to its branches. From a distance it looks like a tree in bloom. Whenever the wind blows, the white blossoms and lacy green branches bow and sway.

The shrine is a regular stop on the city's police patrol. Thieves break into parked cars, and the gutted dashboards that once housed stereo systems, CD players, and GPAs are now empty holes with protruding wires. Glass sparkles on the pavement. Two of Garcia's undercover agents mingle with the crowds. Instead of arresting the bad guys, however, Rissotto, in his novel, has the agents hustling counterfeit bills below the official exchange rate. For him, the shrine is a hoax conceived by Khalid and the Chamber of Commerce. Furthermore, Rissotto renames Father Ortiz as Father Montemor, a leading player in a financial scam designed to enrich the Church at the expense of Americus.

In Rissotto's novel, Father Ortiz is aware of Newell's waning influence, and he is pleased that Catholics, once a minority in Loviers City, are becoming the majority. The undocumented workers are Catholic, and the presence of thousands of pilgrims from around the world is an entity to be reckoned with. Even Wilson's Moby Dickens is affected. He gets requests for difficult to find books by Catholic writers. A new bookstore that sells Catholic tracts opens across the street.

There is a staggering influx of visitors seeking cures. The sick, the crippled, and the infirm arrive by the hundreds. The city builds a hospital near the Virgin Acres. The new taxes on walnut groves are skyrocketing, and Khalid sells the land to developers. The hospital builds short-term and long-term facilities. River water is diverted and purified. There are now hot pools in the hospital annex, where mud baths, massage parlors, and therapeutic exercises are available. The place is known as Loviers Spa. The sick and the hopeful are kneaded and pampered. Doctors prescribe cures, and an army of nurses, pharmacists, and masseuses soothe and massage the infirm. Health stores dispense organic foods and herbal medicines. Services at the new church, Our Lady of Loviers City, run around the clock.

Many of the infirm have been to Lourdes. They come to Loviers City as a last resort, hoping that the newest sighting of the Virgin will provide stronger medicine and a more potent cure. They feel that Bernadette may perhaps not have been attentive to their needs, that the New World, California in particular, the golden land of opportunity, will effect a cure, a cure the Old World has been unable to provide. Already, our Lady of Loviers City has a large room in which the discarded wheelchairs, crutches, and braces are housed. The ailing pass through it on their way to the altar, dip their fingers in holy water, and cross themselves with renewed hope. Charity, it goes without saying, is built into the hospital bill. The tab at the Virgin Acres, where family members are housed for the duration of the patient's cure, is padded with expectation.

Visitors frequently ask who first saw the Virgin. The answers are hesitant because—despite the claims of Squazza, Mingus, and others—no one is quite sure. Father Ortiz steps into the zone of uncertainty by stating that the Pope's visit to Mexico City was a premonitory sign. He says the appearance of the Virgin on the pepper tree was in response to the Church's eternal presence and divine message. He says: "The Virgin is visible to all believers, and the Church welcomes them. Faith in the Virgin is an indelible sign. The heart always has its reasons, which reason may deny. God's revelation is that the eyes of reason and the heart of faith are truly one and the same."

Meanwhile, despite the customary lag between acceptance and publication, *The Atlantic* fast tracks "The Virgin of Loviers City" to publication. In September, Jasmine's story hits the stands. It turns out that she has written it in the first person after all, not in the third as she had originally planned to. The effect is more intimate, more like a true life story than the fiction she had intended to write. Despite the change, she captures aspects of the uncanny. The aura of the supernatural comes across as a testimonial written by someone who has seen the Virgin and felt the grace of God.

The story is a sensation. During the weekends of Palm Sunday and Easter, there is heavy international coverage of the sighting. Jasmine's "Virgin of Loviers City" is the only written first-hand account. The media disseminates her story. Overnight, she herself becomes the virgin of Loviers City, an instant celebrity. Never mind that ever since the Resurrection she and Rudy have been having sex. Never mind that Rudy has risen and ridden. Never mind that the boys at Loviers High call her *Angel from Hell*. She is now "the virgin," and the condition of her hymen has nothing to do with the language of media blitz. The headlines are the truth, and the printed word is God. Jasmine is the new icon, and Father Ortiz's imprecations do little to dampen the fervor. The public is indifferent to the fact that Jasmine is not Catholic or that she and her family are members of the First Unanimist Church. They do not worship at the church of Our Lady of Loviers City.

Newell's skepticism goes from perplexity to dismay. He can't believe that a member of his flock has been elevated to sainthood, not by the Catholic Church, which moves slowly on such matters, but by the public. A national poll reveals that seven out of ten people have heard of the sighting and that five out of ten believe that Jasmine, like Bernadette, should be canonized. Newell is amazed by the electrifying speed of events, amazed that Jasmine has her own website where everybody can read her story and participate in the media coverage. He is convinced that forces beyond his control have taken over, that his vision of Loviers City as a Unanimist enclave has lost momentum. He no longer believes he can disseminate the idea of group cooperation. Henceforth, Our Lady of Loviers City will be the dominant force. Unanimism, cleanliness, and Godliness were a lovely dream, he thinks, but he feels that the new momentum has swung toward Father Ortiz.

Newell feels humbled by recent events. He can't decide whether it's the power of the Virgin or the power of the people, but whoever or whatever is behind it, it is an awesome force. For years, he has been trying to orchestrate people's behavior and has had a moderate degree of success. He and Goodhew had imbued Loviers City with a high degree of consciousness, solidarity and group action, all of which gave the city visibility, All-America status. Now, suddenly, with no help from anyone, unless it's divine meddling, a phenomenon occurs, and the city is turned upside down. It's as though events were self-propelled. How else do you explain the notoriety, the invasion, and the building boom? The First Unanimist Church is still standing, as are the Postmodern Library, the Mission Inn, and the Aggressive Bank of America, but the streets have changed. Asian, European, and Latin-American tourists now wander from store to store, and illegal gardeners work in the suburbs. Loviers City is now the face of the world. The whine of leaf blowers swirls the dust around. No one notices the homeless anymore, and cleanliness may be a thing of the past. Waste abounds. The yellow trucks still make their rounds, but there is a decline in cleanliness. Instead of Godliness, Loviers City is now the city of the Virgin. Houses need painting, driveways need resurfacing, and abandoned cars, here and there, for weeks at a time, gather dust and grime until they are hauled away.

Mingus, like Newell, is amazed at the turn of events. He is angry at the lack of interest in his message of reconciliation. He finds it hard to believe that a girl in black leather, riding a red Ducati, is on the verge of sainthood, that she is the darling of the media. Not long ago, he was on the front page of *The Sun*, and the shooting of the mayor was a cause célèbre. Fickle journalists! Mingus is envious of Jasmine's success and her picture in the paper. He wads it into a ball and tosses her into the toilet bowl.

C.G. follows the turn of events and records them in her diary. She sees the sighting as a response to a hidden need, but she can't decide what that need is. Perhaps it's the desire to believe in the supernatural. She is fascinated by manifestations of group behavior and confounded that thousands of people should see the Virgin Mary in a tree trunk, that thousands of people worldwide should be moved to visit the site. These happenings are of themselves miraculous, and it's the unanimous groundswell that piques her interest.

C.G. thinks of Goodhew and Newell and the ways they directed Loviers City toward Godliness, the way they molded the responses of different groups. She thinks of the Beethoven concert and the poetry contest, both of which, in some small measure, succeeded. These endeavors, however, were the result of leadership and planning, whereas the recent crowds flooding Loviers City are, like a tidal wave, the result of deep seismic activity. The crowds coming and going are motivated by a desire to see the sacred tree and be touched by grace. It's this behavior that piques C.G.'s curiosity and wonder. No one is telling them what to do. No one is urging them to buy a ticket to California. Yet every day, they arrive, check into a hotel, pay the fee, park their cars, walk the path, and stand in the shade of the great pepper tree. They kneel and adore the Virgin. That, thinks C.G., is the miracle. Everything they do is in response to a need: if sick, to be cured; if paralyzed, to walk again; if a sinner, to be redeemed. Whatever it is, there is a desire to be whole, to believe in God's healing power. God is the moving force, and the spiritual energy is palpable. The holy water quenches thirst, the mud baths soothe, and the flickering candles assuage purgatorial pain. What power. Revenues make Khalid happy, and almost everybody adores refreshed. No wonder faith moves mountains. C.G. thinks that it also moves mountains of garbage to Eagle Mountain. Faith also moves people from one continent to another. Once upon a time, you could fly only on a mythical carpet. Now, everybody flies, and the skies are not unfriendly, except for lines, bumps, cramped seats, lost luggage, and late arrivals. It's a small price to pay for flying.

When Rissotto reads Jasmine's story in *The Atlantic*, he knows he can't plagiarize it. The story, like Jasmine, is too hot to handle. All he can do is sit back and say, "I knew her when." She has shot out of his orbit, and he can only follow events as they unfold. He feels like a narrator in a novel who has lost control of his material because one of the characters has assumed a life of her own and no longer listens to him. Jasmine lives.

When the media descends, and the cameras converge on Khalid's house, he is taken by surprise. Throughout the long siege, he and his wife remain incredulous. Leila, however, is delighted, and she basks in her sister's reflected glory. She is "the other virgin," and she is sometimes accosted by reporters who mistake her for Jasmine. Although two years younger, she resembles her sister, and she takes pleasure in dressing like her. When asked if the Virgin spoke to her, she applies Carmex to both lips and says, "Yes." And when asked what the Virgin said, she says: "Peace on earth." Leila's words, as Jasmine's, are printed, and her statements become the voice of the Virgin. Leila is dumbfounded that a prank can become divine, and she concludes that the truth is not to be found in newspapers. She tells her sister about it, and Jasmine says that peace on earth is not a bad answer. Peace is desirable and therefore good—an answer the Virgin herself would have given.

"Suppose you were the Virgin," says Jasmine. "What would you say?"

"Peace on earth."

"See. It fits. Not to worry." Leila looks at her sister, giggles, and hugs her.

Throughout the long siege, Jasmine's liaison with Rudy is on hold—too many reporters, too much activity, not enough privacy. She longs for the unencumbered days of the Rolling Bones, when she and Rudy could meet without being followed, when they could tool through the desert on the Ducati, when they could roll in the grass unseen. Now, at all hours, the media pursues her everywhere: from home to Loviers High, to City College, to the mall, everywhere. Her life is not her own, and she resents the headlines:

VIRGIN ON WHEELS
LEATHER VIRGIN

VIRGIN FOR THE NEW MILLENNIUM
THE TWO VIRGINS
THE THREE VIRGINS
THE-RED-AND-BLACK VIRGIN

Jasmine appears on the covers of *Time, McCall's, The Inquirer, The Intruder, Elle*, and many other magazines. *Playboy* and *Hustler* want to do centerfolds of "the virgin in the buff," but she rejects their offers. They offer more than the ten thousand dollars she received from *The Atlantic*. Have they no shame? To exploit the Virgin? To juxtapose the sacred and the profane? What has happened to public morality? How can they mix heaven and hell? Fame turns her world upside down. Jasmine is confounded and embarrassed. The offers and the publicity offend her sense of proportion. The headlines and the pictures violate good measure. She feels preyed upon, exploited, victimized. Forces beyond her control are buffeting her this way and that, and recent events have dampened the exhilaration she once felt riding her Ducati 750. Rape comes to mind. She toys with the idea of writing a short piece about the loss of innocence but can't find the right tone. Rissotto tells her to read Blake. She does but says she's not ready for that kind of marriage, even though the Ducati has propelled her in that direction, at least in other people's minds. What to do and how to cope? Another dilemma. This time, the horns are sharper than before. Jasmine is annoyed that she is living a scenario not of her choosing. Her parents do what they can to protect her, but they, too, feel vulnerable. In fact, the whole family has become fair game. Each one has been squeezed dry.

Meanwhile, Mingus writes another letter to *The Sun*. This letter defends the wonder of life, human and animal, the born and the unborn. He rails against abortion, against the raising of animals for food, against eating meat—beef, pork, chicken, and turkey, not to mention emu, frogs, quail, and lambs, all animals with or without legs. He says: "The only thing with legs that people *should* eat are tables and chairs. Chew on that, you ingrates!" He says that the treatment of animals is inhumane, that cows before slaughter go into shock, that the raising of chickens in small cages is barbaric, that forced egg-laying in cramped quarters is torture, that there is no such thing as a happy calf or pullet, except the ones living in green pastures.

Mingus says that if abortion is a sin, then eating eggs may also be an offense against nature. Fertilized chicken embryos have hearts, and you can see them beating. He says that people must respect life, not kill it, even insects, ants, spiders, and termites. Everything has its place, he says, and men and women should not meddle with providence or alter God's master plan. To engage in gene control, he says, is a manifestation of pride. Whenever humans challenge the natural order of things, they set the stage for disaster. The depletion of the ozone layer produced cancer, the man-made greenhouse effect is melting the polar ice caps, and, in due course, when the seas rise, there will be global flooding, a sign of God's wrath and of human stupidity. When that happens, all the tankers and all the cruise ships in the world will not be enough to save the animals. "For the millennium we will need a super Noah."

Mingus admonishes his readers, asking them to open their eyes and hearts. He writes, "Face the facts, and change your ways. Stop buying meat and eggs. Every steak not eaten will prolong the life of a steer, and every unbroken egg will save a chick. Think of it! Not only will you lower cholesterol, but you will make it possible for a little ball of golden fuzz to enjoy an existence beyond sunny-side up. Each peep is an innocent 'thank you' to far-sightedness.

"We are also making progress in the endangered species realm. Indeed, all species need protection. Are we not God's creatures? The cats, dogs, and monkeys incarcerated in labs suffer pain. Experimental procedures must stop. We are cannibals and executioners, and eating each other is family practice. We need to venerate life, embrace it, and nurture it. We need to protect the habitats of the Alameda whipsnake, Zayante band-winged grasshopper, Morro shoulderband snail, Arroyo southwestern toad, and the San Bernardino kangaroo rat."

When Rissotto reads Mingus's diatribe in *The Sun*, he is enchanted by its irony, by the fact that Mingus is ready to shoot the mayor, two Council members, one policeman, and anyone else in order to protect animal life. It's like the logic of extreme pro-lifers: save the unborn but kill the doctors. Rissotto thinks that Mingus is a ready-made character for his novel—the perfect specimen for the contradictions of *Americus*. He reads through back issues of *The Sun* for details of the shooting, combines them with Mingus's letters-to-the-editor, and, in the spirit of self-righteousness, he warms to the task, plagiarizing Mingus's intent.

He writes: "It takes millions of years for species to evolve. Surely, it's a criminal act to become an agent of destruction. Change is inevitable but to hasten the extinction of a bird or a butterfly is unconscionable. I appeal to your conscience if you're a Protestant, to your adoration of the Virgin if you're Catholic, to your respect for life if you're a Buddhist, to your group consciousness if you're a Unanimist, to your uncertainty if you're an agnostic, to your certainty if you're an atheist, to your commitment if you're an existentialist, to your sense of wonder if you're a surrealist, to your rebellion if you're a Dadaist, to your sense of the avant-garde if you're a postmodernist, to the new millennium if you're a futurist, to the void in you if you're a nihilist, to your hatred if you're a terrorist, to your ahistorical sense if you're a Zen-Marxist, to your brilliance if you're a scientist, to your humanity if you're a humanist, to your reality if you're a realist, to your sense of the past if you're a classicist, to your bones if you're an anthropologist, to your class-consciousness if you're a sociologist, to Freud if you're a psychiatrist, to your solitude if you're an onanist, to your stamp of approval if you're a numismatist, to your faults if you're a geologist, to your roots if you're a nematologist, to your faith if you're a creationist, to Darwin if you're an evolutionist, to your controlled abstinence if you're an abolitionist, to your other wife if you're a bigamist, to your womanhood if you're a feminist, to your antennae if you're an entomologist, to your king if you're a monarchist, to your sense of time if you're a revisionist, to independence if you're a secessionist, to your shoe if you're a fetishist, to your pain if you're a masochist, to your blue blood if you're a sadist, to your inner worth if you're a racist, to southern comfort if you're a Baptist, to your considerable persuasion if you're an evangelist, to your sensuality if you're a dermatologist, to your many crowns if you're a dentist, to your mobility if you're an orthopedist, to your balanced perspective if you're an ophthalmologist, to the naked truth if you're a gynecologist, to all that's newt in you if you're a zoologist, to your organic self if you're an endocrinologist, to everything in you that's right if you're a pathologist, to the sunflower in your life if you're a botanist, to Mesmer if you're a hypnotist, to your inner depths if you're an ichthyologist, to your orgone box if you're a Scientologist."

Rissotto reads his listings out loud to Wilson. The two men are at the Blue Parrot drinking martinis and chewing the fat, eating chicken fingers, cheese, and crackers.

"What do you think?"

"I like it," says Wilson. "It's clever and wide ranging." The two parrots in their jungle cage squawk. The waitress flutters between tables, takes orders, and ruffles the feathers of her blue miniskirt. "I can't believe what's happened to Loviers City. It was such a quiet town. Now it's a zoo."

"It's a mirror of the future," says Gregor. "A planet in fast forward: visitors from around the world, immigrants, big bucks, and God, not to mention His Mother." Gregor crosses one corduroy leg and sips the martini. "I have another one for you. How about an accordionist?"

"I'd have to appeal to his pleats," says Wilson.

"And an expressionist?"

"To black and white in color."

"How about a machinist?"

"It would have to be his future prosthesis."

"You're into black humor," says Gregor. "One more. What would you do if you were a balloonist?"

"Appeal to China and Khadafy?"

"That's good. Very good. How about a leftist?"

"I'd appeal to his other hand."

"And an absurdist?"

"To his sense of play."

"What about a Hispanist?"

"Only if he's from Spain. However, it's gotta be the Colombian cartel." Both men laugh, drain their martinis, and order seconds. The waitress flutters to the bar and, in no time, wings her way back. "Cheers."

"What if you were a vorticist?" says Wilson.

"I'd burrow into the cortex."

"And an ironist?"

"Someone who was once in the service of Iran-Contra," says Gregor.

"You're getting better all the time," says Wilson.

"One last one," says Gregor. "What would you do with a hypertextualist?"

"I'd go to her website."

"Oh … we're getting gender sensitive! Do you always think of women as spiders?"

"You're just projecting."

"This could go on forever."

"I suppose so. But after a while, you end up beating a dead horse."

"Do you think so? The trick is to find the kernel of truth in the generality."

"True. But sooner or later, saturation sets in. Like what would you do with a saturationist?"

"I wouldn't do anything with a saturationist. I'd let him stew in his juice."

"Ha-ha." Wilson pops a cheese cube in his mouth. Gregor gnaws on a chicken finger. The blue parrots preen, and the waitress smiles as she passes by.

"I like to play with words," says Gregor, "and the meaning of words. But you can't always indulge in games or immerse yourself in the texture of language. *Finnegans Wake* is fine, but who, besides academics, reads *Finnegans Wake*? There has to be suspense, a lot of suspense, to keep the audience alert. The reader wants to know who did it but not right away. That's why I'm rearranging Nicole's murder, not the murder itself but the solution. I'm putting it at the end of the novel, even if Chip Berger is still the guilty party. That way, the reader is kept guessing, and Ziad isn't off the hook, not until the very end. What do you think?"

"You're right. Suspense will sell more copies, if that's what you want."

"It's not what I want. It's what is expedient."

"What is expediency?" says Wilson, sipping his martini.

"I'll bite," says Gregor, chewing on a Frito.

"It's the strategy of an opportunist."

"Will my parody of Mingus never end?" He sips his martini.

"I thought there was more to your novel than suspense?"

"There is. There's the shooter's trial and Squazza's suit."

"What about the sighting?"

"I can't use the sighting."

"Why not?"

"Because Jasmine Khalid got there first."

"I see."

"I was going to borrow her account, but when *The Atlantic* published her story, I could no longer use it."

"I see. So what do you do now?"

"I stick with suspense."

"Expediency?"

"You've got it."

"When is the shooter's trial?"

"Next week."

"And Squazza's suit?"

"Coming up."

THE CULT OF THE Virgin intensifies. Tourists, illegals, and pilgrims arrive from Europe, Asia, Africa, and Latin America. The homeless of Central America now have one more reason to head north. Hurricane Mitch unleashes hunger, disease, and despair. In Guatemala, the people have nothing to lose but their lives. The pull of *el Norte* is audible. The winds have spoken. It's as though this act of God and the sighting of the Virgin were part of a scheme to propel thousands of people toward Loviers City. Every day, the city welcomes more visitors. Hotels and campgrounds are always full. The river bottom is crawling. The faithful advance slowly on their knees toward the image of the Virgin. Khalid's enterprises flourish. The city's coffers swell. The Africanized bees are spreading. Mingus, who has become a prison guru, wields more influence than the Mexican mafia. The millennium is approaching.

Hazel Broom publishes Mingus's *Notes from the Underground*, and *The Sun's* circulation grows. Right-wingers write letters, calling Mingus a savior. Anti-abortionists support the cause. The SPCA joins in. Zealots rally around the new slogan: Zero to Hero. Its ring is reverberating. Vegetarians, animal lovers, and pro-lifers join forces and march on City Hall. They carry banners that say: *FREE MINGUS*. Everyone has heard of Bernard. What will that do to his trial? Concerned Christians gather to lend their support. Reverend Newell and Father Ortiz keep their distance. Goodhew and the Council try to cope. The yellow trucks haul refuse overtime. The Eagle Mountain landfill is filling fast. What will Loviers City do when it is full? Speer, who was never religious, buys a walnut statuette of the Virgin. He prays, regularly.

It is early October, and the millennium is less than three months away. A tide of new worshipers floods a city that was once a peaceful town. The walnut groves, suburbs, and downtown are changing. The lazy feeling of a small burgh gives way to metropolitan frenzy. There are hawkers at every street corner selling millennium trinkets: T-shirts, caps, Virgins, amulets, rosaries, pictures of Christ, religious figurines, Mexican sombreros, and stuffed animals. Khalid hires undocumented workers to sell his wares. Sidewalk cafés open on streets where small stores eked out a marginal existence. French tourists and Latino immigrants are indifferent to cleanliness. Paper wrappers, tossed cups, and empty cans accumulate under the watchful sign of Coca-Cola: *Believe Refreshed*. Although the city's sanitary services are being stretched to capacity, Godliness, despite discards, persists. A feeling of cosmopolitan sleaze oozes over the city, and despite the changes, God still reigns. But the zeal is gone. To make matters worse, the SS gives up, and the squads are disbanded. There is a different mix of students at Loviers High. Vandals break in to lockers. They take everything, even Leila's Carmex. The crows multiply, and once again, they blacken the skies of Loviers City. This year, however, fewer nuts rain down on city roofs. Many groves are sold to land developers. No one denies that the Virgin has brought a bonanza to Loviers City, to all residents tenacious enough to remain in town. The weak, if not the meek, sell their homes and go elsewhere, while those strong enough to face the hordes gain a renewed faith in profit.

The profitmongers, however, must contend with the ongoing influx of the hopeful, the curious, and the pious. In addition to the spendthrift tourists and the exploited, low-wage workers, there is another phenomenon: cults. First, the PORTALS OF PEACE sets up shop, then a group calling itself FOREVER EDEN. They buy old, nineteenth-century mansions near the edge of town. After them, in quick succession, come the PEARLY GATES, KINGDOM COME, and PARADISE REGAINED. Goodhew is concerned, and a nervous Garcia notifies the FBI. Loviers City is welcoming but vigilant. Who wouldn't be, after Jonestown, Waco, Heaven's Gate, and the Concerned Christians? The FBI sends undercover agents to infiltrate the cults. Nonetheless, eager recruits fly in from all four corners. Converts from every walk of life swear allegiance to the leader of PARADISE REGAINED. He professes equality but rules with an iron fist. He controls the cult's funds and every convert's mind. Everywhere, the power of group-think regulates lives, expectations of bliss, and faith. The millennial Virgin becomes everybody's sign of hope and salvation.

The leader of Y2K-GATE says that charity begins at home. He is a well-built man in his fifties with steely gray hair, straight eyebrows, two stern furrows between them, and eyes of fire. When he speaks, thunder rolls. "To give is to please God," he says. "Your new brothers and sisters are now your family, and family comes first. Uphold, do not withhold ... Repeat after me ... UPHOLD DO NOT WITHHOLD. Through the K-GATE together ... Repeat ... TO-GE-THER. Joyfully and holding hands we will enter the Elysian Fields. Once there, happiness, bliss, comfort, and salvation will bless each and every one of you. You are the elect, the chosen few, God's anointed. The year two thousand is at hand. Prepare for the apocalypse, for an astrological shift of cosmic proportions. Its advent signals an occasion of vast realignments. The end of one thousand years. The beginning of another one thousand or, better yet, the second coming. The coming of Jesus Christ. His return may be imminent, and the end of the world may be near. Soon, Christ will separate the sheep from the goats, the righteous from the unrighteous. All this has been foretold. It will not be easy, but our ship of faith will weather the storm.

"You may be edgy, uncertain, and afraid. You cast about aimlessly for meaning. Some of you may wander, lost, in search of spiritual food and solace. Others may swim up and down, like gold fish in a bowl, butting your heads against semi-transparent walls through which another world glimmers darkly. You seek reassurance, faith, and certainty, and you have come together because the Virgin of Loviers City is available for all to worship, resplendent and serene under her green canopy. Enlightenment is at hand, and the year two thousand welcomes you with open arms. Embrace the love. Give thanks and *Alleluia*. You are on the threshold of Heaven's Jubilee. You will hear the trumpets of the Lord. Amen."

The families of converts come to Loviers City hoping to deprogram their loved ones, but it's difficult to contact or connect with alienated sons and daughters. The compounds are inaccessible, even to the closest relatives, and the prodigal offspring are often unwilling or unable to return to former lives. On the home front, no one is rejoicing, and no one is killing the fatted calf. There are no happy reunions. The happiest people are the merchants dancing around the golden calf.

For a long time, Khalid's veneration of the beast has been the stuff of legend, and his financial holdings are the envy of many. To distribute his riches, he sets up trust funds and bank accounts. Jasmine and Leila are now swimming in money. Jasmine wants to give some of it to Rudy, but he refuses. His pride says "no." He says it would be impossible to live with that sense of obligation. He says that getting away from indebtedness to his father was hard enough. Also, for many years, the work ethic kept him indentured to Exxon.

"Never again do I want to experience such feelings of duty. It was worse than prison … and all because of lucre. Filthy lucre. You can buy me beer, bones, and knick-knacks if you like. That's in the spirit of friendship, but anything else crosses the line. When you cross the line, the dead are no longer grateful. If I took money from you, I wouldn't be able to see you again. I like seeing you. So thanks, but no thanks."

The seasons are changing. Halloween comes and goes with new tricksters, candied expectations, and ghostly costumes. The witches' brooms, however, sweep less cleanly. Once again, the orange jack-o-lanterns become the pumpkins of Thanksgiving, and the stores display the signs, objects, and frenzy of another Christmas season. Goodhew flicks the switch on the platform at the Mission Inn for the Festival of Lights. No room at the Inn this year. In anticipation of the millennium, the lights are brighter than ever, the fireworks dazzle, and the crowd is the largest in Loviers history. The Victorian mannequins wave, sing, and nod their heads at the passing multitudes.

C.G. is relieved she doesn't have to direct another poetry contest, but she's glad she organized the first one. "Yankee Stadium," "You the Audience," "Women Arise," and "Homeless" were all worthy efforts. But as for moving crowds, gathering the masses, or capturing the throngs' attention, nothing compares to the power of the Virgin ... or fear of the millennium. C.G. is amazed by the outpouring of believers and impressed by the forces that are shuffling thousands of people from one continent to another, like pawns in a giant game of chess. Not a knight here, a rook there, or a Machiavellian bishop whispering in the queen's ear but armies of people jousting for position on a planetary scale.

Rissotto's novel is progressing: Gomez and his agents distribute thousands of counterfeit bills to unsuspecting tourists who buy real objects and pay for good services with fake money. The imitation of the twenties, fifties, and hundreds is so good that nobody knows the difference. Meanwhile, the Virgin clutches the Infant to her bosom as though to protect Him from such iniquity. The faithful, on their knees, advance toward salvation. But Rissotto doesn't quite know what to do with the phenomenon of the millennium. It looms too real and too large. His playfulness is offended by the serious attitudes of Mingus and the cultists. He suspects that some of the leaders are fakers, but their rhetoric is so similar to the real thing that it's hard to tell the true message from the false one. The cults take out full-page ads in *The Sun*, and except for slight variations, they all sound alike. SOS. REPENT NOW. BESEECH FORGIVENESS. LOVE. PREPARE FOR THE END. JOIN. LIFE EVERLASTING.

Once again, in keeping with his rules for writing fiction, Rissotto changes the names of people and places, including the logos of the cults. He doesn't want his parody of Americus, that is, Loviers City, to end in a lawsuit. Squazza's suit against the city is an object lesson, and Rissotto hopes to avoid financial loss and time-consuming annoyances. He satirizes the cults but deems it prudent to rename them. After some reflection, he chooses five: DOORS OF JOY, PEACE OF PARADISE, VIRGIN GATE, CURTAIN TIME, and HEAVEN'S PREAMBLE. He re-reads the list, pleased, intent on creating a Timothy Leary-like character: Norman Desch, who urges his followers to tune out of the old world and trip into the new one. His pitch is that they, too—that is, their ashes—will, one day, be shot into planetary orbit. All it takes is money.

The beady-eyed alertness of Norman Desch, the leader of HEAVEN'S PREAMBLE, is softened by a short gray beard and square protruding upper teeth—the face of a sixty-year-old gopher. When he speaks, the velvety voice of his conviction wreathes his head with an energy that is a clerical force, transforming his resemblance from a rodent into an unknown species. Desch tells his people that he has rediscovered a biologically effective energy. He says that in many ways it behaves differently from what is known about electromagnetism. He tells his followers that his zorgone source, once denounced as fraudulent by the FDA, exists not only in living organisms but also in the atmosphere. "If you stare hard enough at the dark spaces between the stars, you will see light. Light is a primordial, cosmic radiation, and it is all around us. I have built a box—a zorgone box—that will concentrate this energy and allow you to connect with yourselves. After yourselves, you connect with the divine. I also have a zorgone blanket that folds compactly for easy traveling. When the space ships come, these blankets will be our short-range transporters. We have to be prepared. I expect all of you to sign up for practice in the zorgone accumulators. The bion samples inside will help you to focus the ZORANUR, our antidote to radiation poisoning caused by the deadly lorgone. It is better known as ZOR.

"The zorgone box will help you to escape the weight of gravity and break through your character armor. This armor blocks the development of your higher self. Believe me when I say that I have come to understand more about the real processes of nature than conventional physicists do. When the spaceships arrive, we will have to make calculations according to zorgonometric space-time reckoning. Meanwhile, we have to resist the gravitational pull of disease, psychological malaise, and government-speak. Together, we will break away, free ourselves, and experience zorgonasm—the highest form of group consciousness. It is the ultimate love potion, the coming together of minds and bodies. And it's not something that you take or drink. When you learn how to focus the bions in the zorgone box, you yourselves will be able to generate the zergals, the total power necessary to transport you into the new millennium. In time, and soon, you will feel the primordial mass-free light that fills the universe. Then, you will know that zorgonasm rules all living processes and the lawful behavior of celestial functions. It determines our emotions, our first sense of orientation, judgment, and balance. When you master the craft, and your feelings, you will know God. I promise you that.

"Meanwhile, vigilance and secrecy are essential. At this very moment, our enemies are infiltrating HEAVEN'S PREAMBLE, diluting the force, subverting the cause. Resist the intruders with every fiber in your body. Their only purpose is to re-enslave you, reprogram you, and destroy the power of zorgonasm. May the zions be with you."

The millennium is one month away, and new cults arrive in Loviers City. They buy houses and land. BLUE HEAVEN, JACOB'S LADDER, and the DOORS OF JOY set up shop, each one proclaiming the superiority of its own millennial vision. There are now nine messianic orders herding their flocks into apocalyptic corrals. The Virgin's tears have congealed, but in the sunlight, they shine.

GREGOR ORDERS A LATTÉ at Zeno's and sits down at a corner table next to the roasting stove. Bags of coffee beans are piled on the floor. Kathy walks through the glass-paneled door, tosses Gregor a nod with her blond hair, orders coffee, and joins him at the round table.

"Did you see this morning's paper?" Gregor raises one black eyebrow. "Squazza's settlement with the city? Two point eight million, including punitive damages."

"Good news for Squazza." Gregor lifts his cup and takes a drink.

"Does this mean he's no longer homeless?"

"Who knows," says Gregor. "He may like being homeless."

"How can anyone prefer the streets?" Nora shudders.

"He does."

"How do you know?"

"Jasmine told me."

"Of course. I should have remembered. Her report on the homeless. It was brilliant. One-on-one interviews … a truly in-depth study. I sent her paper to Goodhew, for the Shelter Committee. But he probably filed it, like everything else. She's something."

"Tell me about it." There is a twinge of envy in Gregor's voice. "Everything she does is brilliant, including the story of the Virgin. One day she'll be a well-known writer."

"She already is. And only a freshman. What I don't understand is why she chose to stay here. She could have gone anywhere … Amherst, Wellesley, Princeton. Why City College?"

"She wanted more of my mentoring."

"Seriously, Gregor. Why didn't she go elsewhere?"

"Maybe Rudy Squazza has something to do with it."

"You think so?"

"Or the Virgin."

"Will you never be serious?!" Nora glares at him.

"I am being serious. Everybody else wants to be in Loviers City for the millennium. Why wouldn't she?"

There is a moment of silence, and Nora says: "Been to any good concerts lately?"

"Not since the Rolling Bones."

"That was fun. Let's do it again." She twists her paper napkin around one finger.

"I'll walk you down Main Street. Hear the new musicians?"

"There are some good ones. The guitarist at the corner of the Mission Inn is a genius, and the rotunda amplifies the sound."

"But most of the musicians are lousy," says Gregor. Panhandlers, like the homeless. It's a phenomenon. Ever since the sighting of the Virgin, music has come to Loviers City."

"Question of survival," says Nora.

"Everybody has to eat." Gregor examines the coffee-bean-sacks next to the table. "You know what Victor Hugo once said?"

"I'll bite."

"*L'univers se mange en famille.*"

"That's good," says Nora. "Very good." She arches her back and twists her neck to one side. "The play on worm, universe, and family is word-perfect. How would it go if you were to translate it?"

"I'd say: 'The family banquet is the universal worm.'"

"It's not quite the same."

"It never is. Poetry is always lost in translation," says Gregor.

"Leaves you hungry. Isn't that why Jean Valjean stole the loaf of bread?"

"Yes … and French justice ate him up."

"Aren't we funny today?" Nora smiles.

"Even funnier, I think, is my parody of Heaven's Preamble."

"I'd like to hear it."

"It's a spoof of Theodore Reich's discovery of orgasmic bliss in the nineteen forties, after he was expelled from the International Psychoanalytic Association for being a communist. Did you know that he once said Freud was not satisfied genitally?"

"Pray tell."

"In 1939, Reich got a job at New York's New School for

Social Research. Soon thereafter, he began placing his patients in metal-and-wood boxes. They were known as orgone energy accumulators … supposed to improve their mental health and orgastic potency. He claimed his orgone boxes would also combat cancer. But when the Food and Drug Administration heard about them, the FDA accused him of fraud and sex-cultism."

"You're putting me on."

"No. It's true. In 1954, the FDA requested and got an injunction against Reich. Without a search warrant, they invaded his house in Orgonon, Maine , seized his orgone boxes, and burned them, along with his books. He was then arrested and, in 1956, sentenced to two years in the federal penitentiary in Lewisburg, Pennsylvania. He died there in 1957 of a heart attack."

"You are putting me on! How could the government do such a thing?"

"They did it despite Reich's protestations. He said he was experimenting with natural phenomena. In fact, his boxes had nothing to do with foodstuffs, pharmaceuticals, or cosmetics, you know, the stuff the FDA was authorized to investigate."

"That's as horrifying as the things that were going on in Nazi Germany." Nora screws her face up in disgust.

"Yes … the book burning, the false accusations, prison, death." Gregor makes an all-inclusive gesture with his arms.

"All because Reich advocated potent orgasms?" The tone of Nora's voice is one of incredulity.

"He was a bit of a nut," says Gregor matter-of-factly, "particularly his use of cloud busters. That was a machine designed to protect all of us from hostile UFOs. But in a sense, you're right. Before the sexual revolution in the sixties, sex *was* taboo." Gregor emphasizes the "was." "I remember smuggling a copy of *Lady Chatterley's Lover* into this country in a brown dust jacket. I bought the book in Paris when my parents took me to France. I was in high school."

"It's such a sweet book," says Nora.

"That's not what the sex patrol said."

"My sigh," says Nora. "This country has always had a fascist streak."

"You mean the sexually repressed?! Like the House Managers who wanted to impeach the President?"

"It's a good thing they failed."

"I suppose they had to try," says Gregor. "Fortunately, the country has assimilated Reich's obsession with orgasm."

"How does Reich fit into Heaven's Preamble?" Nora pushes her chair back and crosses one leg.

"He's the historical martyr. Falsely accused, then imprisoned. Dies in government hands. Every good cult needs a sacrificial lamb. Rome crucified Christ, and in a sense, the United States crucified Reich. The difference is that Heaven's Preamble has moved beyond the orgasm. We—and they—know all about it. What's lacking, however, is an integrated self and the absence of double-speak. The Preambulites also look forward to being transported into the next millennium."

"And you say all this is funny?"

"Believe me, Nora, it's funny. As funny as the holy tree. As funny as a wooden Virgin. There's a phenomenon! A tree trunk that looks like the face and body of the Holy Mother. And she becomes a millennial miracle. Give me a break. It reminds me of Reich's cloud busters." Gregor sputters the word "busters."

"You're not a believer?" asks Nora casually.

"I'm a believer, but not that kind. Imagine ... a vague resemblance, hearsay, rumor, and, in no time at all, God and His Mother transform a sleepy town into a world hub."

"But if people want to believe, that can't be wrong."

"I'll reserve judgment," says Gregor.

"If it makes them feel good?" asks Nora.

"Yes, like Reich's orgasm."

"Don't let the pious hear you. They'll hang you for blasphemy."

"Why? Because Christ's conception was immaculate?"

"As pure as the sky is blue."

"Where the flying saucers roam."

"Home on the range …" Nora sings the words. "My parents wanted me to be a singer."

"You have a beautiful voice."

"I liked science more, even though my dad thought science was for men only."

"You proved him wrong."

"I'm happy doing what I do."

"Everybody should be so lucky," says Gregor.

"Do you think Squazza is happy in his homelessness?"

"Jasmine says he is."

"Why do I have such a hard time believing it?" asks Nora.

"You're wedded to creature comforts."

"And you aren't?"

"I didn't say I wasn't." Nora and Gregor stand up, go to the coffee counter, order more latté, and return to the table.

"I think the crows last year were an omen of things to come," says Nora.

"How so?"

"A preamble, so to speak, for the influx of people. Instead of crows, Loviers City has been overrun by wingless bipeds. I find it all very strange. The extraordinary inflow of tourists, migrants, illegals, mystics, musicians, cultists, you name it, not to mention the homeless who were always here and are now more numerous than ever."

"Remember the fight about the parks?" asks Gregor. "Look at them now."

"And our campaign for cleanliness?" asks Nora.

"The Virgin has preempted cleanliness."

"Do you think we should blame the Vatican?"

"Are you going to write a letter?"

"We should ask Jasmine to do it. She's the one who rides Italian wheels."

"One look at her black leather and the Pope would send her to hell," says Gregor.

"But she saw the Virgin."

"Like hell she did."

"I thought you were going to reserve judgment," says Nora.

"My judgment slipped out."

"You're bad."

"Not as bad as the pickpockets, the counterfeiters, and the cult leaders … or Khalid, who sells religious baubles to the pious."

"They wouldn't buy them if they didn't want to," says Nora.

"Loviers City was once a sweet little town," says Gregor. "We had identity. Goodhew and Newell saw to that. In fact, we had an identity of cleanliness. It was almost a national identity. We were Mr. Clean. And every Sunday, on all the television screens, Newell's bells rang in Godliness. It was all so neat and nicely ordered … collective consciousness. Look at us now. Rip van Winkle would never recognize our town."

"You don't believe that," says Nora.

"What if I don't? Newell and Goodhew did. And most of Loviers City, until the crows multiplied."

"That's what I mean by omen."

"You helped get rid of the crows," says Gregor. "Why can't we get rid of the people?"

"People aren't crows."

"D-u-u-h … What I mean is, our color-coded dumpsters once served a purpose, like the flag. Whereas now, Loviers City has become one giant dumpster. Look around. The only discernible order is profit. Money regulates the flow of traffic, all because of the Virgin.

"It would have happened without her," says Nora. "It might have taken longer, that's all. Loviers City is our microcosm. It's the mirror of the future."

"Our real motto should be: *Pay and Pray* … or *Discard Without Regard*."

WEDNESDAY MORNING. GOODHEW PICKS up the phone.

"Hello?"

"David? Hi. It's Alfredo Garcia."

"Hi, Alfredo. How are you?"

"I'm okay, but Rudy Squazza has been shot."

"No. How's he doing?"

"He's dead."

"Jesus. Who did it?"

"We don't know. He was found in a dumpster behind the Pizza Hut on College Avenue."

"When?"

"Early this morning."

"Two days after the settlement. Holy Maloney. Do you think there's a connection?"

"Could be, but we haven't a clue. When we found the body, he was clutching a piece of half-eaten pizza."

"Jesus. Where is he now?"

"At the morgue. When my men found him, he was slumped over a discarded pizza box. The coroner says he was shot twice, and one of the bullets went through his heart."

"Jesus. Did you know he donated all the money from the settlement to the shelter? All two point eight million of it?"

"No."

"The very day he received it. I imagine the lawyer took his cut, but even if it was half, that's still one point four million for the homeless. That's true generosity. Why would anyone want to kill him?"

"You tell me, David."

"No, Alfredo, you tell me. That's why we pay you. I want you to look into this. Do you hear me? Leave no bone unturned. I mean stone. You know what I mean."

"We'll do all we can, David. But I've got to tell you, there's nothing to go on."

"Use your imagination, man. What good are your detectives if they can't apprehend killers?"

"They caught Chip Berger."

"He turned himself in, for Christ's sake!"

"Well, they're not miracle workers."

"Then have them consult the Virgin. Murder is bad for our image. We need solutions, Alfredo, not excuses."

Garcia hangs up, cursing the mayor, but he orders two of his detectives to leave no stone unturned. Meanwhile, word of the shooting spreads from the river bottom to Eagle Mountain. When *The Sun* prints the story, it's already old news.

C.G., Silber, and Wilson meet for coffee at the Loviers Flag Café. They gather every Sunday morning for a friendly chat. The Flag, a café of long standing, is a Loviers institution—and a coffee hole for the elite. Its walls sport a century of memorabilia from the early days of walnut growing: pictures of the groves in sepia tints, the packing houses, the growers, and their equipment. C.G.'s grandfather stands under a large tree next to George Wilson's father. A variety of art nouveau labels for walnut boxes—labels in blue, brown, and green—are displayed on the wall facing the entrance. On one label, a crow holds a sprig of three walnuts. On another, a smiling maiden embraces a cornucopia of walnuts. On a third, a brown road arcs toward a green grove cradled by a range of blue hills. The city flag, set on its pedestal in one corner of the café, curls limply around the pole. Pictures of the oldest growers are on the wall to the left of the label display. Photos of recent growers are on the right. A youthful Ziad is grinning from ear to ear. There are no pictures of Nora Silber's antecedents on the wall. She is from Philadelphia.

"Who do you think did it?" asks Silber.

"Beats me," says Wilson.

"Me too," says C.G. "Why would anyone want to kill Rudy Squazza, a homeless person?"

"A rich homeless person," says Wilson, stirring his coffee.

"But he donated the money to the shelter," says C.G.

"Maybe the assailant didn't know that," says Silber. "Maybe he was unaware of the donation and figured Squazza had money on him."

"That makes sense," says C.G. "If he'd kept some, he might still be alive."

"Or dead," says Wilson. "These days, cooks will shoot you for no reason at all."

"Maybe it was dumpster rage," says Silber, looking at the display of labels on the wall.

"That's all we need," says C.G. "When dumpster diving leads to dumpster rage, we're in big trouble."

"Maybe there's another reason," says Wilson. "There are other scenarios."

"Like what?" ask Silber and C.G. together. They look at each other and smile.

"Like the two ex-officers who beat him up and threw him in the lake. Now they have to pay for part of the settlement."

"That's a plausible theory," says Silber. "Gregor would like it. He thinks the police are always suspect, and he says half of them are corrupt. Do you know that he's writing a novel about counterfeiters? If he were to write about Squazza's death, I'm sure Garcia would be implicated."

"We should put him on the case," says Wilson. But suppose, for the sake of argument, that it's not another homeless person or the ex-officers. Who else would want to do it?"

"It could be anybody," says C.G. through a mouthful of toast. "There are plenty of criminals around. The way *The Sun* splashed two point eight million dollars across the pages of the newspaper was enough to attract everybody's attention. With that kind of publicity, it could have been a doper or a gangbanger. In any case, somebody out for easy money. Whoever did it probably didn't know Squazza had given it away."

"How about Khalid?" asks Wilson, running both hands through his beard.

"What about Khalid?" C.G. drains her cup and sets it down with a clink.

"He hated the homeless. He adores his daughters. And

everybody knew Jasmine and Rudy were an item."

"Everybody?" asks Silber, shaking the white streak in her hair. "I didn't."

"The question is," asks C.G., "did her father?"

"Good question," says Wilson. "But if he did, he wouldn't take it out on his daughter. I would think he'd tell her to stop seeing Rudy."

"And if she refused?" asks Silber.

"Khalid would be mad as hell," says Wilson.

"Mad enough to kill?" asks C.G.

"It could happen," says Silber.

"Maybe it did happen," says Wilson.

"Maybe Jasmine did it," says Silber triumphantly. "Maybe she was jealous."

"Nah," says Wilson, shaking his beard to the right and to the left. "That scenario doesn't ring true. It's not like her to shoot somebody."

"Anyway," says C.G., licking jam off one finger, "we have several plausibilities. As for me, I think some doper did it."

"I don't know," says Wilson. "Khalid can be ruthless. Maybe he thought his daughter had been damaged."

"How do you mean 'damaged?'" asks C.G.

"A pregnant virgin!" says Wilson, arching his bushy eyebrows. "Isn't that reason enough?"

"Maybe in the old days," says Silber. "But on the eve of the millennium?"

"Millennium or not, passionate acts can, and do occur, at any time, at any place," says Wilson.

"I agree with that," says C.G., "but I still think some doper did it. We all know how desperate they can get, when they need money for drugs." A man walks by outside carrying a placard. C.G. watches him through the window as he walks back and forth on the sidewalk. The placard says: *REPENT*.

"I hope Garcia solves the crime," says Silber.

"His track record is none too good," says C.G. "And the force has more to deal with than its bad image."

"They were good at subduing Mingus," says Wilson, looking at the cultist outside the window. "He faces ten years for shooting the mayor."

"That's a big price to pay for your convictions," says C.G. "Particularly when they're so far out." The cultist looks into the café through the glass window and waives his placard.

"You can say that again," says Silber.

"No further out than these guys," says Wilson. "They all have messianic ambitions."

"What is it about Loviers City that attracts fringe groups and odd people?" asks C.G.

"Good question," says Wilson. "Maybe it's the convergence of electromagnetic forces, the crystallization of the ether, and the condensation of collective ideologies."

"That's a good explanation," says Silber. "Takes care of everything, from crows to cults. All the high fliers."

"Their names are wonderful," says C.G. "KINGDOM COME, FOREVER EDEN. Even Gregor is impressed."

"He should know," says Silber. "He's the master of invention."

"A little too masterful, if you ask me," says C.G. "Sometimes his word-play is as far out as the cultists' ideologies."

"That's because he fancies himself as the reincarnation of Joyce," says Wilson.

"Nothing wrong with that," says Silber.

"Not if you're a consummate plagiarist," says C.G., amused.

"He's really a playgiarist," says Silber, "as in play. He loves to play with words. It will be fun to read *Americus* when it gets published."

"Yes," says Wilson. "Then we can figure out who we really are."

"Or aren't," says Silber.

"My guess is we're composites," says Wilson.

"It will be a *roman à clé*," says Silber.

"Who do you think you are?" asks C.G.

"I don't know," says Silber. "I haven't seen the manuscript. All I know is that Garcia figures prominently as Gomez. As for us, the other characters, we'll have to wait and see."

Wilson looks at his watch. "Oops. Moby's calling."

"Me too," says C.G.

"What the Dickens?" says Silber. The three friends stand, turn their backs to the wall-display of nut labels, pay at the cash register, and leave the Flag Café. The sun on the sidewalk is blinding. A big placard walks toward them. It says: *REPENT.*

ONCE CONTENT TO SEE Rudy whenever the occasion presented itself, Jasmine now wants to be with him all the time. She wants to touch him, feel his skin, and run her fingers through his red beard. When she learns that Rudy has been shot, she can't believe it. Three days of happiness has been shattered by a bullet. It's impossible. Such things happen to others, not to friends and lovers. Or do they? It did happen to Nicole. But to Rudy? To such a generous person? It's unfair. Donating his settlement to the Reach Program is not what her father would do. And not only does Ziad despise the homeless, he would never give so much money away, not to anyone. Money is to be used and put to work. The thought of voluntarily parting with it goes against the grain of Khalid's predatory practices.

Before Rudy donated the one-and-a-half million to the homeless, Jasmine's regard for him was high. She admired the simplicity of his lifestyle, his honesty, and his refusal to compromise with mendacity. She accepted him as a free spirit living an unfettered life with no sense of obligation to anyone, except, perhaps, the homeless. She herself could not live on the street, but she accepted his choice, and, in time, their friendship matured into an intimacy of shared feelings and attitudes, regulated in part by their dislike of institutions and authority.

They never mentioned Jasmine's father, but both she and Rudy rejected his values.

After his generous act, her esteem, delicately balanced between friendship and sex, does a heart-felt dolphin roll into a sea of love. She feels its warmth wash over her in waves. It is an astonishing feeling, one she has not experienced before, and she is surprised. If this is love, she thinks, why has it taken so long? Where has it been? Sex is one thing, a delight, and friendship is the pleasure of being together. But love, this love, is a quantum leap into a place that words can barely describe. Her feelings open like the petals of a budding rose, and despite her writerly talents, she feels unable to put them into words. Flora and fauna, as metaphors, seem inadequate to the task, unable to convey the sensations of her body. She imagines exotic places, foods, and smells, but they, too, fail to describe her new emotions. Neither the sun nor the moon, neither daylight nor darkness, nor the depth of the Pacific or the height of the Himalayas can convey the tender immensity of her affection.

Now Rudy is dead. The pain of his absence is as intense as the abundance of her love. Its emptiness is now as vast as a sky without stars. The sea is frozen, the sun is black, and the once easy roll of the dolphin is gone. Fear and trembling replace the frolicsome spirit of her fancy. The warmth of touch gives way to a cold nullity. Rudy's booming laugh is silent, the blue sparkle in his eyes is blank, and his arms are now the remembrance of an embrace without promise.

Jasmine remembers their first encounter in the park—feeding the swans and taking a spin around the lake on the Ducati. She remembers the Rolling Bones concert and their trysts under the pepper tree. They called it their pepper tree. It was under that tree where they first kissed, where, for the first time, they made love on the soft carpet of dried leaves and peppercorns, the cascading branches shielding them from view. She remembers the smell of the leaves and the sun sparkling through those fern-like branches on which the ravens sometimes gabbled, kherred, and mewled while cawing. Rudy always thought that ravens were smarter than crows: "They mate for life," he said, "and after the flood, Noah first loosed a raven from the ark. When it didn't return, he sent out a dove. In Norse legend, two ravens patrolled Odin's realm and returned every evening to perch on his shoulders. Hugin was Thought, and Munin was Memory. And they whispered the news of the land in Raven's ears. In ancient Greece, he was sacred to Apollo, and for the people of the Northwest—the Tlingit, Haida, and Tsimshian—he was a creator of life. That's why we were upset when the City Council voted to kill the crows. They were our friends … more than friends. They spoke to us, they played with us, and they shared our lifestyle. Killing them was like shooting us. I was so angry I set fire to the grass in the river bottom."

"Yes, I know."

"Had it not been for the fire, the Virgin might never have appeared."

And Rudy would still be alive. Jasmine relives the what-if happenings that might have prevented his death. She hears the timbre of his voice. She feels the pulsing of their bodies, his body lying next to hers. And now his body is lifeless: shot like one of the crows and lying in the morgue, waiting for someone to claim it. But no one does. There is no family, no trace, no name, and no address. Rudy is a prodigal son who never returned, a son who remains outside the father's house, a son who refuses the call of other people's expectations, a son content to live off the leftovers of society's abundance. "Reckless waste" is what he called it. And Jasmine remembers the disdain in his voice whenever he talked about conspicuous consumption.

Jasmine thinks that Rudy's lifestyle mirrors his beliefs, and she admires his determination to practice what he preaches by removing himself from a system that is coercive and destructive. She concludes that homelessness may not be the preferred choice for vagrants, but for Rudy, it was a deliberate decision not to participate in the practices of a culture that values money more than life. "Millions of citizens," she remembers Rudy saying, "are persuaded that they must earn a living prescribed by corporate cyber culture: information, communication, medicine, entertainment. The faster the technology, the more dependent we become. Websites, email, Netflix, Facebook, Google, and Amazon—all bringing the world together, shrinking the planet, and encouraging a lifestyle of consumerism. Everybody buys. *I consume, therefore I am.* That will be the new *Cogito* for the millennium. Forget thought. The impulse to buy is already so strong that advertisers do our thinking for us. I think where I am not, and I am not where I think I am."

Jasmine remembers the awe she felt while listening to Rudy's pronouncements. He, she thinks, is a twentieth-century guru and saint. If the sighting of the Virgin means anything, it should commemorate the death of a man who was perhaps the only Christ society deserves. Jasmine feels numbed by Rudy's death, but the more she thinks about his life, the stronger her determination to do something for it, to make it count.

She writes a letter to Dorothy Broom, editor of *The Sun*, in which she praises Mr. Squazza's generosity while lamenting the tragedy of his death. On December 5, in its Sunday edition, *The Sun* publishes Jasmine's letter defending Rudy's engagement in the lives of the homeless. She denounces the practices of corporate America and ends the letter by comparing Christ and Squazza, urging every reader, in the name of the Virgin, to sanctify his death. "He," she says, "is the sacrificial lamb, martyred by a society that has lost touch with life—a society that has turned its back on love."

When Ziad reads his daughter's letter, he is livid. When Newell and Ortiz read it, they agree, for the first time, yet they both denounce the well-intentioned innocence of a teenage writer. They decry the belittling of Christ and the besmirching of the Virgin. Mingus is taken aback by the new challenge to his candidacy for martyrdom. When the homeless read the letter, they feel encouraged. Garcia dismisses it. Wilson is amused.

Rissotto and Konlon are pleased. Goodhew thinks there are more important issues. Silber is touched, and C.G. is impressed with the letter's style and content.

Jasmine rides her Ducati 750 to the Three Lambs Mortuary. Mr. Holcomb, in his shirtsleeves, meets her at the door. He ushers her inside, guides her into the room of last decisions, and offers her a chair. She sees her reflection on the highly polished surface of the mahogany table.

"How can I be of service to you?" asks Holcomb, rubbing his hands. Jasmine expects them to lather. Holcomb continues. "We are here to help in any way we can. Has there been a loss in the family? Perhaps you would like to sign up for our tri-county plan? 'Pay now and die in peace later.' Many of our clients find comfort in the arrangement."

"No, thank you," says Jasmine. "A friend of mine died, and I need information. You may remember my father, Ziad Khalid? Last year he arranged for the burial of an employee, Nicole Sebastian."

"Yes," says Holcomb, still rubbing his hands. "I remember him well. A gracious and generous man."

"He told me that, in addition to burial and cremation, you offer cryonic solutions."

"Yes, we do."

"Please, tell me more about it."

"Cryonics is the ultra-low-temperature preservation of bodies in special chambers. Those who choose this procedure believe that at some time in the future, in three hundred years, perhaps sooner, cell and tissue repair technology will be available. With recent developments in nanotechnology, it will be possible to restore an individual to full-function and health."

"Is this really feasible?" Jasmine looks at Holcomb, wide-eyed.

"Cryonicists believe that as human knowledge and medical technology expand, they will be able to revive the dead and restore people's bodies."

"Wow," says Jasmine. "How many frozen bodies are there?"

"At least ten thousand, as we speak. The challenge is to provide the techniques that will ensure the patient's survival. Future control over living systems should allow fabrication of new organisms and sub-cell-sized repair devices. Cryonicists believe that molecular repair will also revive clients who are waiting in cryonic suspension." Holcomb sits up in his chair and straightens his back.

"That's cool," says Jasmine. "Immortality, at last. I'm dying to become immortal."

"Now you can," says Holcomb. "Will this be for yourself, or someone else?"

"Someone else. Maybe me, in the future."

"Excellent," says Holcomb. "We are here to serve."

"My friend has no immediate family. I'm here to make the final arrangements."

"Where is he now? Or is it a she?"

"He's at the morgue."

"Good. It's important that the body be refrigerated. Otherwise, the cells decompose, and when that happens, regeneration is impossible. Do you know how much time elapsed between his death and transport to the morgue?"

"No, I don't."

"Well, for cryonics to work, the time-lapse must be minimal. May I suggest that you find out. Meanwhile, this is for you." Holcomb slides a brochure across the table. "It will help you make up your mind." *Cryonics: Death and Resurrection.* Jasmine thumbs through the pages.

"Thank you very much. I'll call you." When she gets home, she reads the brochure and then calls the morgue. She says she's related to Mr. Squazza and wants to make arrangements for the funeral. She asks when he was shot, when he was found, and how long it was before the body was put in the freezer. She notes the details and says she's making funeral arrangements with the Three Lambs Mortuary. She dials Holcomb.

"Mr. Holcomb? I have the information on Mr. Squazza. The

morgue believes he was shot sometime between 9:00 p.m. and midnight. His body was discovered about 7:00 a.m., when the trash collectors made their rounds. He didn't go into the morgue's freezer until 10:00 a.m.

"That's about twelve hours," says Holcomb, "give or take a few. I hate to say this, but for cryonics to work, we need to get to the person within one or two hours after death. Sooner, if possible, because after ischemia, deleterious changes occur in the cells and tissues of the body."

"Ischemia?"

"After death, the blood no longer circulates. For clients who have signed up ahead of time, a team arrives on the scene and does what we call 'a remote whole body washout.' The body, thus perfused, is packed in ice and transported to the cryonics center. Clearly, in Mr. Squazza's case, that has not been done. Despite the promise of nanotechnology, a twelve-hour delay is pushing the limits of the assembler. Future cell repair is unlikely. The cells have already been degraded, and although we could go for cryostasis, a resurrection in the future would probably be impossible."

"I see."

"It's up to you, of course, but under the circumstances, I would not recommend cryopreservation. Would you want us to make other arrangements?"

"Yes. In that case, my second choice would be cremation."

"Very well. We'll arrange to transport the body, but you will need to come by again and sign some papers."

Too bad. Jasmine thinks of Rudy's body suspended in liquid nitrogen for three hundred years, waiting for the day when advances in nanotechnology will repair cells and rejuvenate tissue. She thinks of assemblers, disassemblers, nanocomputers, and nanomachines capable of reviving the body. It seems impossible, almost too good to be true, that at some future date it will even be possible to repair the brain, restore memory, and resurrect consciousness. After her death, she would join Rudy in the suspension chamber where, shielded by her endowment fund, they would float through time together, waiting for the miracle of reanimation. What a dream—when ancient bodies will be valuable antiques, animated treasures worth their weight in gold and silver. Think of the insurance … and the premiums. What an industry—worthy of Loviers City's highest goals. Recycling at its best, saving space in cemeteries and mausoleums. But what happens to the soul? Is it in limbo, or is it frozen, unable to fly to heaven or go to hell? Hey, maybe cryogenics offers a reprieve, a second chance for sinners who might have gone to hell but who, having tasted death, so to speak, will think twice before pursuing their evil ways.

Jasmine is disappointed and dejected. The thought of life with Rudy in the future, even after her death, has tempered her grief. But now, with the hope of reanimation gone, her grief returns. It seeps into her body, draining her energy and sapping her faith. She thinks of Newell's reassurance that, after death, loved ones will see each other in heaven, but she's not sure she wants a disembodied soul. In heaven, she wants her Ducati, the Rolling Bones, and Rudy's red beard. Maybe that's why the cultists are so intense. They believe in the end of the world and the resurrection of the body. Maybe if she joined PARADISE REGAINED, the space ships would reunite her with Rudy. Jasmine fantasizes the possibilities. She thinks of Rudy's comments about sacred trash and the Hindu belief in recycled souls, as opposed to Christianity's throwaways. In Christianity, souls are used only once before they go to heaven or to hell. Hindu souls, on the contrary, are ultimately recyclable—just wipe and reuse. A reasonably imperfect soul can still give an eternity of use—just put it in the Blue Toter. Jasmine smiles wryly at the thought of Rudy's soul in another body. She is tempted briefly, just in case, to preserve his head, so that he will always be there, like Julien Sorel in his cave, surrounded by candles and Italian marble. But Rudy had none of Julien's ambition. He was neither red nor black. Rudy was a prototypical anti-hero, and Jasmine is not a romanticized Mathilde. Cremation it will be. And she will preserve the ashes.

She remembers Rudy saying that Buddhism encourages the mixing of the ashes of the dead with cement in order to provide a lasting sculptural image of the deceased.

Rissotto introduces Jasmine to Horace Quickendhal, a sculptor at City College. His faded overalls are covered with smears of plaster. He is a burly man in his late forties with blue eyes, a beard that looks like a crow's nest, strong shoulders, big hands, and a body that seems accustomed to lifting heavy objects. Slabs of marble lean against the wall. Busts of bronze and plaster sit on a table, looking at each other. In one corner, there is a pile of iron tubing. Jasmine shows Horace two pictures of Rudy—one full-face and one in profile. She says she would like his ashes mixed into a cement likeness. Horace says that he will make a plaster bust first, to see if she likes it.

Wherever Jasmine goes, she thinks of Rudy. Things, places, sounds, and smells remind her of him. Whenever she rides the Ducati, she feels his arms around her waist. When she hears the tok of a raven or the kher-r-r of a crow, she thinks of the birds mewling in the pepper tree. The sight of a dumpster depresses her no end, and the smell of pizza revulses her. She plays PYRE ON THE MOUND on her hi-fi and thinks of the ROLLING BONES, Irwin Meadows, and yellow balloons. Her void is now a state of mind, and its emptiness feels like a dumpster, with only memories to fill it. She thinks of Rudy dumpster diving. Thinking of him is all she has. Every mnemonic moment is a treasure she holds on to, fiercely.

Jasmine, again, remembers the first time they made love under their pepper tree. She remembers his lips and hands, his kind words, patience, and refusal to compromise his values with those of a derailed social system. She admires his mind and the logic with which he handled information. She remembers the change in his looks—neater beard, cleaner clothes, more frequent showers, and a happier laugh—after they met. She herself was still in rebellion against authority, whereas he had passed beyond it. They were both angry at life for not being what it should be.

But whereas she was still thrashing around, he was in a state of acceptance, willing to change what he could, accepting of the rest. Donating one-and-a-half million dollars to the shelter was, in part, an act of atonement for setting fire to the river bottom. It was his separate peace. Jasmine loves him for it and admires his courage. Waves of sadness well up within her and tears wet her cheeks. She feels sorry for herself, angry and lost, unable to sort through the emotions pulling her this way and that.

Jasmine thinks of Rudy's future bust. The thought restores her sense of balance, and the idea of placing the bust in a public place offers hope. His likeness will remind people of his charity. She thinks of putting it on a pedestal in front of the shelter but rejects that idea. Only the homeless would see it. There, it would not have much of an impact. In front of the Postmodern Library? No. The City Council would never approve of that, nor would the First Unanimist Church. How about the parking lot, next to the path leading to the sacred tree? That might be a good place. There, thousands of pilgrims would see Rudy's bust. A plaque would bare an inscription commemorating his generosity. His bust would be a fitting representation of poverty and selflessness, a reminder of forgotten possibilities in a consumer culture that values money above everything else. It would be a visual prelude to the visitation of the Virgin. His bust would also be a memorial to the tree and to their love. All she has to do is persuade her father.

Persuading Ziad will be a Herculean task fit for an Amazon. For Ziad to acknowledge that homelessness is a virtue, and poverty divine, would be like reversing the flow of Niagara Falls. Although a First Unanimist in faith, Jasmine incorporates the Virgin into her pantheon of saints. She crosses her fingers and hopes for a miraculous intervention. If the Virgin can move millions of people, Ziad should be a pushover. But it's Her millions against his. Jasmine imagines the Virgin hovering over Niagara Falls. A rainbow is her halo. She hears the thunderous roar of falling water and feels its misty spray on her cheeks. Suddenly the roar stops, the spray settles, the rainbow vanishes, and the water flows upward, like a video clip in reverse. Time reverses itself, and if the reversal lasts long enough, Rudy will return alive and the Mohicans will repopulate the banks of the river. Jasmine thinks that if the Virgin can perform miracles, this will be Her test. But she worries about her period. She has missed two, and everything, she thinks, hinges on the third.

How should Jasmine broach the subject with her father? How can she convince him to display Rudy's bust at the far end of the parking lot? Should she ask outright, beg, cajole, have a tantrum, what? Dare she reveal her love for Rudy? What if she's pregnant? There are too many ifs, none of which is likely to influence the old man. The only sure way is to appeal to his pocketbook. But is there anything about Rudy that would ever appeal to her father? There was a time when he was ready to deport him.

On December 9, Jasmine drives her Ducati to the crematorium. She enters a vaulted chamber next to the oven where a man wearing a dark blue smock says that after the body is cremated, the bones will be ground and the ashes placed in a bronze urn. He shows her an octagonal object eight inches high and five inches in diameter. Another man opens a door and wheels out a gurney with a long cardboard box on top. The attendant removes the lid of the box, and there, in it, lies Rudy, his eyes closed and his body wrapped in a white sheet. Despite his red beard, he seems diminished. Jasmine places the palm of her left hand on his cold forehead, bends over, kisses him on the lips, and, after straightening up, says: "I'm ready." She is startled by the loud sound of gas igniting in the oven and looks into its aperture with wild eyes. She turns abruptly and walks out of the vaulted room. The glare of sunlight is blinding.

The following day, Jasmine picks up the urn at the crematorium, straps it to the back of the Ducati, drives home, goes directly to her room, puts on a CD of the ROLLING BONES, and turns up the volume. PYRE ON THE MOUND. The four walls of her room reverberate. The sound mourns the memory of the man she loves. She sits on the edge of her bed, staring out the window at the walnut trees. She dives into the past.

Quickendhal calls to say that the cast is ready for her inspection. Jasmine rides the Ducati toward his City College studio. She violates speed limits. In the studio, on a table in the middle of the room, is Rudy—an immaculate, white Rudy, beard and all. His hair has white plaster ringlets. Jasmine is enchanted. She feels a great weight lifting, and for the first time since Rudy's death, she feels less vulnerable. She runs her fingers over his nose, eyes, and lips. Yes, he's all there. She hugs Horace Quickendhal and says: "The bust is wonderful. Please proceed without delay."

He replies: "I'll need the ashes."

"Oh, the ashes. Don't go away." Jasmine runs out of the studio, jumps on her Ducati, breaks more speed limits, and returns with the urn. She enters the studio. "When will it be ready?"

"In a couple of days. I'll call you."

"I can't wait." He smiles, and his blue eyes and crows' feet deepen.

"Have you considered bronze? I could save a pinch of ash and mix it in. More than a pinch would spoil the casting. Bronze, you know, is more durable than cement, even when you coat the cement with sealant. I'll give it a coat myself, before you pick it up, but you should reapply sealant every two years."

Jasmine has been so intent on following the Buddhist formula that the idea of bronze has not occurred to her. "Of course," she says. "Bronze, by all means. I'll place the cement bust in the garden and the bronze one in the parking lot."

"You can have the plaster one too, but it will cost you."

"I don't mind."

"I'm kidding. It's the bronze that's expensive."

"Either way, cryonics was going to cost a fortune. Ten thousand on a bronze is a bargain."

"The Greeks used to paint their statues. You yourself could paint the plaster."

"Really?" Jasmine thinks of flesh tones and a red beard. "Please make another plaster cast, with a pinch or two of ash." She shakes the urn, listening to the rustle of ashes and bone.

"Sure."

"You're a miracle man!"

"If you say so. But casting bronze will take longer."

"That's okay. I can wait."

Jasmine calls City Hall and makes an appointment with the mayor for December 13. Despite his busy schedule, Goodhew makes time for Khalid's daughter. Is she not a celebrity, the author of "The Virgin of Loviers City?"

"What can I do for you?" says Goodhew, smiling broadly and dimpling his rosy cheeks. Jasmine explains her project. She describes the bronze bust, its placement, and the plaque:

RUDY SQUAZZA.
BENEFACTOR.
LOVIERS CITY.
1962–1999.

Would the mayor consider making a brief speech at the dedication?

"But I don't want my father to know who's behind this," says Jasmine.

"Oh?"

"Please don't mention me. Like ... say ... pretend the placement is in the best interests of Loviers City and my father's pocketbook."

"But your father hates the homeless."

"Yes, I know. But if the idea comes from you, he'll listen." Goodhew smoothes his walrus mustache with the middle finger of each hand, rubs his chin, shifts in his chair, and finally says: "What the hell. Squazza donated one-and-a-half million to the city. A dedication speech is the least I can do. Your father has his plaque. Now, you and Squazza will have yours."

"Oh, thank you, thank you." Jasmine hugs the mayor.

"When it's ready, let me know."

"I will."

Goodhew calls Ziad: "An anonymous benefactor is donating a bronze bust of Rudy Squazza to the city. This person wants it placed at the head of the path leading to the sacred tree. Is that okay with you, Ziad?"

"No way," says Ziad. "No homeless bust is going in my parking lot."

"But Ziad, you yourself donated twenty thousand to the homeless. There is even a plaque honoring your generosity."

"Forget it, David. I don't want Squazza on my lot."

"I understand your feelings, Ziad. But the word is out. The press knows about the bust, and the Council thinks your lot is the best place for it. How would it look if you appeared to trash Squazza's generous donation? One-and-a-half million is not chicken feed."

"How much was it?"

"One-and-a-half million."

"Jesus."

"Can I count on your support, Ziad?"

"This is blackmail, David."

"No it's not. It's public relations." The two men argue back and forth, pushing, pulling, persuading, squirming, and cajoling, until finally, when it seems there is nothing more to be said, Khalid agrees. "You won't regret this, Ziad. I'll owe you one."

When Jasmine learns that her father has agreed to the dedication and that he will not oppose the placement of Rudy's bust in the parking lot, she thinks a true miracle has occurred. She sees Niagara Falls resume its flow, the rainbow in the mist reappears, and the roar of time resounds. Jasmine sends a note to the mayor thanking him. She writes: "I admire your persuasive powers. You are truly a great man." Goodhew reads the note, smiles, and thinks of the irony of a city dream undermined by the Virgin. Loviers City may be famous and its residents may be getting rich, but its new civic spirit is unanimous only in the pursuit of lucre.

Jasmine asks Quickendhal about a marble pedestal, and after considering different hues and grains, she selects a brownish pink one with black specks. "It will go well with the bronze," says the sculptor. "Your plaster cast is also ready … and so is the cement one."

"I'll take the plaster one now, but can I leave the cement one?"

"No problem."

"How long will it take to get the marble?"

"A week or so."

"That's cool. But you know, for the cement, I prefer gray."

Jasmine puts the plaster bust in the back of her mother's Land Cruiser, braces it carefully with blankets, and takes it home. On the way, she stops off at the hardware store.

Jasmine still hasn't gotten her period. It's been almost three months since the last one. Is she pregnant? She buys a pregnancy kit, reads the directions, and follows procedures. When she's done, the color is pink. She laughs, then cries. What to do? There are always options. Is she happy or sad? Concerned or dejected? She's not sure. She'll need to see a doctor, and if she's pregnant, then what? To have or not to have?

The gynecologist, an African American woman, confirms the pregnancy.

"Are you married?"

"No."

"Do you want the baby?"

"I don't know."

"Whatever you decide, if you choose to terminate the pregnancy, the sooner the better. Time is of the essence."

Jasmine goes home, takes Rudy's plaster bust out of the closet, places it on the desk in front of the window, and opens the paint cans. With a flat wooden stirrer, she mixes the pink and brown paints in a bowl and begins. Gradually, the brush paints Rudy's forehead, cheeks, nose, ears, and neck. Little by little, except for the hair and beard, the white gives way to flesh-colored tones.

When the paint dries, Jasmine does the lips, then the red hair, and the beard. The blue eyes are last. Uncanny. She studies the face, shades the cheekbones, and adds a few wrinkles. Voilà! A living resemblance. Would Rudy want a child? She'll never know. The question is, does she? It's a big decision. She looks at the calendar … one more week till Christmas. Then, she'll decide. She circles November 29, the day of Rudy's death. She arranges six honey-colored candles around the painted head, lights them, and, for a long time, stares out the window at the walnut trees. The candles burn, each with an orange flame.

It's hard to believe that Christmas is at hand. There are presents to get and things to do. Quickendhal delivers Rudy's cement likeness, and Jasmine accompanies him to a remote corner of the garden where he sets it up on the gray marble pedestal. It stands five feet, six inches tall and can be seen only if you walk from one end of the garden to the other. Before leaving, the sculptor informs Jasmine that the bronze bust will be ready for New Year's. Jasmine picks two gardenias, inhales the fragrance, and places the flowers on the pedestal next to Rudy's head. She looks at his eyes and, with the fingertips of her right hand, caresses one cheek. She opens the garden gate and walks through it into the walnut grove. The walnuts on one tree have not been harvested. Some nuts, with their husks still on, have fallen to the ground, forming a ring around the base. The husks have perforated and dried into a burnt umber, revealing the lighter shells inside. Other nuts have split open and are now germinating in the furrows. Jasmine feels the warm December sun on her shoulders. She kneels and picks up a sprig of elongated, pale-green leaves. Except for the four-inch terminal leaf that forms the stem's tip, the six leaves below it are arranged two-by-two in augmenting lengths.

Jasmine picks up a walnut, peels the dry husk from the shell, and closes her hand around it. It feels warm and solid. She tosses it in the air and catches it. She picks up another walnut husk, peels it, and, with both hands, tosses the two nuts in the air, catching them alternately. She looks at the ring of walnuts around the tree and at the earth in which the trunk is embedded. She thinks of the seasons and the rhythms of life and death. She thinks of the seed in her womb, and she thinks it is a boy, perhaps a boy who will grow up to look like Rudy. Yes, let Christmas be a time of joy.

LOVIERS CITY IS PREPARING for the millennium. C.G. wishes she and Tony were on the Concorde jetting between Paris and New York. They could celebrate two New Years and two millennia. She thinks of the people on cruise ships in the Caribbean and the Mediterranean, dancing into the Y2K. She thinks of revelers in all the capitals of the world, in all the cities of the world. She thinks of parties in hotels, clubs, restaurants, homes, and hamlets. She thinks of the world as one millennial machine, one big unanimous engine welcoming the year 2000. She thinks of celebrations in Shanghai, Tokyo, Jakarta, Sidney, Moscow, Tehran, Cairo, Ankara, Budapest, Helsinki, Stockholm, London, Toronto, Mexico City, Lima, Rio de Janeiro, Rome, Madrid, Tunis, Cape Town, Sofia, Bucharest, Oslo, Lagos, Addis Ababa, New Delhi, Kabul, Beijing, Vienna, Berlin, Brussels, Copenhagen, Algiers, Athens, Jerusalem, Baghdad, Auckland, Santiago, Buenos Aires, La Paz, Tierra del Fuego, and Kamchatka. She thinks of the bears, the wolves, the lions and the elk—all the animals in the world, humans included, consciously and unconsciously grunting, howling, roaring, and snorting their way into the twenty-first century. She thinks of the bugs, the birds, the fish, and everything that walks, creeps, crawls, swims, and flies—everything moving, inching, rolling, and sweeping its way forward in time, through all the dimensions, through all the spaces and interstices of the infinitely large and the infinitely small, from field, to quanta, to string, all of it moving inexorably down the historical path of a man-made chronology. Only Rissotto, Quickendhal, and

Jasmine think of time as circular. C.G. thinks of Tony. Her New Year will be with him in Austin.

As for the cults, BLUE HEAVEN, FOREVER EDEN, PORTALS OF PEACE, and the others, they bide their time, knowing that the end is near, less than a fortnight to the end of the world. Then, the arrival of God's space ships will separate the sheep from the goats, resurrect the dead, and reward the faithful, all in the name of Jesus Christ. So much for cryonics and the big three-hundred-year-sleep, so much for unbelievers who will receive their just and skeptical deserts, so much for the ungodly who should have seen the light and fallen to their knees in repentance, and so much for a Loviers City that tried to be Godly but failed. The cults will prevail, and their unanimous message is the only true message. God and the comets will see to that. It will be a true kingdom built on the ruins of the old millennium. The hotels in Loviers City are full. Virgin Acres is full. So is the Mission Inn. The festival lights blink. All the clubs and restaurants are booked. So is the Pepper Corn. The faithful rally in the streets. The Hare Krishnas walk down College Avenue in their saffron robes. The homeless buy more rotgut and occupy the gazebo of the Postmodern Library. Garcia's force is on ready alert. He will delay his confrontation with Goodhew until 2001. Our Lady of Loviers and the First Unanimist Church have scheduled midnight services. Father Ortiz and Newell are writing sermons. The City College auditorium is selling tickets for its all-night, sci-fi film festival. Mingus is writing another letter to *The Sun*, even as he frets about doing time until the year 2024. Rudy's killer cleans his Saturday night special. The FBI agent who has infiltrated the PORTALS OF HEAVEN sends a coded message to headquarters saying that the group has ordered fifty pairs of immaculate Nikes.

All eyes are on the clock. Three hundred and thirty-six more hours. Twenty thousand one hundred sixty minutes. One million, two hundred nine thousand, six hundred seconds. Think of it. Each ticking moment bringing you closer to the end.

Everybody's pulse quickens, skips a beat, fibrillates, runs

hot, runs cold, and pulses. Glasses overflow, bells chime, and people yell. Billions of voices shout and chant, welcoming the millennium. People dance, skip, and hop. They eat and drink, looking forward to the final countdown. Global energy bubbles over and the moment of transition is at hand. One century ends and another one begins. The event is full of uncertainty and promise. For weeks, the pundits have been recapitulating the past and rehearsing the future. Newspapers, journals, television, and websites overflow with commentary, evaluations, and prognostications. The cultists say it's the end of the world. Skeptics say it's just the beginning. Billions of words and thousands of ideas circulate. The planet is now one entity thinking of itself, its past, and its future. Hyperconsciousness encircles the globe. The oosphere is saturated. Anima reigns. Intelligence, stupidity, avarice, faith, cupidity, idolatry, indifference, and zealotry orbit the earth. They spin webs of unanimity, influence, wonder, and appeal.

It's a planetary party. Think of the refuse worldwide. It's a staggering amount of garbage, enough to sink all the barges in the seas. The toters of Loviers City—the *Blue* and *Brown*—will certainly be full: empty bottles of champagne and beer, cups, straws, confetti, streamers, ribbons, banners, balloons, hats, horns, and masks. The yellow trucks will try to make their rounds on time. The giant brushes, too, will swirl before the rotten smells unfurl. Eagle Mountain will receive its waste. At dawn, the crows will rise and fly and gorge, the bees will buzz, the pepper tree will shudder in the wind, and the Virgin's tears will also flow.

ABOUT THE AUTHOR

Ben Stoltzfus is Professor Emeritus of Comparative Literature and Creative Writing at the University of California, Riverside. He is a novelist, translator, literary critic, and internationally recognized inter-arts scholar. He has published twelve monographs of literary criticism and received many awards: Fulbright, Camargo, Gradiva, Humanities, Creative Arts, and MLA. He has published five novels and two collections of short stories. *Romoland*, a pictonovel written in collaboration with artist Judith Palmer, was also published by 39 West Press in 2017. Stoltzfus's most recent collection, *Falling and Other Stories*, was published by Anaphora Press in 2018. He lives in Riverside, California with Judith Palmer, his wife.